A SHORE THING

PORTIA MACINTOSH

B

Boldwood

First published in Great Britain in 2026 by Boldwood Books Ltd.

Copyright © Portia MacIntosh, 2026

Cover Design by Alexandra Allden

Cover Images: Alexandra Allden and Shutterstock

The moral right of Portia MacIntosh to be identified as the author of this work has been asserted in accordance with the Copyright, Designs and Patents Act 1988.

Every effort has been made to obtain the necessary permissions with reference to copyright material, both illustrative and quoted. We apologise for any omissions in this respect and will be pleased to make the appropriate acknowledgements in any future edition. |

A CIP catalogue record for this book is available from the British Library.

Paperback ISBN 978-1-80557-314-2

Large Print ISBN 978-1-80557-313-5

Hardback ISBN 978-1-80557-312-8

Trade Paperback ISBN 978-1-80656-174-2

Ebook ISBN 978-1-80557-315-9

Kindle ISBN 978-1-80557-316-6

Audio CD ISBN 978-1-80557-307-4

MP3 CD ISBN 978-1-80557-308-1

Digital audio download ISBN 978-1-80557-310-4

This book is printed on certified sustainable paper. Boldwood Books is dedicated to putting sustainability at the heart of our business. For more information please visit https://www.boldwoodbooks.com/about-us/sustainability/

Boldwood Books Ltd, 23 Bowerdean Street, London, SW6 3TN

www.boldwoodbooks.com

For Kim,
my wonderful mum

1

'Remember: you're all here to score tonight!'

Oh, boy. It's going to be like that, is it?

It's strange because you think you know where you are in life, both personally and on the timeline of the history of the world, and then you discover something that rattles you.

Don't get me wrong, I know that thirty-two isn't old by any stretch of the imagination, but I am finding myself noticing things that I never thought would happen. Take music, for example. You think you're young and hip and you've got your finger on the pulse until one day when you venture into the top-streamed chart and you realise that not only do you find songs actively annoying, but you hardly know who anyone is. In fact, the only songs you do know are songs that were around when you were younger, ones that have been remixed to appeal to a younger generation.

To be honest, it's that kind of realisation that's on my mind tonight, because something I had thought of as fairly standard (although still deeply unpleasant) is tonight being touted as some quirky retro event from a bygone era – speed dating.

I guess it makes sense, everyone is so chronically online these days – myself included – so naturally dating apps are one of the first stops on the road to romance (if you can stomach staying on a bus full of creeps, ghosters and sleazes, that is).

Meeting people in real life only feels more and more impossible as you get older. Not going on as many nights out seriously limits how many people you meet, and how much you work means less and less time to actually try to meet people out and about – which only leaves the potential to date people from work, and that's never a good idea. Well, what happens when you break up? I can't even imagine the awkwardness of having your ex around you all the time, especially when you're trying to do your job – the thing that pays your bills. You just can't mess with that. I kept bumping into my most recent ex at my local supermarket, we weren't ever serious but seeing him felt so awkward, so I did what any sensible, mature grown woman would do – I started shopping somewhere else.

So, fair enough, I guess that means events like this are a way to go, I just feel so weird about it being pitched as something retro. If something I tried in my twenties is now retro, I must be getting on.

I'm not looking forward to it this evening just like I wasn't looking forward to it back then either. To me, speed dating is a bit like playing Russian roulette. It's sitting at a table, potentially putting yourself in danger, because God knows who you're going to meet. Every round could be the worst-case scenario. The best you can hope for are the duds. The blanks. Have I mentioned that I don't have high hopes for this at all?

Whether it's an ironic return or not, speed dating is back. I suppose I could try to be grateful that it keeps the process streamlined, but you can't always rush these things.

Tonight you only get a matter of minutes with each man

(which is the last thing a girl wants, usually). Minutes don't exactly give the earth time to move – it's definitely not long enough to work out if someone is boyfriend material or the kind of bloke you'll see crop up on a Netflix true crime documentary.

I'm here, I'm dressed up, I'm sipping my £25 cocktail, sitting on a stool so high I might have to pursue one of these men just so he'll help me down. We're in one of those painfully trendy London bars where the furniture is more style over substance and the drinks are more credit card than coin prices. This one is called Room. They also own a restaurant called Eat. Why am I letting that annoy me?

The organisers have done their best to make it romantic, just, I don't know, almost sarcastically so. Candles, roses, sexy jazz music playing softly, love-heart-shaped balloons almost everywhere you turn. And of course all of the drinks have stupid names like a 'Happy Ever After' and a 'Magical Night' – as though either of those things feel remotely possible tonight.

It's hard not to be cynical when the air is thick with the smell of booze and cheap aftershave... that said, the fact that I don't feel at all ready to move on romantically could be coming into play here, like a reflex to keep myself safe. But I'm here now, and the 'fun' will be kicking off soon, so I just need to get it over with. You know what they say: when in Room.

Our host tonight is a very enthusiastic woman called Julie – a woman who never should have been given an amp, because she hasn't quite grasped the idea that the microphone is to remove the need to shout, not something you need to shout into to make it work. I'm not quite sure what she's doing to generate such excruciating noises from the speaker, but I'm sitting right next to it and the high-pitched sounds and the crackling make me flinch every time. Shit, I've caught her eye. And – great – she's coming this way.

'Is everything okay?' she asks me, approaching me with a degree of caution. The kind that makes me wonder whether these things usually kick off. 'You look a little... crazy.'

Way to boost a girl's self-confidence, eh? Because men just love crazy.

'Oh, I'm okay,' I reassure her. 'It's just the feedback.'

I'm lucky she isn't talking to me through the mic right now, given that she's leaning on the amp while she chats to me, or the noise would be even worse.

She sighs.

'Look, I'm sure there are many things they could write down about your personality or your appearance, why you might not be for them, but everyone is different. Different folk like different things. People are into all sorts – I've seen it all, trust me. Someone is bound to like you.'

Oh, fantastic, she thinks I'm worrying about the feedback I'll get from my speed dates, not the screeching sound she keeps inadvertently forcing out of the speaker.

'Thank you,' I say politely.

She heads off back to her post, smiling like she's done her good deed for the day, oblivious to the fact that I'm trying to trip her up with the daggers I'm shooting her way. Because what did she mean: there are many things they could write down about your personality or your appearance? She can't know my personality, obviously, but she can see me. What's wrong with the way I look? What could anyone possibly take that much issue with that they wouldn't even give me a shot? I'm dressed up, made-up, I've done my hair. I look like I've made an effort and that's what people want, right? Except now I'm second-guessing whether I'm too big or too small, if my nose isn't right, if I have eyebrow blindness (again – I seem to come down with a case every couple of years). Why am I even considering this? As

I've said, I don't care. I'm not here to impress or disappoint anyone (although Lord knows I'm anticipating the latter now), I'm here to get this over with. I'll be back home before I know it, in bed, reading a book or watching TV, with a huge cup of tea, all on my own, just the way I like it.

But first...

'Now, I need you all to be open-minded, okay?' Julie bellows through the mic. It's hard to believe she's ever done this before. Hosting an event, using a mic, speaking to people generally... 'If you like what you see, score highly, if you don't, stick it in the feedback,' she continues.

God, I hate that. I really hate that. Is that really necessary? Fair enough, not everyone has to like everyone, but I don't know how much any of the women sitting here at these tables need written feedback to support the low scores they might get from the line of men queued up at the side of the room. Then again, I don't know what's worse, reading why you got a two out of ten for personality, or never knowing why.

I scan the crowd of men as they all find their starting tables. The event is for young, fun, sexy singles who are up for anything. And me, I guess, because as I'm sure you can tell, I'm not feeling all that fun or sexy, I'm up for very little, and to be honest when I'm in crowds like this I don't feel all that young any more, even though some of the people here are clearly older than me. Sometimes youth feels like a state of mind. My grandparents are in their eighties and you'd never guess. Good spirits (my gran would say positivity, my grandad would say whisky) and infallible optimism are all it takes. My cynicism, pessimism and general 'can't be arsed' approach must stick a decade each on me. We'll see if anyone mentions it in the feedback, if I even read it.

I glance down at my scorecard. A neat little grid where I'm

supposed to jot down names, scores, notes and ultimately either tick a box for 'yes' or 'no'. Can it really be that easy to find love? I seriously doubt it.

The bell rings and a man plonks himself opposite me, inadvertently pushing the table far enough to make the candle flicker. The loud screech of the legs on the floor makes everyone look at us for a second.

'See, we're already the most checked-out couple in the room,' he jokes.

I know I'm certainly checked out.

'I'm Brad,' he tells me.

Of course he's called Brad. Men with muscles like that always have a cool-guy name, don't they?

He raises an arm to push his hair back, oh-so blatantly flexing his bicep as he does, setting out his stall from the off.

His T-shirt is so tight you could mistake it for being sprayed on – it's distracting, but not in a sexy way, I'm finding my eyes darting from seam to seam, waiting to see which one splits first.

'Do you have a name?' he prompts me. 'Or have you forgotten it?'

I don't think he's joking. In fact, I could swear he gave a subtle nod to my hair – my blonde locks. Does he think I'm dumb? If either of us looks like we could have forgotten our name, it would definitely be him. If not his name, then definitely how to spell it.

'Cleo,' I tell him.

'Looking at my arms, huh?' he says with a grin.

I am, but not for the reason he thinks I am.

'Well, I bench 315, squat 415, deadlift 550,' he tells me, not that I understand a word of it. 'And most important of all, the one I'm sure you're interested in – hip thrust, 650.'

It's only his wink that tips me off to this clearly being some kind of sexual thing and – ew.

'Do you go to the gym, Cleo?' he asks.

'I used to,' I reply. 'My local had a café that did this amazing baked potato. They took it off the menu, I was gutted.'

'What's your PB?' he asks.

'My PB?'

'Your personal best,' he adds.

'Oh, right,' I reply. 'Two.'

'Two?' he repeats back to me. 'Just two?'

'Just two?' I clap back. 'I was pretty hungry, but three baked potatoes is a bit excessive.'

His face falls. It doesn't take mine long to follow.

'Ah, you didn't mean the food.'

'Erm, no... no, I didn't.'

Brad looks at me in a way that reminds me that: be yourself is not good advice when it comes to trying to attract most men.

'Yeah, I mostly just went for the café,' I tell him.

'I couldn't even tell you if mine had a café,' he replies. 'I take a shake, so...'

Well, that's this conversation dead in the water. I need to get it back on track.

'So, do you watch much TV?' I ask.

'Sometimes, at the gym...'

Bloody hell, is it always the gym with him?

'What about reality shows?' I press on. 'Do you enjoy shows like *Love Island* or *Welcome to Singledom*?'

'I've never watched *Love Island* but that *Welcome to Singledom* is all right,' he says. 'That's the one where the couples have to survive on a deserted island?'

I nod.

'Yeah, I like that, because the lads have to be strong and

sharp and that,' he says. 'The lasses just have to be hot and pick the right bloke. I reckon the girls would be fighting over me, don't you think?'

'Oh, yeah, of course,' I reply.

'I think it might be the same tonight,' he says, puffing up his chest. 'So, if you want me, better say something to sell yourself now...'

The buzzer sounds, prompting the men to move on. Saved by the bell.

As much as it pains me to do it, I make a note to say that, yes, Brad has made the shortlist. Hopefully the only way is up.

The next man to sit down in front of me is wearing a T-shirt with a bunch of different cryptocurrencies on it. It's not looking good, is it?

'Hey, I'm Callum, everyone calls me Cal,' he tells me as he makes himself more comfortable.

'I'm Cleo, hello,' I say back.

'Are you looking for a man in finance?' he asks with a wiggle of his eyebrows.

I'm not. Not at all.

Callum might work in finance but he isn't very tall and his eyes are brown.

'I'm looking for a man who likes to take risks, who is looking for an adventure,' I reply.

'Risk is a big part of my job,' he says. 'I'm this close to making my first mil.'

He holds his finger and his thumb about a centimetre apart and smiles like I might be about to fall at his feet. There's a Shania Twain song for moments like this, and it isn't 'You're Still the One'.

'Cooooool,' I say, holding on the word a little longer than can possibly be sincere. He's oblivious though. They're all always oblivious. I meet men like this all of the time and it's always the same old story. Sometimes I wish I could mix things up a bit. 'Could you live without Wi-Fi?' I ask, moving things along.

'Wi-Fi? What? No, of course not,' he says – now he's looking at me like I'm an idiot. 'Why would I? Why would anyone? Don't be so stupid.'

Gosh, I just love it when men call me stupid.

'Not being dramatic at all, I'd rather die,' he continues and I believe him.

The buzzer sounds and Cal leaves. Big fat no for Cal. It's also a no for Bart, the poet, and Ellis, the introvert, forced to come here by his friends. Mike, the personal trainer and part-time theme park character gets a yes, despite bragging to me about how dressing up as a cartoon dog is a great way to 'pick up mums' and women who want to 'rub his belly'. I think Mike might need putting on a different kind of list too – more of a register, if anything.

I don't know if tonight feels a little more bleak than usual or if I'm just so, so sick of looking for Brads and Mikes. Every conversation cements for me that there is in fact no one out there for me. Not one man on this planet I can stand spending more than a few minutes with.

Looking at my form, I can see that the next speed date is the last. Just one more man, one more boring conversation, one more short burst of disappointment and then I can go home.

'Hi,' he says.

I look up. He's taller than the others, broad-shouldered but without looking like he's inflated segments of his T-shirt like a lot of the gym bros do. His dark brown hair is blown back, and it looks almost too good, the kind that requires a routine and products, and he's got enough stubble to pass as a beard, but not so much you can't see the dimples in his cheeks when he smiles.

I'm surprised, not by how good he looks, but by how good I think he looks. I don't usually get anything at first sight apart from annoyed, but this guy has actually caught my eye.

'I'm Lockie, nice to meet you,' he says, sliding into the seat opposite me.

I feel... I don't know. Like I need to remind myself to play it cool? But I don't, at all, I just need to talk to him, find out if he's what I'm looking for, and put a cross or a tick next to his name.

'Cli'm Leo,' I say. Nope, try again, Cleo. 'Sorry – I'm...'

My voice trails off. What is wrong with me? Maybe I'm just tired. Lockie laughs.

'For a moment I thought that was a request,' he replies cheekily. 'I'm a Leo. You are?'

'A sceptic,' I tell him. 'Whatever I am, it reckons I'm an optimist, and enthusiastic, and... nah.'

'I meant your name,' he says through a big grin.

'Right, yeah, sorry, of course you did,' I reply, finally getting a grip. 'I'm Cleo.'

I notice his eyebrows raise slightly.

'Nice to meet you, Cleo,' he replies.

'So, what do you do, Lockie?' I ask.

'Really?' he replies with a chuckle. 'We're doing this? Okay, tell you what, why don't you guess what I do?'

The urge to be a little cheeky is too hard to resist.

'You look like you lift things,' I say.

'Only the mood,' he replies.

'Carry things, then... a waiter?'

'I've been told I serve before, but not like that,' he says.

'Astronaut,' I reply, going for something completely different.

'Well, now you're just making fun of me,' he claps back. 'I think I'll keep you guessing.'

'Fair enough, then I'll do the same,' I reply.

'So, what brings you here, Cleo?' he asks.

'The same reason you're here,' I reply.

'Any bites?' he asks.

'None yet, but the night is young,' I tell him, my flirtatious tone still very much there.

I don't actually have to flirt with the men I meet. Interesting that I'm choosing to.

The bell rings, signalling the end of our seven minutes, and I'm almost angry about it.

'Tell me something about you that would surprise me,' I suggest.

'I have two degrees,' he begins.

'Really?' I squeak.

He laughs.

'Really – why, are the people you usually meet at these things dummies?'

'Well... yeah,' I confess. 'But I don't mean, like, they're bad at maths, because I'm bad at maths. One guy tonight called me stupid.'

'Well, he was definitely a dummy then,' Lockie replies. 'I hope you didn't give him a high score.'

'Not a chance,' I confirm.

'Do you think you'll give me a high score?'

'Higher than him,' I joke.

For a few seconds we just look at each other, in comfortable silence, and smile.

This time, instead of the buzzer sounding, music starts playing – 'Can't Help Falling in Love' by Elvis Presley.

'That's your lot,' Julie bellows down the mic. 'But we've got a bit of a song to end the night so, if you found the one, now is your chance to have a little dance while I see if we have many matches.'

Almost over. Almost...

'Do you want to dance?' Lockie asks me. 'One girl was a bit intense – she started asking me what I wanted to call "our" kids. Help me out?'

I laugh.

'Okay, sure,' I reply.

It's just one dance and then I can get back to business.

Lockie takes me by the hand and leads me out onto the dance floor. We move our bodies closer together. He wraps one arm around my waist, I drape one around his neck. We join our other hands, holding them close. Lockie is so much taller than me so it feels right to rest my head against his chest. We just sort of snap together, instinctively, and move gently to the music.

It's been a long time since I slow danced with a man – it's been a long time since a man held me full stop. It's hard not to melt into his big, strong arms. This buff, funny, dreamy, intelligent man. Honestly, what is he doing at speed dating?

I feel a tapping on my shoulder. Oh, great, it's Julie.

'Cleo?' she checks and I nod. 'Can I borrow you?'

'Erm, yeah, okay,' I reply.

I follow Julie over to her desk.

'I've just realised who you are,' she tells me. 'The one scouting for the reality dating show?'

'Yeah, that's me,' I reply.

'They told me I should pass on details for the people you wanted,' she replies. 'So... any luck?'

'Just a few,' I reply. 'Brad, Mike and... and...' Should I? 'And Lockie.'

'Great,' she says. 'I'll slip them the info with their matches.'

'Great,' I say back to her. 'Then I guess I'll get going...'

I look over at Lockie as he chats to some of the other guys here. I want to go over, talk to him some more, but that's not why I'm here, I'm not looking for men for me – God forbid – I'm looking for men for the show. I work for *Welcome to Singledom* and part of my job is finding contestants to take part in the survival dating show. It definitely takes a certain kind of person, to want to take part in the show, but people seem to love to watch it.

I should leave but... I don't know, maybe Lockie could be good? A nice change, to have someone a bit smarter, not your usual gym-going, content-creating, full-of-themselves top shaggers we usually cast.

Would he even want to take part in a show like that though? I guess we'll find out, when Julie hands over my details, but for now I'd better go. I'm not here for me – I'm never here for me. I can't even think about putting myself out there, not after what happened. Best I focus on finding love (or showmances, most of the time) for the contestants.

Love is the last thing I'm looking for.

2

Don't get me wrong, I love living in London, but London in January is a sure-fire way to work out the optimists from the pessimists.

I think it's probably because, even though December is cold and dark, all the bright lights and sparkle of Christmas take the edge off. The decorations, the beautiful shopfronts and markets, the Winter Wonderland – come January, all gone, just the empty spaces and bad weather. The sky looks extra gloomy today, although it could be how I'm feeling. It's one of those days where I wish I could have stayed in bed but instead I'm trekking across the city, weaving in and out of crowds of people who probably also wished they didn't have to get up today. It's cold and it's wet. Not even my emotional support latte is doing much to take the edge off.

I toyed with the idea of a New Year's resolution, and the best thing I could come up with (other than continuing to swear off men) was to stop spending £10 on a coffee and a croissant on my walk to work. You might think I've failed, because I have a coffee, but I got a cookie instead of a croissant, taking the price from £10 to £8.50. Saving £1.50 a day for – what? – 260 working days a year, that's an annual saving of £390. I'll be on the property ladder before I know it!

Sarcasm aside, I don't really buy into that 'new year, new me' crap. There's just no way that singing 'Auld Lang Syne' and counting down with Big Ben can suddenly usher you into being a better person. Plus, why wait for the end of the year to be better? You can do it any day. Or you can stay who you are, unashamedly, because really, is the world going to change if I drink less coffee? Probably not for the better, I can be a grumpy cow without caffeine (yes, this is me on caffeine – I know, I'm a delight).

There's a reason I am the way I am. Last year was… well, it's not worth talking about, let's just say I've no desire to look back at it too closely anytime soon. It's in a mental box marked 2025 that I have no intentions of opening for a while.

The only thing that is new this year is that someone is on my mind – Lockie. I know, I only interacted with him for like ten minutes, and it was for work, but he made quite the impression. I think it's a work thing though. I just think he would be so much better than the usual kind of bloke we cast. I'm professionally thinking about him, I swear. I'm not attracted to him… well, no, okay, I'll admit he's gorgeous, anyone into guys would think he was gorgeous, but it starts and stops there. I think Lockie is a catch – but for work.

I work in casting, on *Welcome to Singledom*, a reality TV survival dating show. Think something like *Survivor*, or *Naked and Afraid*, combined with something young and sexy like *Love Island*. We plonk single men and women on an island where they have to couple up to survive. It's survival of the fittest – you want to find yourself a partner who can help you not only survive until the end but, for the big finale, there's a public vote to win too. If a couple simply survive together then their prize is nothing more than bragging rights. But if the public vote says viewers think it's true love, then the winning couple get £100k to share. Of course, most of the contestants these days are on there to find fame and fortune, not love, so the prize money is by the by compared to the sponsorship deals they can bag themselves after the show. This is why I think someone like Lockie would be great. These days it's always influencers and wannabe Z-listers who think the show will raise their profile, and if it wasn't this show, it would be a different one. It's always the same gym bros, the same girls – who often quite literally have the same face, because they tend to go to the same celebrity surgeon for their TV-ready faces.

It's no secret that ratings have been dipping over the years. We've gone from must-watch, everyone's-talking-about-it TV to almost like a parody of ourselves. A rite of passage for fame-hungry, veneer-clad, beautiful people who go to secure their collabs with clothing retailers like ABO, or to get a free hair transplant, or whatever. It's not churning out household names and nation's sweethearts like it used to. The post-show deals are drying up, reserved only for those who make themselves the main characters, and it just all feels so contrived and soulless. This is why I think we need to switch it up, to go back to people who are more real, people like Lockie. People with more than just drive and a ring light. People with substance, with intelligence. People you want to watch, on a show where anything could happen, where anyone could win.

All of the above is why we're trying something new with the casting this year – my idea, of course. Going out and about, meeting real people, asking them if they want to take part. I'm sick of scanning Instagram for who is popular, or being approached by agents with 'the next big reality star'. I'm not sure how much luck I had at the speed dating – Lockie felt like a great catch, but Julie passed on my details to everyone I requested, and I haven't heard from him yet. We'll just have to wait and see.

Transitioning from the cold street to the lobby of The Cactus building, where OutOfTheBox (the *Welcome to Singledom* production company) is based, the warm air wraps me up like a big hug – not that the vibe here is at all cosy. It's all chrome and glass, with security guards eyeballing you suspiciously as you pass through the barrier, and then obviously everyone is coming here for work, so the place is just a blur of stressed-out people clutching coffee cups (or smoothies – I always notice an influx of smoothies in January).

I'm lucky enough to catch the lift solo, which means I can check out my make-up in the mirror, make sure my hair hasn't frizzed in the winter air. It's a brief pause, the only bit of calm I get during my workdays, before the doors open and it's more chaotic than ever. People are always running around with clipboards. I work here, and I'm never really sure why, but we always feel right on the edge of an emergency. There are live TV shows recorded here – everything from quiz shows to rolling news channels – so I always imagine it's something wild, like a major story breaking, rather than a particularly difficult quiz show host insisting his decaf coffee has caffeine in it and he wants someone fired.

I suppose one of the best things about working with people who want to be famous, instead of people who already are, is it means they're so eager to please – they want to make you happy, not get you fired because you watched them eat.

We're kicking the day off with a meeting so I head straight for the meeting room. Inside, I find Tara and Jamila scrolling TikToks together while they wait to get started. They're both a bit younger than me, in their mid-twenties, but for some reason they feel a lot younger than me – or, more specifically, I feel a lot older than them. Sometimes the Millennial vs Gen Z divide feels too real. Every now and then I'll have no idea what they're talking about, or they'll give me a look that makes me feel like I'm a thousand. It's not that I'm especially uncool, or out of touch, but sometimes I'll reference something from the nineties and they'll remind me that they weren't born.

'Cleo!' Tara says with an adorable squeak when she sees me. 'How did it go last night? Did you meet anyone fit? Anyone perfect for the new season?'

Jamila looks up from her phone, raising an eyebrow in anticipation. Tara is the friendly one, Jamila is the cool (verging on cold) one.

'I'm thinking from the smug look on her face that she did,' Jamila says dryly.

I'm not in love with being told I have a smug face, but it's nice to have something good to report back. Something to get excited about.

I hang up my coat and sink into a chair.

'I don't know if he's on board yet but I think I've found someone kind of perfect,' I tell them.

'Perfect?' Tara repeats back to me. 'My gosh, Cleo, tell us everything. Come on, spill. Name, age, location, job, hobbies, follower count, the size of his—'

'Morning,' Simon, the showrunner, says as he joins us. He throws his breakfast, a bagel with tuna and cheese (I could never, not first thing in the morning), down on the table like he's mad at it. Luckily it's well wrapped, because no one wants to have this meeting over a fishy table. 'I'm only hearing good news today. If you have anything bad to tell me, I highly suggest you resign.'

He's joking but he isn't. Simon isn't a man you want to get on the wrong side of. Of course, when you're pleasing him, if you can somehow worm your way into the position of his favourite (he always has one – and only one – favourite) then your working life is a dream. For everyone else it's kind of a nightmare, especially when the show is on the ropes, and the viewing figures just seem to keep going down and down. Do you know what, I think he's fired someone (not necessarily anyone who has done anything wrong though) each time the show has taken a hit in ratings. This year that person can't be me.

Simon is in his forties, but he almost defies age, he's demographic-less, he's too into his job to be anything but a vehicle for TV. It used to be that anything he touched turned to gold, but with *Welcome to Singledom* on the rocks, his reputation is getting away from him and he's not happy about it. Of course, it's not his fault, it's the incompetent staff, the dull contestants, the idiot viewers who don't know what's good for them. It's anyone's fault but his.

In my opinion the show isn't failing because of the fault of any one person or any particular thing, it's just that as we've moved from season to season it's become a bit samey, a bit predictable, and I think people just need to see something new, something to get them interested in the show again.

'Cleo has found us someone perfect,' Tara tells him.

'He's different to our usual type,' I'm quick to add, before Simon gets his hopes up.

'Different?' he says, narrowing his eyes at me. 'We don't want different, and we definitely don't want perfect – we need a villain.'

Simon is of the opinion that it's easier to get viewers to hate a contestant than it is to get them to love them.

'I mean he's perfect for the show, for mixing things up,' I clarify. 'But to have a villain, you need a hero...'

'Okay, go on, tell us about your perfect hero,' he says as he unwraps his bagel. The sarcasm in his voice is unmistakable but it's not worth me correcting him again.

'I think the viewers need someone to get behind, someone they like, someone they can care about,' I explain. 'Like this guy, for example, is sharp, funny, genuine. Intelligent too. He feels real. Viewers could actually root for him.'

Simon tilts his head like he's considering it – am I finally getting through to him? Am I making him see that we need to give people someone they want to tune into, rather than someone they love to hate?

'What's Mr Perfect's name?' Tara asks. 'I'll look out for him, in case he replies. Did you give him a card?'

'The speed-dating organiser did,' I reply. 'His name is Lockie.'

There's a pause. Then they all burst out laughing.

'What?' I dare to ask, but I'm not sure I want to know. You know when you can just tell that people are laughing at you, not with you?

'You're joking,' Jamila says. 'Right?'

'I'm not,' I reply, confused. 'What's so funny?'

And right on cue, the door swings open, and of fucking course, in he strolls. Lockie.

He's dressed a little more casually today, in a dark green, muscle-hugging Ralph Lauren jumper and a pair of black trousers. He's carrying an iPad and a smoothie. Of course he's one of the smoothie lot.

My stomach drops.

'Well, well,' Simon says, grinning. 'Speak of the devil. Cleo's just been telling us that she met the most perfect man last night. And that man... was you.'

Lockie's grin widens. He looks positively flattered.

'Oh, really?' he says, glancing at me. 'I'm perfect, eh?'

I wonder if my face is as red as it feels. I feel so hot you could fry an egg on my face – which is a funny coincidence because, boy, do I feel stupid right now.

'That's... not exactly what I said,' I mutter, trying to will the embarrassment away.

'Close enough,' Jamila says unhelpfully. 'I can't believe you thought Lockie was there to date. Didn't anyone tell you he's joining you in casting?'

Oh, no. Oh, God, no.

Lockie drops into the chair opposite me, in such a cool-guy way, leaning back like he owns the place.

'Cleo is just joking around,' Lockie says. 'We met last night, had a good chat.'

I narrow my eyes at him. Obviously I didn't know who he was but... did he know me? Was he messing with me?

'All right,' Simon says, clapping his hands together, moving us along. 'Let's talk plans. New season, new angle. Cleo reckons we need more "real" people – whatever that means. Lockie? Give us your expert opinion, for the love of God.'

'We need top-tier influencers. Micro-celebs. People who'll bring their followings and stir up drama,' Lockie replies. He doesn't even hesitate.

'How can you be so sure?' I shoot back, quicker than I should.

'Because Lockie used to work on *Made in Yorkshire*,' Simon answers for him.

Oh, fab, Leeds's answer to *The Only Way is Essex* and *Geordie*

Shore. Made in Yorkshire, a show known for 'scripted reality', aka manufactured storylines. It's the worst one for it.

'We're abandoning reality?' I check, irked.

'No, we're embracing storylines,' Simon continues. 'That's what Lockie is here to do. Craft storylines.'

'But that's not genuine,' I protest.

'It is actually,' Lockie pipes up. 'I just... guide the facts. Present them in the most entertaining way. Audiences want fireworks, not dull authenticity. I don't make anyone do or say anything they wouldn't normally do, I just help them get to their own conclusions – and act on them – much quicker. At a better pace for TV.'

'So, you manipulate them?' I clarify. 'That's not ethical.'

'No, how many millions of viewers we've lost, that's what's not ethical,' Simon insists.

I mean, where to even begin with that one? A comment so dumb, it would actually kill my brain cells if I were to challenge it.

'I'm telling you, people are sick of all the fake stuff, we shouldn't be leaning into it, we should be pulling away from it,' I insist.

'In my experience—' Lockie starts.

'In your experience, everything is fake,' I interrupt him. 'Nothing is real.'

Simon waves a hand.

'All right, kids, enough,' he tells us. 'Cleo, you find me your "real people". Lockie, you get me influencers and celebs. Try all the usual channels for casting, plus anything else you can come up with, and then we'll see who brings me the best contestants for the job. How about that?'

'May the best man win,' Lockie says, trying to sound like a good sport.

'She will,' I reply, backing myself.

And on that note the meeting moves on. Schedules, budgets, brand tie-ins. I barely hear any of it. I'm too busy trying not to burst into flames every time Lockie flashes that smug grin in my direction.

'Okay, let's leave these two to try to find a way to play nice,' Simon tells Tara and Jamila. 'Or not. Whatever gets the best results.'

They leave us alone, just the two of us, sitting at opposite sides of the meeting table, staring at each other like we're facing off. How are we supposed to be working together and competing? How is that going to work? And what the hell is his problem, sitting over there, smiling?

'What?' he asks with a chuckle.

'You know what,' I reply.

'I really don't,' he says. 'Unless you're just annoyed that I have better ideas than you...'

'Okay, first of all, you don't,' I'm quick to remind him. 'But what I'm talking about is last night. You knew who I was, didn't you?'

'Well, yeah, because I'm smart,' he replies.

'Then why did you act like it was a date?' I ask.

'I thought you were doing a bit,' he tells me. 'I thought you knew I was the new guy and you were messing with me. But now I know how much you fancy me, that you were flirting with me – Cleo, I'm flattered.'

'Oh, get over yourself,' I snap.

He laughs at me, which only annoys me more.

'I thought you were just another bloke, show fodder, someone I could use for work – I wasn't there to flirt,' I insist.

'And yet you ended up dancing with me,' he reminds me. 'Something to think about.'

He holds his hands in the air as he gets up from his seat.

'I mean it,' I tell him. 'I am not interested in you at all – beyond professionally.'

'That's a start,' he says, amused. 'I'm looking forward to working with you. It's going to be fun.'

Fun? Ha. It really isn't.

As he strolls out, casual as he walked in, he hums the tune to 'Can't Help Falling in Love' – the song we danced to last night.

Oh, it's not going to be fun. It's going to be infuriating. I don't want to work with him, I want to murder him.

I guess I'm stuck with him – but I don't think this office is big enough for both of us.

3

Considering casting days are such a big part of my job, you'd think I'd have them down to a fine art by now.

The problem is that so many people turn up, all with their own idea about what they think I want to see, what they need to do to secure their spot on TV. What I see is rarely what I want though. People try too hard to be entertaining when the real beauty of reality TV is finding the right people, not the loudest or the most outgoing, and putting them together. Figuring out that mix is what makes me so good at my job – and it's not at all like what Lockie does, which is purposefully putting people together who will clash and then putting them in situations that will cause trouble and then whipping them up, telling them what to say and do, and then leaving them to it. Yes, everyone signs disclaimers saying they're up for anything, and yes, 'that's entertainment', but I really can't get on board with pulling the pin on an emotional grenade and just lobbing it in amongst them. Call me sad, but I do like to think we can help some of these people find love as well as fame.

Casting days are where hope goes to die. I always count my

blessings that I get to be on this side of the table, choosing people, rather than on the other side of the room, desperately hoping someone picks me. I love working in reality TV, even with all its faults, but I could never, ever take part in one of these shows. The thought of surrendering control and putting myself out there for all to see, handing over every piece of me for people to dissect online – no, no, no. I couldn't hack it. I'd sit on social media, searching my own name, not because I love myself but because sometimes (like most people) I don't, and you can always trust the online public to let you know what they think is wrong with you.

You would think it was a glamorous process but it's sort of bleak. We're in a rented conference suite above a budget chain hotel, the kind of venue that usually hosts Alan Partridge-type seminars and careers events that usually just trick you into signing up for an MLM sales opportunity that almost always ends up costing people money, not earning them it. The carpet has that suspicious sticky feel when you walk across it, the kind that makes you wonder how it got that bad, but you also really hope to never find out the answer. The walls are a shade of yellowy cream (I suspect they didn't use to be) and the lighting is so harsh, you better hope you've primed, contoured and fixed yourself within an inch of your life. Lights like these don't just showcase little imperfections, they actually manifest ones you don't really have.

And yet... this where stars are born. Sort of.

'Well, this is glamorous, isn't it?' Lockie mutters, as he takes his seat at our pop-up table. We're like Simon Cowell and Sharon Osbourne – just for horny influencers instead of wannabe singers.

Lockie looks so laid-back, like he's a guest here, and this is a luxury resort.

'It is what it is,' I reply, skimming applications on my iPad. 'It gets the job done.'

'Ah, yes,' he says, smirking. 'Nothing says TV and "true love" like a flickering light and the faint smell of damp.'

I ignore him and glance at the line of hopefuls stretching out outside the room. I can see a bunch of them, through the windows, and I can already tell it's the same old, same old.

Lots of fake tan, white teeth, surgically plumped-up lips – and I'm not even just talking about the girls. Even the men feel the pressure to be perfect.

Tara mans the door with her iPad, calling people in like she's working the door at a very exclusive nightclub.

Lockie and I are waiting at our table, sitting in silence now, for our first hopeful. And then the hundreds if not thousands that will follow.

The first contestant shuffles in.

'Yo, I'm Rick,' he says proudly, flexing in a T-shirt so tight I think I just saw a few of the stitches pop. 'I'm a PT and fitness influencer.'

'What's your follower count?' Lockie asks before I can even open my mouth.

'Eighty-five K on Insta. Hundred and forty K on TikTok,' Rick tells us casually.

Lockie's eyes light up.

'Decent numbers,' Lockie tells him. 'Congrats.'

I force a smile.

'And what are you hoping to get out of the show, Rick?' I ask.

'Exposure,' he says immediately. 'Brand deals, a few more followers. Oh, and maybe a girlfriend.'

He tags that on at the end, like he thinks it's what I want to hear, but even if it was, he would need to actually mean it.

'Maybe?' I repeat.

He shrugs.

'Depends who's fit – have you signed up any worldies yet?'

'Not yet, but the day is young,' Lockie replies with a laugh.

The rest of the interview doesn't produce anything eye-opening. He's just another typical contestant, there will be a thousand more like him passing through here today – and, I know, if it ain't broke... but *Welcome to Singledom* is broken. Doing the same old, same old and hoping for a better result isn't going to help.

'He's great,' Lockie says when it's just the two of us. 'He's self-aware. He looks the part. He's got his options wide open.'

'He's muscles and teeth and he's going to make a play for the hottest girl – until a hotter girl comes in,' I reply.

'Which brings drama,' he replies.

'Which brings nothing new,' I correct him. 'Nothing worth watching.'

The next few blur together in a haze of the usual. A girl who called herself a 'future entrepreneur' but, when pressed on what that meant, couldn't tell us, beyond saying she's going to 'get her bag' when she wins. A man in a comedy suit who insisted he DJ'd in Ibiza but then admitted, under the mildest questioning, that he just made the playlist for his last lads' holiday. And then there was the woman who burst into tears when we asked her what her greatest strength was, before insisting it was her 'emotional strength' while wiping her eyes on her sleeve.

Lockie puts a tick next to each of their names.

'She's messy. People love messy,' he whispers after the crying woman leaves.

'She's vulnerable,' I whisper back. 'And this show will eat her alive.'

'Exactly,' he says – but then he catches himself. 'Cleo, she said it herself, she's emotionally strong.'

'She sobbed it,' I correct him.

'And maybe this is what she needs to make her fantasy a reality,' he replies.

'My God, you're the most delusional one here,' I point out.

'And you're the grumpiest,' he replies. 'You're the best example of what we're not looking for.'

'And you are?'

'Someone recently said I was perfect...' he teases.

Yeah, before I knew what a bellend he was. But I'll keep that to myself for now.

I just roll my eyes.

Next up we have Damien, a twenty-six-year-old with awkward body language, hair covering his eyes (but I can still tell he's struggling with eye contact), dirty trainers – not the usual type we get at all.

'Hey, I'm Damien, I work in IT support for a bank,' he tells us, his voice low and soft.

'So why are you applying, Damien?' Lockie asks.

'My mates put me up to it,' he replies with a shrug. 'They sort of dared me so... yeah... here I am.'

I cock my head curiously.

'So, why did you go through with it?' I ask. 'If your mates were telling you to do it, why did you listen to them?'

He just shrugs as he searches for the words he's looking for.

'Because I'm always overlooked,' he says eventually. 'No one ever sees me so... this is a way to get seen.'

Huh, that's interesting. Usually people applying like being seen and want to have more eyes on them, but Damien just wants to be noticed for a change, even if it means taking himself out of his comfort zone. This wouldn't be elevating for Damien, it would be life-changing. Character-building. A chance for him to find himself – not just get himself a job on Insta flogging supplements.

'What do you think you would bring to the island?' I ask.

'And to the show?' Lockie adds.

'I think... honesty,' Damien replies. 'I don't want to play games, I just want to be myself, see how it goes.'

'We play a lot of games on the show,' Lockie reminds him.

'I didn't mean like that,' Damien tells him, his cheeks flushing lightly. I know he didn't, and I'm sure Lockie did too. 'I'll play those games – I just don't want to mess anyone around.'

'That's great, Damien, thanks so much,' I tell him.

The second he's out the door I turn to Lockie.

'Don't look at me like that,' he says with a laugh.

'Like what?' I reply.

'Like you're going to say we should cast him,' he says.

'I think someone like Damien, someone real, and genuine, who could actually get something out of the experience is exactly who people want to see – they want someone they can root for,' I point out.

'And this is exactly why the show is flagging,' he replies. 'He would be so boring. You heard him say he'll actively avoid drama. So unless he's going to be dishing out IT tips while he's sandwiched between two girls in the hot tub, he's not going to have any survival skills.'

'IT is a modern survival skill,' I suggest.

Lockie snorts with laughter.

'If anyone on the island ever needs an IT skill to survive, I'll eat my hand,' he claps back. 'It's a desert island.'

'Right, except it's not, is it? Because large parts of it are rigged up with cameras, lighting equipment, microphones – it's a TV set. And the luxury room, where said hot tub is, attached to the studio where all of us are. It's not actually a deserted island, you know.'

'It is this year,' he corrects me.

'Erm, what?' I reply. 'What do you mean, it is this year?'

'The crew won't be stationed on the island this year,' he says, still not really giving me much more information.

'Of course we will,' I insist. 'That's how it works. We stay close. Usher them around, if anyone unlocks the luxury suite we let them in, we prep the new additions there and put them in at the right times. Even Simon lives on the island, to oversee everything.'

He shakes his head, smug as ever.

'Not any more,' he corrects me. 'I convinced Simon that the stakes need to be higher.'

'Higher?'

'Yeah.' He leans back in his chair, oh-so proud of himself. 'This year, the crew's staying offshore. On a boat. Out of sight. That way, the contestants are truly deserted.'

I just stare at him.

'Or,' I say finally, 'we could just edit it to make them look deserted. Like we've always done without issue. That's literally what editing is for. You know this is a TV show, right? It's not real.'

'But if they feel alone,' he says, his eyebrows raising as his eyes widen, 'they'll act differently. Raw. Unfiltered. Like rats in a maze, only sexier.'

Presumably anything is sexier than that.

'You're a sicko,' I tell him plainly.

'Aw, thanks,' he replies. 'I just love my job. Shall we see another person?'

I really, really don't like the idea of being stationed on a boat. It's bad enough that we have to take a boat to the island, I get terrible seasickness, but to find out I'm supposed to be working on one for the duration of the show? That's crazy. I have to find a way to veto this.

We go through more interviews, and they're almost all as expected. The influencers, the wannabe celebs, the people who think it will launch their careers if they turn up and showcase their talents like singing or magic tricks. I'll admit, it's hard to find a story here, a narrative that will drive the show and keep people tuning in. I suppose that's why he's here, Lockie, to manufacture some story, but I hate the idea of that too.

'He seems like he might have jealousy issues,' Lockie says after another potential (with zero potential) leaves the room.

'Yeah, good luck getting him through the mental health check,' I reply.

'We could prep him to pass,' Lockie thinks out loud.

'You're kind of horrible,' I say.

'And you're very naive,' he claps back with a laugh.

I swear, he thinks I'm flirting with him, as opposed to insulting him to his face.

We stare at each other until the next hopeful comes in: a woman with long extensions, lashes you could sweep the floor with, a red body-con dress that looks like it was sprayed on.

'Hiya!' she practically sings, slipping into the chair with a flip of her hair. Her eyes flick straight to Lockie. 'Well, hello!'

'Hi,' he replies with a cheeky smile.

'So I'm Mel, and my brand is, like: a sexy nightmare in red lipstick and high heels.'

'Sounds more like a dream come true,' Lockie tells her with a smile.

It's already a no from me. We've been there, done that – every girl who takes part in the show these days thinks that they can become the main character by being a nightmare contestant. Of course, Lockie writes down yes almost instantly.

'So, tell us why you want to be on the show,' I prompt her.

She giggles, leaning forward so far I'm surprised she doesn't topple out of her seat... or her dress.

'Honestly? I just know I'd smash it,' she says confidently. 'I've got the looks, the banter, and like...' She winks at Lockie. 'I'll just do, like, whatever it takes. I'm great entertainment.'

'You read the disclaimer, right?' he says. 'You're aware that anything goes – anything can be filmed, anytime?'

'Oh, deffo,' she says, waving a hand like it's nothing. 'Anything goes is my motto. You'd be amazed what I'll do... Film me anywhere. Film me on the toilet, if you need to. Some people like that.'

Lockie laughs and jots down a note that I can't quite see.

'Well, we stop short of filming you on the toilet,' he tells her. 'But the contract does say that the island is being filmed constantly, day and night, and all footage is released for TV. So, as long as you're good with that.'

'Hundo-P,' she replies.

Hundo-P...!

'Well, Mel, I think you'd be fantastic,' Lockie tells her.

'Squeeee,' is the excitable sound she makes back at him.

When she finally totters out, leaving a cloud of perfume and a trail of body glitter in her wake, I turn to him.

'Really?' I say in disbelief. 'That's your idea of fantastic?'

'She's fun. She's confident. She's not afraid to play the game,' he replies.

'She kept telling you that she'd do anything to be on the show,' I reply. 'She told us that we could film her on the toilet – that's desperation. She can't actually want us to broadcast her on the toilet...'

'First of all, we wouldn't do that, the majority of people wouldn't want to see that,' he replies, in a way that suggests that, if more people did want to see it, he'd be all over it. 'And anyway, desperation makes great TV.'

The assistant ushers in the next contestant before I can reply, a tall bloke in a jumper and jeans. Not jacked, but handsome in an unassuming, quiet way. He sits down without fuss, resting his hands on his lap like he's here for a job interview.

'Hi,' he says. 'I'm Jon. Thanks for having me.'

Points already for politeness.

'Thanks for coming,' I say warmly. 'So, why do you want to take part?'

'I want to see how far I can get using my brain,' he says matter-of-factly, cutting to the chase. 'I'm not the biggest or the fastest, but I think I'm strategic. I'd like to test myself. See if I can out-think the competition – see how far I can get.'

Now this I like the sound of!

'What kind of strategies do you have up your sleeve?' I ask.

'Forming alliances. Reading people. Convincing the stronger guys to do things for me. I figure brains can always manipulate brawn. Maybe the women will be drawn to that for a change,' he points out.

I can't help but smile. This is good – something fresh. And he even said 'women' instead of 'girls' or 'chicks', which I like too.

'I think you could bring something different to the show,' I tell him. 'What do you think, Lockie?'

He's been quiet. Perhaps that's a good sign.

'So physically, you'd struggle,' Lockie tells him. 'You think you can talk your way into winning, but that might not go down well. People like to see one of the boys – loyalty. Can a lone wolf really win?'

'He's smart. He's got a game plan. That's exactly the kind of angle we need,' I say to Lockie in a hushed-ish tone. 'No one ever has an actual strategy.'

'It's reality TV, not chess,' he replies. 'You get fireworks from fire and explosives, not logic.'

What am I even supposed to say to that?

We let Jon go, like he's our child and we're sending him to his room to save him watching us bicker in front of him.

'I'm just saying, we won't be able to push him into a story-line, if he's that smart,' Lockie says.

'There are no storylines to push people into,' I point out, irritated. 'People have free will.'

'You'll have free will too. To go down the jobcentre when this series gets cancelled because you cast Mr Shy and Mr Smartarse,' he says through a grin.

'Because Little Miss Watch-me-on-the-toilet is going to save the day,' I reply.

I can't imagine the two of us agreeing on anything.

By six o'clock, I'm knackered. My eyes feel bleary as I look over my notes scrawled with names, pros, cons and the occasional doodle. Lockie, of course, still looks maddeningly fresh, like he could do another eight hours without so much as a coffee to pump him up.

'Well,' he says, with a satisfied sigh, 'that was fun.'

'You thought that was fun?' I check. 'It was closer to torture.'

'Torture for you maybe,' he replies. 'But I'm new to this, it's a challenge for us, and every person we met was looking at a potential plot for the series. Someone here today is going to win the show, I can just tell.'

'Right,' is all I say. 'Well, we're done for the day, and I'm tired and starving, so...'

Lockie stretches, arms above his head, shirt pulling taut across his shoulders in a way that is hard to ignore.

'Want to grab dinner?' he suggests.

My stomach lurches. For a split second, I'm tempted –

although I'm not sure why. I guess our speed date was good but, I don't know, now I know him, and he's my colleague. It's probably not a good idea. He is the enemy, after all. The man who is going to ruin my show.

'I've got lots to do tonight, so I'd better go straight home,' I say. 'But thanks.'

'No worries,' he replies. 'I'm sure some of the others will be up for it.'

Oh, of course he wasn't asking just me.

I pack up my notes quickly, avoiding his eyes, and head out into the cold evening air. The city buzzes around me – buses hissing, people hurrying, chatter – the only thing louder is the growling of my stomach.

Was it the right thing to do, saying no? It was just dinner, and we do need to try to find a way to work together. I need him onside, really, if I'm going to stop him hijacking this show with his 'scripted reality' – dinner could've been... strategic.

But it's too late now. I said no, I've left the building, it would seem crazy to change my mind.

Plus, if anyone has learned not to get too close to anyone at work, then it's me. I found out the hard way.

4

Simon is about as dramatic as a person can be. He's worked in TV all his life, so naturally he looks at everything through rectangular vision. Everything is a storyline. Optics are all that matter. Grabbing and holding as many people's attention as possible is paramount. Whether he's putting on a TV show or filling his car with fuel, he knows how to get and keep eyes on him. It's just lately, I don't know, it's like he's losing his touch, and rather than depend on me to figure out how we revive a show that I used to love, he's bringing in the big guns – the man with the big guns – Lockie, thinking he's going to save the day. So obviously being called into his office for an emergency meeting feels like being asked to sing a solo, naked, in front of ten Simon Cowells. This is just one Simon, and I don't have to sing, and Lockie will be with me – sarcastic yaaay – so there's only so bad it can be. Right?

The blinds are drawn tight, muting the sounds and sights from the streets below and the buildings that surround us. Simon is sitting at his oversized desk – a desk with nothing but a single glass of water and a dagger-shaped letter opener in the centre of it. Knowing Simon, honestly, I would not be surprised if he had summoned us in here to play some kind of twisted game – like, I don't know, drink the poison or stab the other person. Some kind of test of character. The only reason I confidently know that's not what is happening is the fact that there are no cameras in here. If something really bad was going to happen, Simon would most definitely be filming it.

'Thank you for joining me,' he says blankly as he analyses the back of his hand, almost like he has a script on there he's about to read from. 'So... the thing I want to talk to you about... is...'

Simon is so into TV he delivers news like he's announcing who is going to be evicted from the *Big Brother* house next.

'Cleo...'

Well, that can't be a good omen.

'Erm, yeah?' I reply, without a shred of confidence.

It startles me, to hear my name, while Lockie sits next to me comfortably as ever.

He's leaning back in his chair with his legs crossed, his right ankle casually balanced on his left knee, like he's in a hotel lounge instead of a crisis meeting. He's annoyingly easy-breezy, and for some reason that makes me sit up straighter, as though I can win points for professionalism just by perfecting my posture. Although I'm probably just coming across as more uptight than usual.

Simon clears his throat before he continues.

'This season of *Welcome to Singledom* is critical,' he says. 'The last two years, our ratings have dipped. Viewers want more. Our competitors are snapping at our heels. If we don't deliver this year, and I mean really deliver...'

The look on his face says that it's not good. The look on Lockie's is still unwaveringly chill.

'So, Cleo, I know you want to go for depth and sincerity and show real people's real emotions,' he continues. 'Lockie, I know that you want to up the chaos, bring the drama, isolate people and drive them cr... into storylines.'

He was going to say 'drive them crazy' which, yeah, is exactly what Lockie is planning.

'The thing is...' Simon continues. God, I wish he could just spit it out. 'Cleo has worked on this show a long time, she knows the viewers well, and if she thinks—'

'I still need to tell you my latest idea,' Lockie interrupts him.

I wouldn't dare interrupt Simon.

'Oh?' Simon replies, intrigued.

'So, no offence to Cleo, I'm sure she knows what she's doing, but I'm just thinking for pulling in the viewers – new viewers, big numbers of viewers – her approach is all wrong. So I started wondering about the opposite: what wouldn't Cleo do?'

I want to push him off his chair right now.

'Go on,' Simon prompts him.

Oh, stunning! He's hearing him out.

'Real people are a gamble,' Lockie says, planting both feet on the floor, leaning forward in his seat. 'What we need are people who are going to pull in the big numbers, and we need that from night one. So, what about we have the new and improved *Welcome to Singledom*, and we give it a new name. Or, rather, a subtitle. *Welcome to Singledom: Survival of the Fittest.* Not only are contestants going truly remote, with no crew members on the island, true desertion, but... we don't cast new people, we cast legends – reality TV legends. I'll get you the biggest names from our rival shows, the hottest reality TV stars of the moment – all of them millions of followers online – and I'll give you the best season you've had.'

For a moment Simon just stares at him.

'You were saying, Simon...' I prompt him, trying to get him back on track, because I'm sure he was just about to say that he trusted me with a show that I know like the back of my hand. Not Lockie with his fake drama and general disregard for people's well-being.

'Yes, okay, so the person whose approach I'm going to go with, who is going to lead us into a new era, bringing us success and awards and more viewers than we've ever had before is...' Now he's acting like he's announcing the winner of *Britain's Got Talent*. 'Lockie!'

'Yes!' Lockie says.

Noooo, is all I can think. He's just swooped in at the last minute, dazzled Simon, made me look rubbish. I get it, I do, his ideas are big and flashy and – who knows – maybe it really will work. But we're getting further and further away from what the show has always been about.

I bite the inside of my cheek, trying to keep my thoughts and feelings to myself. Simon has made up his mind, and what Simon says always goes.

Lockie grins. Not too wide, not obnoxious – just enough to give off that air of modest-but-still-smug.

'I really appreciate the vote of confidence,' Lockie begins his acceptance speech, 'and I won't let you down. You'll see – this year's show is going to be spectacular.'

'So, you're happy to crack on with the new plan, Cleo?' Simon checks – as though it might be optional. It's only a choice if I choose to no longer have my job.

I force a nod. My disappointment tastes bitter in my mouth.

'Of course,' I manage to say. 'If that's what you want.'

'It is,' Simon says firmly. 'I think it will be great, if the cast is made up of recognisable faces. And with Lockie in charge of storylines – sometimes it takes a spark to start a fire.'

'I couldn't agree more,' Lockie says. 'I've already got a list of contacts who'd kill to get their clients on board. We can halt all casting efforts – if it's people we've seen on TV, we know we're getting gold, so I'll have their agents book them in. People with built-in followings, the right kind of chaos vibe for the show, all single – or willing to be. We'll go viral before the first show even airs.'

'That's what I like to hear,' Simon says, clapping his hands together with a loud slap. 'We're back in the game, people. Go make it happen!'

Well, that's that then. I can like it or lump it.

As I gather my notes, tucking my pen neatly into the spiral of my pad, it's hard not to wonder how many more seasons I have in me. It's been a slog, with the viewers dwindling and the mood shifting from fun to something more stressful. But now not only will I be doing things in a way that I don't want to do them, I'll be taking my orders from Lockie. I'll have to do whatever he wants, because it's what Simon wants now too. But is it what the viewers want? Only time will tell. And if the ship is going down, well, it's always felt like my ship too. I may as well be on it when it does.

5

If there's one thing reality TV thrives on, it isn't romance, or drama, or even copious amounts of alcohol. It's product placement.

Nobody really talks about that side of it, of course, but it's capitalism that pays the bills, so we rely heavily on adverts, sponsorship deals and oh-so subtle (or oftentimes not at all subtle) product placement.

The drama sells the show, but the advertisers keep the lights on. That said, it's not always easy, to work in product placement on a show like *Welcome to Singledom*, where contestants are marooned on a desert island. It's easy enough with bikinis and swim shorts, pretty much the only clothing anyone wears while participating, but it's not so easy with things like protein powders and fake tan.

Still, like I said, capitalism makes the world go round, and it's been months since Lockie and I started working together. Almost all of the plans are in place. The only things left to sort are this and the contestants we're going to drop in as the show goes on. Lockie, who has been running the show pretty much, is of the opinion that we need to deep-dive into the lives of our contestants. We haven't even met them, given that they're all TV regulars, their agents have sorted everything out, but oddly I feel like I know them. We're cyberstalking them, seeing if they have any exes who might want to get involved, or if we can work out what kind of people push their buttons. It's all part of Lockie's biiiig plan. I still hate it.

Have we been working together? No. Not at all. Don't get me wrong, we're getting things done, I'm doing his bidding, but we're more like rivals than colleagues. I'll be glad when this season is over, because it will be a hit or it will be a flop, and then we'll know who was right, me or Lockie, and, I don't know, I'm not sure which is worse, or which would make me more likely to stick around.

So it's just me and Lockie, in a room full of swag, trying to work out what products we can feasibly place within the show that will seem natural, not like an ad.

'The good news is, with the contestants being influencers, they'll already know how to flog most things,' Lockie says as he rifles through boxes.

'Yeah,' is all I say.

'You look awfully miserable for a woman holding a giant inflatable duck,' Lockie jokes. 'Looks like you're both feeling... deflated.'

I laugh politely.

'Well, I think he's going to stay that way, I can't see him working with the island aesthetic,' I point out.

The island does have the most beautiful pool – man-made for the show – that looks like a lagoon with a beautiful waterfall. Floating around on a giant duck might be nice, but it's not exactly in keeping with the survival vibe, is it?

'True,' he says, rubbing his hands together with the enthusiasm of a person who is about to unwrap their birthday presents. 'Shall we start with the swimwear?'

He holds up a bikini so barely there you could mistake it for a sample of the material they use to make bikinis – not an entire one. It's bright orange, with little beads on the spaghetti straps, and a similar little cluster of beads that will form a heart right at the top of the butt crack of whoever wears it. That's probably the part that covers the most.

'I cannot imagine wearing nothing but this kind of thing for weeks,' I blurt. 'Weeks and weeks of thongs and trying to avoid nip slips.'

'Both of which make great TV,' Lockie jokes. 'Swimwear is easy, and it pays well, and contestants are always thrilled to get free clothes.'

'They're hardly clothes,' I point out. 'They're hardly swimwear. Not practical at all, for surviving on the island.'

'Practical isn't sexy, is it?' he reminds me.

'Neither are UTIs,' I clap back, throwing a plastic-feeling thong at him. 'It gets chilly at night. The ones who can't get fires going are going to suffer – the ones who can need to worry about being flammable.'

'They'll be fine,' he insists.

I shoot him a look.

'You're an expert at sleeping outside, are you?' I ask.

'I once camped at Glastonbury,' he replies through a grin.

'That's not the same,' I say.

'You're right, it was so much worse,' he replies. 'All that mud and rain, and the communal toilets – God. These guys are going to be in paradise.'

The funny thing about *Welcome to Singledom* is that no one actually knows where the island is. Sure, if you use your brain, you can probably figure out that it's a private island in the

Caribbean somewhere, but we've always made it a thing that no one really knows, like we're dropping them in uncharted territory. And yes, it's a set, we've constructed things to look real that weren't there before, but the climate is real, the weather is real, the bugs are real. Yes, we're on hand to keep everyone safe (well, we usually are, this year we're going to be offshore on a bloody boat) but there's a reason everyone has to sign an 'anything goes' release form.

I sigh, drumming my fingers against the table, scanning the ridiculous products in front of me. Sun cream, swimwear, a protein powder that smells like sick. Some products are easy, sun cream makes sense, but whipping up a protein shake? Not so much.

I grab a box and see the words 'adults only' on the lid.

'Well, well, well,' Lockie says, reading it over my shoulder. 'Now this one I've got to see inside.'

Curious too, I open the lid and... wow.

'Oh, hello,' he says, pulling out a bright pink feather boa.

'No,' I say quickly, reading his mind.

'Yes,' he insists, shaking it out and looping it around my neck. 'Actually, better not, it clashes with your angry red face. What about on me, any better?'

He strikes a pose, lips puckered.

'Looks good on me, don't you think?'

'You look like the person you get for your hen party when all the other sexy men are fully booked,' I point out.

'So I'm a sexy man,' he replies.

'Absolutely not,' I insist.

He grins, then plunges his hand back into the box like it's a lucky dip at a very questionable village fair. This time he pulls out... a pair of novelty handcuffs.

'Is that...'

'It is!'

He dangles them from one finger, the polished silver metal sparkling under the ceiling lights.

'Brilliant,' I mutter. 'Just what every contestant needs on a deserted island. Forget food, shelter, or water – a way to take hostages.'

'I think we all know they're not for that,' he reminds me. 'These are for... solidifying the connections.'

Welcome to Singledom is all about making connections so, in the luxury suite that couples can unlock a night in, there is a bed, champagne, chocolate – and usually a selection of silly toys. Handcuffs are a new one though.

Then he pulls out something even worse – a skimpy nurse's outfit, all white lace and red crosses. He holds it up against his chest, raising his eyebrows.

'What do you think?' he asks.

'It's giving Joker from *The Dark Knight*,' I tell him. 'Only more unhinged.'

'Here's the male option,' he says, pulling out a white thong with a fake stethoscope hanging from it.

'You're joking!' I say.

'You're blushing,' he replies.

'I am not,' I insist.

I definitely am though, I can feel it.

The pile grows – silk blindfolds, a suspiciously shaped, definitely oversized silicone something or other that I quickly drop back in the box, and finally, a box of glow-in-the-dark body paint.

'Now this,' Lockie says, shaking the paint, 'is TV gold. Imagine the night-vision cameras.'

'We're supposed to be helping people fall in love, or even lust

– not promoting comedy dildos and glow-in-the-dark body paint,' I protest. 'That's not sexy, is it?'

'Respectfully, I disagree, sexy can be funny,' he replies.

'Maybe the way you do it,' I tease him.

'I'm serious,' he replies, laughing too. 'It's supposed to be fun. When you're with someone and you're so comfortable, and things go wrong, or really right, and it's just... something to smile about, or laugh about. I find it really hot, when a woman laughs.'

I can't help but smile at how much I like that – and flush at how much I secretly want it. God, I've missed that, having someone to be silly in bed with, and it's not just a sex thing. You know those nights where you stay up late laughing and being goofy, talking about everything and nothing, and then suddenly realising it's 3 a.m. but not caring because you've never felt so much joy? It's been a long time since joy was on my radar. Sex too. And now here I am with Lockie and a box of sex toys and suddenly the atmosphere feels less funny, and not at all worky... more charged with... something.

I shove the lid back on with more force than necessary. Yes, I am quite literally putting my feelings back in a box, banishing them there, with no intention of thinking of them again for as long as I can. Mostly because, as much as Lockie is irritating me professionally, I can't deny that we had that spark when we first met, that I felt attracted to him – well, I wasn't to know he was the reality TV Antichrist, was I?

'I'm sure we don't need to paw through this stuff,' I say.

'Shame,' he says lightly, but there's a glint in his eyes that I can't quite figure out.

'That box is a HR disaster waiting to happen,' I tell him. 'And a PR nightmare, if we give the lot to the contestants.'

'Why are you so scared of a bit of drama?' he asks. 'Anything remotely entertaining – it's like you're allergic to it. Where has the girl from the speed-dating night gone? She was great.'

'She was working,' I point out.

'You're working now,' he reminds me. 'What if I were to order you to let your hair down? To put on the feather boa, to go out for a drink with me...'

I think for a moment. Does that really sound so bad? No, but it does sound risky.

'Then I would remind you of what I just said, about HR,' I reply. 'Not everything has to be chaotic and dramatic and sexy.'

'You think I'm all of those things?' he checks cheekily.

'I think you can't function without all of those things,' I correct him.

'Chaotic and dramatic and sexy make great TV,' he says simply. 'And great TV gets great ratings. People don't sit in the office talking about the reality TV contestant who has their head screwed on and makes decent decisions, they say: did you see the one who ate her breakfast in nothing but a feather boa while those two guys ended up wrestling in the ocean?'

'You're out of your mind,' I point out.

'Out of my mind and effective,' he corrects me.

And the worst part? He's right. Stuff like that really will get people talking – but is it sustainable? And is it the kind of show I want to work on? Will I be proud of it?

By the time we finish sorting through the rest of the boxes, my head is pounding. There's still an entire stack of potential crap, but the office clock is crawling past 6 p.m. and I'm starving.

Lockie stretches, arms above his head, shirt riding up just enough to flash skin. Of course he notices me noticing, because his grin widens. I swear, the more chill he seems, the more uptight I get. It's like he absorbs good vibes from people, taking them for himself, leaving them hollow. Or perhaps that's just me. Everyone else seems to enjoy him.

'Dinner?' he asks casually.

'What?' I blurt.

'Dinner. You, me. Food. I'm thinking pizza. I'll wear the feather boa, if you like, I'm quite fond of it,' he jokes.

I hesitate. For a second or two I actually imagine what it would be like, to go for dinner with Lockie – the two of us at some little Italian place. Pizza, glasses of wine, a lit candle flickering between us. It doesn't sound awful.

But no. Absolutely not. Because he's the enemy, professionally, and I don't know how to navigate that. I have to put my job first and here at work we do not get on. How could we possibly get on outside of work at the same time?

'We'd better not,' I say, hoping that will be the end of it.

'Why?' he replies.

'Because I have the sense not to mix work with... whatever this is.'

'Low-key flirting?' he offers with a smile.

'It's more like bickering,' I correct him.

My face feels hot. Are we bickering or flirting or both? Sometimes it's a fine line.

'Like an old married couple,' he jokes. 'I just thought speed-dating Cleo might enjoy it, rather than office Cleo...'

'That's okay,' I reply. 'We're the same person, so...'

'Pizza for one it is,' he says, smiling to let me know it's okay. 'I'll see you tomorrow then.'

'Yeah, see you tomorrow,' I reply as I head for the door.

Why does he keep asking if I want to hang out? Why do I keep saying no? Was it the right thing to do? It probably was. It has to be.

Back in the 'adults only' box with the lot of it. And I'll do everything I can to avoid opening the lid again.

6

The office looks so different at night. Not just when it's dark, because it's always dark before the end of the day when it's winter, but when it's late enough for almost everyone to be long gone. I don't know anyone else that's still here apart from me and Lockie.

It's quieter, darker, more honest somehow – and yet kind of eerie too. It's always so frantic during the day that at night it feels abandoned, like the zombie apocalypse came while I wasn't paying attention – if anyone would have to work through an apocalypse, you just know it would be me. Desks abandoned, swivel chairs sitting empty, everything casting long shadows under the few lights that are on. Even the cleaning team have been and gone and now it's just me and Lockie, takeaway pizza, and the entire internet to sift through.

Lockie drums his fingers on his laptop in rhythm with the buzzing fluorescent bulb above us. It's kind of maddening. He catches me glaring at him.

'Sorry,' he says with a chuckle. 'I was trying to drown out the noise from the light. I'll turn it off.'

He pops up from his seat and flicks off the overhead light. The remaining light comes from a weak desk lamp and the glow from our screens.

'This place is depressing at night,' I say with a sigh.

'Depressing?' He looks around like I've just insulted his home interior. 'It's romantic, if anything. Eating dinner, a gentle glow – typing slurs and usernames into social media to see if any of our contestants need giving the last-minute boot.'

'Oh, yes, so romantic,' I say sarcastically.

He grins, as pleased with himself as always.

We've been at this for hours – one last-minute round of contestant vetting before Simon signs everything off tomorrow. It's mindless work: combing through social feeds, googling names, making sure no one has a secret OnlyFans or used any unsavoury language in an online spat back in their school days. One of the blessings, when it comes to casting people who have already been on TV, is that usually these things come to light the first time around. I would be surprised if we found anything, but best to make sure, we need this series to go without a hitch.

Lockie sits back next to me, the glow of his laptop uplighting his face like we're telling ghost stories. He looks irritatingly awake, while I'm propped up on one elbow, scrolling through Instagram profiles that all blur into one parade of fake tans, Turkey teeth and gym selfies.

'This guy,' I say, gesturing at my screen. 'He seems like he's going to be trouble.'

Lockie leans forward to peek. Our heads almost touch, and I'm suddenly aware of how close together we're sitting, and how warm the office feels. Yes, summer is finally settling in now that we're in June, but it's not that. There's just this heat between us.

'Trouble's good,' he says. 'That body is made for slow-motion walk-ins. He'll have half the cast eating out of his hand by day three.'

I frown.

'He always seems so arrogant.'

'Exactly. He's perfect,' Lockie says.

Perfectly unbearable, perhaps.

'It's funny, because if you were into guys, you would sound complimentary – if not slightly pervy – but because you're not, I don't know, you talk about him like he's some sort of specimen,' I explain.

'He is!' Lockie jokes, pretending to fan himself.

'I'm just not sure what you see in him... or anyone,' I reply.

'Cleo,' he sighs, as if explaining the obvious to a child. 'The audience loves arrogant. They hate them, they scream at the telly about them, call up all of their friends to chat shit, but they keep watching. That's the point. It's like when we were at the auditions, and we trialled talking to people separately, and I wanted that fitness model, and you wanted the soup kitchen guy.'

'Benny? He was great,' I insist. 'He volunteered, raised money for charity – he ran marathons.'

'Benny who ran marathons was the fitness model,' he corrects me.

'No, he was the guy who volunteered,' I reply. 'He ran marathons for charity.'

'Describe him,' he prompts me.

'Tall, blonde undercut, athletic, kind smile,' I say.

'That's Benny,' he replies.

'Yeah... I know. I just said,' I remind him.

'No, I mean that's my guy too, and your guy – they were the same guy,' he tells me. 'We must have argued about who was better for like forty minutes. It was the same person.'

I laugh.

'So... we actually agreed on someone?' I say.

'Yep!' he replies.

'Well, for what it was worth, because we had to abandon new people in favour of your big idea to use only reality TV stars. Do you remember Elle, from a couple of seasons ago?'

'Elle? Oh, yeah, Elle Shaw? The influencer?' he replies. 'I watched the show that year. She was my favourite.'

I nod. She was everyone's favourite – everyone male anyway.

'Yeah, well, she's heard from her agent that we're doing this, and she is hounding me on Insta, begging to take part,' I tell him. 'I've told her, we're not considering ex-contestants any more, just other reality stars – we don't want anyone to have a tactical advantage – but she won't let it go. She's actually starting to get quite mean. She says we'll have words at the launch party – because of course Simon invites all the ex-islanders. I'm going to have to spend the whole night avoiding her.'

'Well, that should be easy, given that it's a masquerade ball,' he replies.

'Yeah, I heard someone had that great idea for this year – I thought it might have been you,' I reply. 'You seem like the kind of guy who likes to orchestrate a misunderstanding.'

We both reach for the last slice of pizza at the same time, his hand brushing mine, warm, casual, lingering just a second longer than you would expect before we pull back. It's like we're playing chicken – I think I'm the one to move first.

'You can have it,' I tell him.

'You can, if you like,' he replies.

'No, no, it's fine,' I insist, pushing the box toward him slightly.

'We should share it,' he suggests.

'It's not a milkshake with two straws or a big plate of spaghetti,' I reply.

Lockie laughs.

'As into both of those things as I would be...' he jokes. 'Here. I'll take the top half. Seeing as though you don't eat your crusts.'

'There's nothing wrong with not eating crusts,' I protest.

'Do you cut them off your sandwiches too?' he checks playfully.

'I'll cut your crusts off, if you don't back off,' I say through gritted teeth, but it's a playful reply. I sort of like the banter, sometimes, although other times I really do want to murder him.

'Sorry, sorry,' he replies.

I try to keep cool but my pulse betrays me, thudding louder than it should over something so silly.

We eat in silence for a minute, chewing, getting back to the task at hand, pretending we're not flirting with the idea of flirting.

It's Lockie who breaks the silence, of course.

'So,' he says, wiping his mouth with the back of his hand. 'Since we're already invading the contestants' private lives, what about ours?'

I give him a wary look.

'Ours?'

'Yeah, I heard a rumour today, about an office romance – *the* office romance, apparently.' He smirks. 'One of the girls was telling me how you and your ex were like the main characters of the place, the ones everyone shipped.'

The words hit like a punch to the stomach.

'Yeah, well, it didn't work out, because it turns out he couldn't be trusted,' I say flatly. 'And I don't want to talk about it.'

His smirk falters, softening into something else.

'Fair enough,' he replies.

'I'm very anti-workplace romance now,' I say, setting my stall out. 'They're a terrible idea.'

'Not always,' Lockie replies. 'Statistically speaking, some of the best relationships start at work.'

'Statistically speaking,' I counter, 'so do most affairs, divorces, and HR investigations.'

He grins. 'That's just all part of the story, right?'

'Everything is a story with you – do you ever have a day off?' I clap back.

'No,' he says plainly. 'But I have had an office romance too, and mine didn't work out either, so I do know where you're coming from.'

'Oh, right, well... I'm sorry to hear that,' I tell him honestly. 'What happened?'

I know it's rich of me to ask, when I'm keeping my own secrets to myself, but I get the impression he wants to talk about it.

He hesitates, then shrugs.

'She cheated,' he says eventually. 'At the Christmas party. It's a tale as old as time. You know what these industry parties are like – drinking games, spin the bottle, truth or dare. Harmless enough when it's inside the game. But...' He swallows. 'I caught her kissing one of the show's stars out in the smoking area. She said it was no different to doing it in the game, that I was being a baby but... the trust was gone.'

I feel a pang of something in my chest.

'I'm sorry,' I say.

He shrugs again, but you can see in his eyes that, in this moment of sincerity, he's not his usual laid-back self.

'It is what it is.'

'Still,' I say, 'once the trust is gone, it's hard to get it back. Not just with that person. With anyone – with everyone.'

He looks me in the eye and his gaze lingers a second longer than it should: softer; more cautious, suddenly.

'I'm doing my best,' I say softly. 'To go with your ideas. But it's not easy to trust there, either.'

He sits up a little straighter.

'Then let me make my case properly,' he replies. 'Look, I know it seems shallow, stacking the cast with reality TV stars, but these people, they know the game. They create chaos naturally. We probably won't have to script it – they're used to being good TV. We just set the stage and let them do their thing.'

'And hope it doesn't blow up in our faces?' I reply.

'It won't.'

I narrow my eyes.

'Sometimes you have to trust someone,' he says.

'Except... I remember on *Made in Yorkshire*, that house fire,' I say. 'One of your tricks, I assume?'

He bursts out laughing.

'Cleo. That was a real fire,' he tells me. 'Nothing to do with production. Some idiot knocked over a candle.'

I'm not sure if I believe him.

It's not fair how easy he makes it look – just existing. He sits there, confident, charming, believing in his ideas like they're gospel. I don't know where he finds his faith.

I want to believe in his idea too, it's just so hard to trust him, when I don't really trust anyone. I meant what I said – once trust breaks, it doesn't just snap with one person. It infects everything. Every relationship, every partnership. Even this. Especially this.

I really do want to trust him. I want to believe that his chaos theory will work, that he's not just another pretty face coasting on male privilege and bravado. But I can't help bracing for the moment it all burns down – literally, if that house fire was anything to go by.

And all of the above is just trusting him professionally. I daren't even think about anything else.

'Still,' I say, 'if you take it too far, or it doesn't work out – that's it. I'm revolting.'

His lips twitch.

'You're not that bad,' he replies.

I roll my eyes.

'Not that kind of revolting.'

'I know, I know,' he teases, and I can't help laughing too.

He's funny, I do like that about him. That laugh-a-minute vibe is what keeps life light. It's hard to frown about everything when you're always laughing with someone, even in the darker moments.

'I'd better put my mask back on, you actually look like you don't hate me right now,' he jokes.

'You're not all that hateable right now,' I tell him. 'Never mind your metaphorical mask. You'll have a real mask on tomorrow.'

'Ahh, yes, the masquerade, can't wait,' he says, pulling a bit of a face.

'Our pre-show launch parties can get pretty wild too,' I point out. 'It must be a TV thing. But God knows how people will act with anonymity.'

He leans in just a little, I'm sure he does.

'It's a good way to let someone know how you feel,' he points out. 'Without… exposing yourself.'

'Always better to do that without exposing yourself,' I reply, deadpan.

He laughs, the sound low and warm.

'Not like that. But then again…' He pauses, watching me

closely. 'Sometimes your gut feeling is right. And you should just ask. I should just ask.'

'Ask what?'

'Dinner,' he says. 'After the party. You, me, somewhere that isn't here – and a food without crusts.'

My instinct is – of course – to say no, like always. Keep it safe. Keep the walls up. And yet he keeps asking. Plus, he's right. I have to trust someone at some point. Maybe Lockie is the one – the one I should trust, that is. I've been kidding myself, pretending there isn't something here, simmering beneath every argument, every brush of hands. I could try... maybe...?

'Okay,' I hear myself say out loud. Somehow I feel like my lips acted before my brain had truly finished overthinking it.

Lockie smiles.

'Great,' he says, leaning back again. 'It's a date.'

It sounds like it is, and the worst part? I think I'm looking forward to it.

7

I'm late. And I know what you're thinking: Cleo, why did you spend so long doing your make-up for a party where you'll be wearing a mask? But I have my dinner date with Lockie after, and I wanted to have the best chance of still looking my best, at the end of the night, when the masks finally come off.

I'm not the only reason I'm late though, oh no, because whenever I want things to go right, that's when they go wrong. My bus broke down too. I ended up sitting there for ages, waiting for a replacement service, clutching my *Eyes Wide Shut* mask, until eventually I resorted to getting a taxi, and walking the last little stretch. So here I am, huffing and puffing down the street, pounding the pavement with my platform heels.

Tonight just... feels like it matters more than it usually would. Not the party itself, not really – I've been to so many of these things and it's always the same endless supply of champagne, arse-kissing and bad choices.

It's a good chance to get into a good spot with Lockie – we're going to be living on a boat together, which would be better if we were on more level terms, but... I don't know, going to dinner with him, putting some trust in him, it feels like a step that I need to take, to finally get some closure, to move on with my life.

I really did spend an embarrassing amount of time getting ready, standing in front of the mirror, talking myself in and out of alternate dresses, because the one I bought just felt so big and fancy and I went from feeling a million dollars to thinking I looked like a kid playing dress up to realising it was the only thing I could realistically wear if I wanted to fit in. Which reminds me, I have to put every item of clothing I own back in my wardrobe before I can go to bed tonight.

I'm wearing a floor-length black slip dress, simple but clinging in the right places – aided by one of those oxygen-stealing undergarments that round up all your lumps and bumps. I opted for a big, chunky platform heel, because I thought it would give me the height needed to make my legs looks longer and slimmer, but also a good base for planting them on the floor. I'm not my best in stiletto-type heels and the last thing I need is to stack it in front of everyone.

Then of course I have my mask – can't forget that for a masquerade ball – but the pièce de résistance has to be the ridiculous pink feather boa from that cursed box of adult-only promo supplies. Well, Lockie said he liked it, so I think it will really make him laugh. Plus, you know, I want him to know that I'm thinking of him, that I heard him when he said he liked it – this is my version of a white flag (it's just pink and feathery instead). If he can make an effort then so can I. And, no, I'm not usually this brave, not even before I got my heart broken, so this is a big deal. I'm putting myself out there and I've no idea what's going to happen, but I'm hoping several glasses of champagne will help.

I reach the venue, my stomach fizzing with nerves, and hand over my ticket. The bouncer eyes the boa but says nothing. Oh, right, because at a party where everyone is wearing a mask, a few pink feathers are worthy of raising eyebrows.

Inside, the masquerade is in full swing. It's like stepping into another world: chandeliers dripping light across the ballroom, the air thick with perfume and booze. Everyone's masked, faces half-hidden behind satin, sequins, polished metals. You just know a bunch of people already had these masks at home... for various reasons.

Women glitter in floor-length gowns, the men are all scrubbed up well in tuxedos – I guess it's nice, to have a reason to dress up now and then.

There's a string quartet playing fancy versions of pop songs, which I like, and you can't look anywhere without seeing a server with a tray of food or drinks, which I love.

The vibe is reality TV meets *The Great Gatsby* meets some kind of bougie swingers' party. I'm here for it. Well, I am now – late.

The party has definitely hit its stride. Everyone looks like they're having a great time, camera crews are hovering discreetly, and already I can see people vying for attention, and potential airtime. The thing is we don't really broadcast it, sometimes we put a few snippets of this online but, for the most part, the party is just a party. A reason to get drunk and touch each other.

Speaking of which... I'm looking around for Lockie but I can't see him anywhere. It's a big room, full of a lot of people, but the masks are obviously making it a lot harder.

A camera crew pass me, briefly pointing the camera at me, which I hate – I'm almost glad to have the mask on. My heart pounds but I don't think it's the cameras, it's Lockie, I'm excited to see him. I've tried to let my guard down a bit, to make just enough room to let just a bit of him in (that didn't sound quite so bad until I finished the thought) but my defences have come all the way down, it was that or nothing, so I guess it's that.

I've nothing to worry about, that's what I need to remind myself. It's a dream night. The kind of night with an atmosphere that sweeps you away, dazzles you, makes you feel like you're taking a little bit of a break from real life.

My heels feel like they thump against the polished marble as I look around the bar, letting my eyes adjust to the different lights. That or I can feel my heartbeat in my feet as well as every other part of me.

I catch sight of myself reflected in a mirror along one wall. For a second, I almost don't recognise the woman staring back. The floor-length black slip dress clings in ways I usually shy away from, simple but unforgiving, the kind of cut that makes you either shrink or stand taller. Suddenly, I feel sort of pumped up. Nervous, but quietly confident. Do you know what? I even think my feather boa looks fab. I'm making it work. It's draped around my shoulders, absurd and loud, nothing like my usual style, but I'm not acting like my usual self tonight.

I decide to grab a glass of champagne from the bar, whether it's Dutch courage or a prop to make me feel more like I've settled in I don't know, but it can't hurt.

Then I notice it, that familiar Leeds accent, the voice of the former contestant who has been sending me voice notes all week begging me to let her be one of the surprise contestants we add in as the show goes on. Elle Shaw. I've told her no time and time again, and she's been getting quite mean, but it is what it is. Hopefully she doesn't recognise me with my mask on, she'll probably just start asking again.

'Of course I did what I had to,' she's saying, her tone dripping smugness. She's got her arm hooked with another woman who is eagerly listening to her tale, her mask glittering like a disco ball under the chandeliers. A drink practically dangles from Elle's fingers (she must have had a few already) as she tosses her head back and laughs, high and triumphant. 'I was determined to get back on this show and now I have. A clever combination of manifesting and giving men what they want. Oh, they're so easy to manipulate. This little card right here is my meal ticket. And all it took was a few minutes behind that curtain over there.'

'What?' I blurt.

Normally, I'd roll my eyes and keep walking. She's been begging to get back on the show, DMing anyone with even a sniff of production authority, pitching herself as the saviour of the show. But she says she's back on the show, and that card in her hand, they're the business cards Lockie and I carry, to give out to people we meet who might be good for the show. It has the direct number to the casting line, which we only give to people we want.

And I know I didn't give her it.

She's waving it around like it's her plane ticket to paradise – I suppose it is.

'Where did you get that?' My voice comes out sharper than I mean, slicing through the music.

'What's it to you?' she asks.

I take my mask off, so she knows it's me. As she realises it's me her smile twists into something even more smug.

'Cleo. Hi, babe,' she says. 'Turns out I didn't need you after all.'

'Where did you get that card?' I ask. 'Did you say you're going to be on the show?'

She shrugs, lazy but satisfied. 'Let's just say you're not the only one who controls casting these days,' she replies. 'And other people are much easier to persuade.'

Is she... is she saying what I think she's saying? She's got a card, from Lockie, so she can waltz into the show after, what, a fumble behind the curtain? Is she mad? Is he mad, come to think of it? Oh, God, he did say she was one of his favourites from an old series. I thought he was joking, or just... ahh, I don't know why I expected any different from anyone involved. This is showbiz, sex is like the main currency, even now, even when you hope and pray that old practices are out, safeguarding is in.

'Look at you, judging me,' she replies. 'And yet you were happy for me to have sex on your island, for ratings.'

Heat floods my cheeks. Anger, shame, humiliation all tangle together, scorching me from the inside out.

I want to march her straight over to Simon, Lockie too, and tell him this is how Lockie is making decisions, with what's inside his boxers, not his head. But, of course, Simon has had his own issues over the years with, shall we say, taking advantage of his position. Even if he's doing better now, you just know he'll go to bat for golden boy.

Instead, I bite my tongue so hard it hurts, and walk away before I say something I'll regret.

It's not her I'm mad at, is it? It's him. Lockie. The stupid motherfu—

Not looking where I'm going, I crash into a man and a woman who are dancing.

'Cleo,' he blurts.

His dance partner wanders off.

I know it's Lockie from his voice and his build. He knows it's me because my mask is off.

He looks almost alarmingly good in a tux – sharp lines, sleek mask, hair slicked back to make him look the part.

A crooked smile hovers at his mouth, like he's been waiting for me all night.

I look at him, then at his dance partner as she walks off, then back at him.

'I actually don't know who that was,' he says with an awkward laugh. 'I thought it was you, when she started dancing with me. You've saved me a lot of embarrassment. I can't believe you're wearing the feather boa, I love it. It suits you.'

There's just no way that's true, is it? That he thought it was me. She had long blonde hair, and I know it's dark in here, but that's about where the similarities start and stop.

'She's like a foot shorter than me,' I reply.

'You're taller than usual,' he says. 'Nice shoes. Want to try them out on the dance floor?'

'I just bumped into Elle Shaw,' I say, raising my eyebrows.

'Ahh, you heard, huh?' he replies, running a hand through his hair. 'I didn't think you'd be happy.'

I laugh angrily.

'We'll make it work,' he reassures me.

'Are you serious?' I clap back.

'It's not a big deal, come on, let's get a drink,' he says.

'I'm good,' I tell him. 'I'm going to the bathroom.'

'We're still on for dinner later, right?' he checks, sensing something is wrong.

'I'm going to have to pass,' I say plainly, trying to keep my nerve and my cool.

'What? Why?'

He sounds genuinely baffled. Is he that deluded? I know, we're nothing to each other, and generally anything goes at these parties, but how could he think I'd be happy with Elle Shaw worming her way in?

He reaches out to me but I sidestep him before he can say another word.

I can feel his eyes following me as I walk away but I don't

look back. I can't. Because all I can think is: I was about to trust him. I was about to let him in.

How could I be so stupid? I'd let myself believe, for a moment, that there was something real underneath all the sparring. That maybe, if I let him in, it wouldn't be a disaster.

And now here I am. Humiliated. Angry. Disappointed – I think that's the worst one.

8

Airports – a transitional place, a waiting room as you head from A to B. How you're feeling can very much shape how you see a place. To some, airports are fun places. You can drink, relax, buy yourself a giant Toblerone while you wait to take off. Or... it's limbo. A place that suspends you in time while you wait anxiously to get your long-haul flight over with.

I'm not usually an anxious flyer – I've done this one a bunch of times now – but it's not the flight I'm worried about, it's the company. Plans were in place before Lockie showed me his true colours, so I was happy for the two of us to sit together. Speaking of being stuck in no man's land...

I'm just waiting. Sitting underneath a flickering fluorescent light that seems to follow me wherever I go. I've been through security, had a few coffees, made sure my devices are charged up for the flight ahead. Because when you're feeling anxious, if all else fails, you can always bury your face in your phone, right?

I feel scruffy and tired already, like the cost of travelling is being stripped of your dignity. Well, you get searched, treated like a potential criminal, made to wait, you get tired and scruffy and sweaty dragging your stuff around.

And yet – of bloody course – I've just spotted Lockie and he looks like a jacked Ralph Lauren model. He's impossible to miss, looking like an England rugby player on his way to an important game. He's standing in front of the aftershave counter, spritzing tester bottles on his wrists like he's in an advert. Two sales assistants are watching him like he's the answer to all their prayers. He tilts his head, offers them a smile, and it's enough to set them off, giggling like teenagers. Look, I get it, he's a good-looking man, and the last thing I need is for him to smell even better, but knowing what a creep he is goes a long way to dampening the initial attraction I had to him. Even when I realised he was my work rival, I still had that attraction to him, but now, ugh, now he turns my stomach.

I duck behind a display of sunglasses, hoping he won't catch me staring, but I knock a pair to the floor and it makes just enough noise to grab his attention – because of course it does.

He doesn't wave, doesn't call out. He just smirks at me – amused to have caught me peeping at him.

We don't speak but we're barely more than a few metres apart as we go through the motions, eventually arriving at the gate, ready to board.

Just look at him, leaning against the pillar near our boarding gate like he's secretly posing for the paparazzi, but trying to look like he isn't. He's got his shirt collar open, giving him a sort of considered but casual vibe, his jacket is slung over his shoulder, and he's got one hand sitting just inside his pocket. And of course his sunglasses are hooked on the neck of his shirt – frankly, I'm astonished he doesn't have them on, if he thinks he's sooo cool.

Two women in the queue glance his way, whispering to each

other. I don't have to lip-read to know it's probably something about his jawline or his broad shoulders or how perfect his hair is.

Meanwhile, I feel like a toad. Hair scraped into a bun that's already coming undone, mascara smudged because I rubbed my tired eyes, and I realised my hoodie had a mark on the sleeve just too late to do anything about it.

Isn't this just setting the tone? He looks so good, and so happy and chill, and I'm a mess and I'm stressing and... and... and it's going to be such a long few weeks together.

And now we're boarding, so I have no choice but to stand next to him. Lucky really, that I can't do anything that will put me on a no-fly list, or he might be in trouble.

'Hi, Cleo,' he says casually. 'Ready to rock?'

'I guess so,' I say with a heavy sigh.

Boarding is chaos, as always. The narrow aisle is clogged with impatient people, everyone fighting for overhead bin space. Toddlers are crying – and there's already a businessman ranting under his breath about it. The air smells lovely, but just a little too much, like everyone hit up the duty-free samples, and it's overpowering the space. Just what you need, when you're trapped in a box.

I'm clutching the book I've been reading like it's a parachute. Reading romance novels feels almost sarcastic at the moment, but it feels like an exercise for my brain, a way to keep working out my love muscle for when I need it. Once again, none of those words seemed like they were going to sound so dodgy until my brain put them in that unfortunate order. At least we know my dirty mind is still working.

And here he is, Lockie, ready to invade my personal space. He's in the seat next to mine, because of course he is. We booked these seats before, when we were working well together, thinking we could do some planning on the plane. We may be in the premium economy seats, or whatever they call the ones that are not the cheap seats, but they are still just seats, side by side, with no escape.

The seats are decent – plush leather, decent legroom, and champagne is already being handed out. Lockie is what's making it feel claustrophobic.

'Don't look so disappointed,' Lockie says as he slides into the window seat, making himself at home. 'I promise not to hog the armrest.'

The last thing I'm worried about is elbow room.

He knows something is up, he must, because I've gone ice-cold with him. The thing is, I don't think he thinks he deserves it, I don't think he believes he did anything wrong, so he's just going with it. Letting me be frosty, being insufferable back. Either starving me of attention or annoying me with it. I don't know which I want. He can't win, of course he can't, because I'm just so mad that I almost let myself trust him, and so relieved nothing went further than it did.

We don't really speak at all while we take off. It seems like it takes ages to get to altitude, to get to a point where we can relax (sort of) and get this show on the road.

A flight attendant appears almost right away. She's tall, blonde, looking fantastic in her perfectly pressed uniform. I have a lot of time for the fashion. Her smile is professional, but when it lands on Lockie, it lingers. Just a fraction too long.

'Hello,' she greets him – or maybe it's both of us, I'm not sure. Her voice is velvet. 'You're with the TV show, aren't you? They said we were transporting a large TV crew today.'

The crew all fly together, on public flights (we're on a budget these days), but the contestants travel there individually, to avoid them seeing each other. No one taking part gets to meet anyone else who is going to be on the island until they're actually there and the cameras are rolling.

Lockie's grin switches on instantly, like the light above our heads when anyone calls for assistance.

'That's us,' he replies. 'I'm the brains behind the casting team.'

Ha!

'Could I have a bottle of water, please?' I ask her.

She nods subtly as she leans over to take out empty champagne glasses.

'That's impressive,' she tells Lockie. 'I'll bet it takes a lot of skill.'

He shrugs modestly.

'It pays the bills,' he says with a smile.

As soon as she's gone I scoff.

'What?' Lockie asks.

'I was just wondering when the dictionary changed the definition of brains,' I point out.

Before Lockie can reply, the flight attendant returns with a bottle of water. She hands it to Lockie, not to me. Then she leaves.

'Wait, I—'

'You can have mine if you want,' Lockie offers, holding out the bottle just enough to make me have to reach for it.

'Thanks,' I say, reaching out to take it.

He pulls it away, playfully, before eventually handing it over.

Another flight attendant appears with two more glasses of champagne – presumably one for me, rather than two for Lockie.

'Here's to a long, fun, relaxing flight,' he says, dimples forming in his cheeks because he's clearly taking the piss.

I don't rise to it, I just clink glasses with him.

The engine hums beneath us, that low, constant vibration that means you just can't quite forget that you're in a metal box drifting through the sky.

'You couldn't make this up,' I say, mostly to myself.

Lockie doesn't miss a beat.

'I could make it up,' he says proudly.

'And I suppose you're proud of that,' I reply.

'Well... yeah. What's wrong with that?'

'Erm, it's unethical, for one thing. Pitching something as reality TV, all the while it's just you coming up with storylines.'

'You do the same job as me, I'm just more open about it,' he replies.

'I don't script them!'

'You do in a way,' he replies. 'You put the right people in the right place – or the wrong people in the wrong place – to make drama. You mix the chemicals to create a reaction and then watch things blow up. That's the same.'

'That's not the same,' I clap back. 'I'm not feeding them lines.'

'No,' he says, 'but you're feeding them the ingredients for them.'

'We're never going to agree on this,' I point out. 'Or anything.'

'I think we're both doing the same job, we want the same results, we're working on the same show,' he reminds me. 'We'd do well to get on the same page.'

'Of the same script?' I reply. 'Never.'

He leans back in his seat, turning his head so he's looking at me.

'What would you have done without me this season?' he asks.

'Oh, yeah, right – I don't know how I would have survived,' I say in my best damsel-in-distress voice.

'No, I'm actually asking,' he says. 'What do you wish we'd done differently?'

'I wanted real people—'

'We're not using robots,' he says with a laugh. 'These are real people. Okay, they've been on TV before, and I get why you have a problem with Elle, and I'm sorry—'

'Can we just leave it?' I say – it's my turn to interrupt him. 'We're here now and I don't care. I just want to get this over with.'

'And I just want to make it the best season yet,' he replies. 'That's all.'

'By trying to script every single part of it?' I check, sarcasm in my tone.

'Not every part,' he replies. 'Or I would have made you much easier to work with.'

'Everyone else loves working with me,' I point out.

'I thought we were—'

'Well, you thought wrong,' I say, shutting him down.

I try to ignore him as best I can. I attempt to distract myself with the in-flight entertainment. Flicking through endless thumbnails of movies I've already seen or have no desire to watch. When I finally settle on something, I feel his gaze.

'What?' I snap.

'You're really going to watch that?' He nods at the screen.

'What's wrong with romcoms?' I check – not that I'm all that interested in his opinion.

'Well, from a storytelling point of view, they're sort of boring,' he replies. 'Everyone knows how they're going to end.'

'But that's the beauty of it,' I tell him. 'They uplift you, give you hope. By the end everything is perfect, everyone is happy. It's a good message to take with you.'

'I'd go for something with action – high stakes, explosions...'

'Yes, just what we need when we're on a plane, fab idea,' I say sarcastically.

He starts lightly drumming his fingertips on the table in front of him, just to annoy me, I'll bet. It's sort of working. I just need to do my best to ignore him.

The cabin dims, some people try to sleep, others keep themselves to themselves quietly. But I can't relax. I can't ignore that he's right next to me, and that I'm so annoyed with him. His elbow keeps brushing mine, or I feel him moving in his seat, or just... ugh, hearing him breathe. Why does he have to keep doing that?

At one point, as I tug my own blanket tighter, his hand accidentally catches mine. The contact lasts less than a second – but it's enough to feel it. To feel like I'm connecting with him, like there's still a little something between us. But it's nothing magical, it's just two hands knocking, exchanging energy, then separating again.

I think the thing that is rattling me the most is facing up to the fact that no matter how many times I remind myself that the flight is well on the way, that it will be over soon, it's the realisation that when we land we'll be sharing a boat together. I don't care how big it is, it could be a cruise liner, it just feels like there's no escaping him.

The first jolt of turbulence rattles me in more ways than one.

Lockie doesn't even blink. He leans back, calm as ever, as if the plane shaking is to create a massage chair, just for him, whereas I can't help but squeeze my blanket until my knuckles turn white.

'Are you scared?' he asks, his voice low so that only I can hear.

'No,' I lie.

Another jolt, harder this time. My hand shoots out before I can stop myself, clutching the armrest – and his hand, which happens to be there.

He glances down, then up at me. No smirk this time, no snide comment. Like he's going to let me have this one.

I quickly drop his hand.

'Sorry, I didn't mean to do that,' I insist.

'Sure,' he replies, turning back to the window.

Maybe I did, maybe I didn't. Either way, I kind of wish I hadn't let go.

9

I don't know what I was expecting when it came to the boat we'll be running the show from. Something modest, probably. Practical. I had a sort of fishing boat in my mind, with peeling paint and nets still dangling off the sides.

What I wasn't expecting was this. A yacht – it might even be a superyacht, although not quite a mega-yacht. Let's not get carried away.

It's pristinely white and squeaky clean, multi-tiered, the kind of vessel you see billionaires hanging out on for a holiday. It's honestly absurd and I kind of love it.

'Now this is a production budget well spent,' Simon says, clapping Lockie on the back as we board.

'Is it?' I ask, dragging my suitcase up the gangway. 'Is it a good look, us living it up on a yacht, leaving the contestants on the island alone?'

'Of course it is,' Simon replies.

Well, that's that then.

Lockie's excitement is almost boyish, the way his eyes light up as we step aboard. And for a moment I wonder if all his big talk about raising the stakes, about putting contestants through hell, was just a scam to bag himself a few weeks on a yacht.

'Welcome, welcome, welcome!' Simon says, arms outstretched like we're on his boat. 'Can you believe it? Isn't she magnificent?'

Lockie nods appreciatively.

'She's a beauty,' he replies.

Ick. I try not to roll my eyes.

Simon ushers us around for the grand tour. Every surface sparkles, like the whole thing is brand new – maybe it is. There's a lounge bigger than my entire flat, a dining room lined with crystal glasses and perfectly polished cutlery just waiting to be used, a gym – not that I'll be spending much time there. I half-expect him to show us an infinity pool somewhere, but I suppose when you're in the sea, everywhere overboard is the infinity pool.

But the crown jewel – according to Simon, and as we all know, whatever Simon says goes – is the control room. A room lined wall to wall with screens, feeds already rigged up to the cameras scattered across the island. Even though it looks like a ghost town at the moment, the footage looks intimate, intrusive. It sends a shiver down my spine.

'Twenty-four-seven,' Simon says proudly, patting the desk like it's his firstborn. 'Every angle, every moment. Nothing gets missed – all here on the luxury of this yacht. No more roughing it on the island.'

We were hardly roughing it on the island, in our purpose-built crew quarters, but here we are.

Finally, Simon shows us to our cabin. At first I sweat, at the thought of sharing a room – how could that be? – but we're not, we're sharing a living space, which has multiple cabins coming off from it.

'I thought you two might like to be close,' Simon says cheerfully. 'Close-ish… for working.'

I manage a sort of strangled noise that might pass for gratitude. In my head, though, I'm already picturing myself cannonballing overboard just to get away from Lockie.

Before I can say anything, Simon's phone starts buzzing. He glances at the screen.

'My weather guy,' he says, as though that's a perfectly normal thing to utter. 'I should take this.'

And with that he takes off, leaving the two of us alone.

'His weather guy?' I repeat after a beat.

Lockie drops his bag on the sofa.

'Haven't you heard?' he replies.

'Heard what?'

'About the storms,' he says as he makes himself comfortable.

I blink.

'Storms? Sort of but… we're not getting storms here, are we? The weather is perfect.'

I glance out of the window to remind myself that there is in fact sunshine outside – the perfect kind, where it's bright, warm, but nothing too sweltering or muggy.

'Perfect for now,' he replies. 'But we're closer to storm season than we usually are.'

'I wonder if that's because someone delayed the start of the show, by making us do a bunch of dumb shit,' I point out.

'Thanks,' he says with a smirk. 'Look, it's fine, it should miss the island, we've got a storm bunker for absolute emergencies. We'll probably feel it more here, on the yacht.'

'Oh, stunning,' I say sarcastically. 'I'm going to get some air – while I can.'

'There will be plenty of air when the wind picks up,' he jokes after me.

Up on deck, the sun beats down, golden and warming, the sea a sheet of glass stretching forever in every direction. It's too perfect, too still.

I rest my hands on the warm metal railing, stare out at the horizon. It's hard to believe that somewhere, out there, storms are brewing. That this ocean can rise up, and the sky can fall down, dark and violent, without warning.

But then again, with Lockie around, a storm never feels that far away.

10

'How would you like to keep your jobs?' Simon asks me and Lockie.

We haven't even unpacked yet and we've been called into his office – yes, he has an office already, with another comically big desk.

Simon looks like he's had about ten double espressos and a major breakdown – usually it's only five double espressos and a minor breakdown, so something must be wrong.

How would I like to keep my job? Honestly, the answer changes minute to minute at the moment. If TV wasn't so impossible to get into, and I didn't have an addiction to paying for rent, utilities and food, then I probably would have quit already.

'So,' he says, clapping his hands. That's always a bad sign. 'There's bad news. Worse news. And… an opportunity.'

Oh, God, I don't like the sound of this at all.

'The bad news is that we've only got four contestants ready to start filming later, and we're unlikely to get anyone else,' Simon begins.

'Four?' I echo back to him. 'Which four?'

'Honey, Camilla, Ozzy, Tony. That's it,' he replies.

'Starting with less than eight throws the whole thing off,' I say. 'We could manage with six, without too much rejigging, but four is impossible.'

'What's the problem?' Lockie asks.

'Flights delayed, storms, bullshit.' He waves his hands around, like he's trying to swat his problems away. 'And the worse news? We need to start filming this evening. I can't push it. The sponsors, the network, the money...'

'You said there's an opportunity?' Lockie says. 'A solution?'

'Yes, both,' Simon says. 'The opportunity is for you two and the solution? Also you two.'

It takes me a second.

'Wait, what?' I practically squeak.

'You're going in,' Simon says. Honestly, the game has a lot to answer for, because it's led this man to believe that everyone has to do everything Simon says. 'I need the two of you to pose as contestants – not just pose though, that would be unethical. I need you to actually be contestants.'

I laugh wildly, disbelieving – because I refuse to believe it.

'No. Absolutely not,' I insist. 'I'm not prancing around in a bikini, sleeping on the island, pretending to flirt with Essex Tony while I try to shield my eyes from the sunlight bouncing off his exceptionally white teeth.'

'Well, I think I'd make a brilliant contestant,' Lockie says. 'I could win, if I wanted to.'

'Steady on,' Simon says. 'I don't need you to win, I need you to fill a gap. As soon as we have our real contestants, we'll see that the two of you are the first couple voted out. I need you to save the show, not take it over. You will, however, be real contestants. What do you say?'

'I've already said,' I point out.

'Who else am I going to send in with Lockie?' Simon asks me. 'Tara is engaged, Joanne is old, Fay has a face for radio – you're the closest thing we've got to a looker. I know it's not ideal...'

Phenomenally offensive on so many levels.

'Simon's right,' Lockie says, placing a hand on my arm. 'It's not ideal, but it works. Plus, think about it – we'll see what it's like from the inside. We'll know exactly what the contestants feel, we can get a better idea of how to do a better job. It's a good opportunity.'

'It's a nightmare,' I blurt.

'It's television,' Simon replies. 'And it's an order, really, when you think about it. No contests, no show, no need for you to stay in your jobs.'

And when he puts it like that...

I sigh, defeated.

'We'll give you both backstories, true but careful, no one will know or care who you are,' he says. 'You'll blend right in and then be gone before you know it. Just survive until reinforcements show up.'

'Survive,' I echo. 'That's not ominous at all.'

Lockie shifts closer, dropping his voice like he's telling me a secret.

'Come on, Cleo, it would be good to know what the contestants really go through,' he says. 'This is the only way. Besides, you don't want to be the reason the whole show tanks before it even starts...'

Ugh, he's right, I know he is, but this just sucks in so many ways.

'Aaaaand,' he adds, a grin tugging at his mouth as he holds on to the word for longer than usual, 'at least you won't be doing it alone. I'll be there too. We're in it together.'

I hate that a tiny part of me feels steadier for hearing that.

Simon, sensing the crack in my resolve, pounces.

'Think of it as method research,' Simon says. 'And we'll pay you, of course, same as we pay each contestant for each day they spend on the island. It's more than usual this year, given that everyone is already known.'

'We're in,' Lockie says. 'Right, Cleo?'

'...Right,' I eventually add. It's like my lips don't want to give up the words. 'But if I end up with some kind of slow-motion bikini malfunction going viral, you will all regret it. The edit better be kind.'

'The edit is always kind,' Simon replies – which is a total lie and he knows that I know it.

'Don't worry. You'll steal the show,' Lockie reassures me kindly.

My stomach flips, equal parts dread and another feeling I refuse to label right now.

'Perfect. I'll get wardrobe on it,' Simon says. 'And contracts. Then you're contestants of *Welcome to Singledom 2026: Survival of the Fittest*.'

Lockie looks thrilled, he really does, a bit of drama is his favourite thing, after all. Me? I like to make it, sure, but not be a part of it. I'm going to be the dullest contestant this show has ever seen, the public will boot me off so fast it will make my head spin. Here's hoping Lockie feels the same once he's on the island.

11

Working on the show for so long means I've eaten, slept and breathed *Welcome to Singledom*, season after season, to the point where I could give even the superstars a run for their money. In fact, if I ever end up on *Mastermind*, I know exactly what my specialist subject is going to be. Well, *Welcome to Singledom* or the original *Gossip Girl* series, I reckon I could clean up there too.

I've watched people arrive here year after year – nervous, tanned, teeth so white they could warn ships away from the rocks. I've seen megastars being made, people getting voted off the week they arrived – I've even seen contestants removed for unacceptable behaviour. The thing is though, everything I know, everything I've experienced, everything I've seen – it's all been from behind the camera. My experience in front of the camera is non-existent and my desire to be there is even less.

Even if I had the confidence, I'm just not the show's type on paper. I don't look, sound or act the part.

'All right, islanders! Let's get you show-ready,' Dan announces, smirking. 'You're about to live the dream! Let your face know.'

Dan works on the show and today his job is to prep me and Lockie, ASAP, for our island debut. What he's failing to realise, however, is that one person's dream is another person's nightmare.

His enthusiasm makes me cringe, because he can't be serious, he knows that I work on the show, that he can't pump me up like he does the other contestants. The only plausible thing he could be right now is sarcastic, and I've got no time for it.

Lockie is taking it like a champ, probably just to make me look bad.

'So, you know the drill,' Dan begins. 'The public loves a good first impression – big smiles, flirty banter, make it look natural, yeah? You're contestants, so act like it.'

'Got it,' Lockie says – I swear, he's excited about it.

'You need to survive together,' Dan continues. 'Challenges, twists – you've got to back each other up, until the new arrivals turn up. You want the viewers to like you, to believe you have enough chemistry to put you together, but don't be too memorable, or too hateable. We all know it's the favourites and the least favourites who the public keep in the longest.'

'Has a villain ever won the money?' Lockie asks. 'I've seen bits of the show, here and there, but I've never seen that.'

'One time, one villain ended up in a couple who won the popular vote,' Dan tells him. 'But to win the money the public decide whether or not you're in love. You only win the money if they believe it's love.'

'Well, we don't need to worry about that, do we?' I interrupt. 'Because our plan is to get in and get out.'

'And do your best not to fall in love with me,' Lockie instructs me with faux seriousness, pointing an accusatory finger my way.

'Oh, it's going to be such a struggle,' I say in a breathy voice. 'I just don't know how I'll resist you, I really don't.'

Dan just laughs.

'So, I know you're not the usual type, but I'm sure you know the lingo to blend in,' he continues. 'You know when you're being mugged off, when you're grafting, when you're cracking on... You know getting a pie-ing from doing bits?'

'I've worked on this show long enough to know a *snake* from a *sort*,' I remind him.

'Doing bits is a new one to me,' Lockie says. 'Bits of what?'

'Bits of what you think,' I tell him.

'Comedy?' he replies.

'I'm sure it is the way you do it,' I joke.

A stylist wheels in a rail of swimwear – the brightest colours in the smallest styles. It's hard to say if they're eye-catching or invisible.

'Right, Cleo, this looks like your size,' the stylist says, grabbing a bikini for me.

Looking at it in my hand, this looks like no one's size.

'Where's the rest of it?' I joke.

'Lockie, these are for you,' she says, ignoring me, handing him a pair of trunks.

Because the men get to feel comfortable, of course.

'Try them on,' the stylist instructs us.

I cannot believe this is happening.

We head into a cabin each (for which I'm very grateful), and I put on the barely there bikini, then stare at my reflection under harsh light. To be honest, it's not the light that's harsh, it's my own self-criticism. I'm all for everyone wearing whatever they want, no matter what society says... except me. How am I going to feel comfortable in this? My skin is pale, my hair is flat, and the bikini might look my size but it doesn't act it. I tug at the material, trying to make sure all bases are covered.

When I walk out, Dan looks me up and down.

'You're looking very... white,' he tells me. 'Like... the ghost of a Victorian woman who died of something incredibly draining.'

'Thanks,' I say plainly.

'We could sort you a spray tan,' the stylist helpfully suggests. 'We can do a quick coat or two – just make sure to keep dry, while it develops. I can contour your body a little, if you're worried...'

I wasn't worried about that. I am now.

'I'm fine, thanks,' I say, folding my arm across my chest, trying to protect my body.

Lockie comes out wearing his swim shorts. He looks ridiculously good, hot as any contestant we've ever had. He looks comfortable – then again, his shorts are made of so much material that you could make at least ten of these bikinis.

'Right,' he says, clapping his hands. 'Ready to humiliate ourselves?'

'It is what it is,' I say, borrowing a phrase that is always overused on the show.

Standing here half-naked feels so weird – like being in your underwear at work.

I can feel Lockie's eyes on me. Not in a gross way, just... noticing. And I don't know whether that makes me feel flattered or panicked. Probably both – something to worry about later, though.

'Are you going to offer me a tan?' Lockie asks the stylist. 'Can you spray me on an eight-pack?'

He must have overheard that when he walked out.

'No, you'll have to settle for the six you have,' she tells him flirtatiously.

'Oi, not in front of my show girlfriend,' he pretty much flirts back.

'Ugh, don't flatter yourself,' I blurt.

'I have to flatter myself,' Lockie jokily replies. 'You won't do it for me.'

'As hot as I think this angsty banter you seem to have is, it's not going to play, not the way we want it to,' Dan chimes in. 'If you're going to sell yourselves as a couple, get paired off, but then voted out, it needs to be real but boring. They need to see you fancy each other. They want a bit of heat! Stand up...'

Dan steps between us. We both get on our feet – one of us less enthusiastic than the other.

'I need flirty. I need sparks. Touch each other like you're obsessed,' he instructs us. 'You need to seem genuine and compatible. We don't want this to seem sus.'

'But it is sus,' I remind him.

'So try extra hard,' he patronises.

'I'll recite poetry, Cleo can gaze at me in slow motion...' Lockie jokes – at least I think he's joking.

'That's not going to make anyone horny, is it?' Dan reminds us.

'I don't want to make anyone horny,' I quickly insist.

'Yes, you do,' Dan says. 'Him. Lockie. Make him horny.'

My face scrunches up at the thought.

'Grab him,' Dan suggests.

'Where?' I blurt.

'His arm, you dirty cow,' he says with a laugh.

I do as I'm told and I feel beyond awkward. Lockie tries to smoulder at me playfully, but he looks more like he's got trapped wind. I roll my eyes and let go.

'Eye contact,' Dan urges, 'look at him like you want to kiss him.'

'Look, Dan, with all respect, I don't think we need this,' Lockie tells him. 'It'll be all right on the night.'

'Are you sure?' Dan replies. 'Because this is giving me the ick.

Cleo, I think it might be you, you're too wooden, you're not... I don't know... I might have to tell Simon, I can't see this working.'

'Just... watch,' Lockie tells him.

Lockie approaches me slowly, looking down at me, with just a hint of a smirk creeping across his lips. He places a hand on the back of my neck.

'You're going to be a good girl, aren't you, Cleo?' he says, his voice gruff and oh-so sexy. 'You're going to do what it takes, right? We're going to do what it takes.'

He pulls me closer with the hand that's on my neck, bringing my body to meet his. The skimpy swimwear means it almost entirely skin-on-skin contact. I just gaze up at him, my mouth partly open with a combination of shock and, to be honest, reflex.

'Right?' he checks, his face close to mine.

'Right,' I practically breathe back at him.

'And that's how it's done,' Lockie tells him, dropping me, stepping back, switching off whatever he just switched on. Like it was nothing.

'Okay, well, that's too good, if you want voting out first,' Dan points out. 'So just... something in the middle, yeah?'

'Yeah, okay, great,' I say, composing myself.

'One more thing, just a formality,' Dan says, pulling contracts out from nowhere. 'You need to sign these.'

I take it from him and eyeball it suspiciously.

'It's the same ones as the real contestants sign,' I tell Lockie. 'Anything goes, all footage can be used, no exceptions.'

'Well, you will be real contestants,' Dan reminds us. 'It wouldn't be fair, if not.'

I don't know how happy I feel about signing it. It basically absolves the production company of all responsibility, and also allows them to film whatever they want, so whether a contestant falls off a cliff or has a nervous breakdown. It's all for the telly.

'Yeah, okay,' Lockie says. 'Pass me a pen – the show must go on.'

His last few words hit me. The show must go on.

Lockie signs his without hesitation. I hover for a moment, pen in hand, knowing he's right, I just wish it didn't have to be this way.

But then I sign.

The sooner this is over, the better. I've got my bikini on, I'm working on my smile – inside I'm screaming though.

This is going to be hard – especially if Lockie keeps being so annoyingly sexy.

12

The way the island smells is ingrained in my memory. Stepping off the little boat, onto the jetty, the salty sea is what hits me first, then the leaves, and finally that sun cream smell you only seem to experience naturally on holiday. From a bottle, this fragrance would cost a fortune.

It really is a beautiful place. A picture-perfect scene pulled right off a postcard. White sand, turquoise water, palm trees gently swaying. It's like looking at pure paradise, but this paradise looks back. Even before I spot the cameras hidden in the tree branches, I feel them. Watching. There's nowhere to breathe without an audience.

There are cameras almost everywhere. I forget how many there are exactly but every accessible inch of the island is covered. As we walk past one – one of the security-style ones – I hear the sound of it panning, being remotely operated, capturing footage of us. I'm not sure if I'll be able to get used to that noise, the sound of the cameras stalking us, watching our every move. Capturing the audio feels even more intrusive. All contestants – including me and Lockie now – have to wear a wristband. It's a very clever piece of tech. It runs off solar power, so it never needs charging, and it contains GPS so that contestants can always be monitored – that way, we can't lose anyone (not that we ever have). But the main reason we use them is because they contain a little microphone, that connects to receivers all around the island, so that we can capture every sound. And for 'safety' once the wristbands go on they can't come off, not without the key. I feel so claustrophobic, with it on my wrist. One of the show's main features is that it has a live feed so, from the moment the show starts, that's it, game face on.

Lockie and I exchange silent glances as we walk, I'm nervous whereas he looks more excited. And then they separate us. Lockie disappears one way with a handler, me the other. My stomach twists. I know it's for the entrance, but suddenly I hate the idea of not having him by my side.

'All right, Cleo,' Will, the handler, says as he reaches out to untwist my bikini strap. The straps are so impossibly thin, like spaghetti, and I appear to lack the elegance to keep them in place. 'You're up in thirty,' he continues. 'Just remember: smile, breathe, walk out confident. They're going to love you.'

I don't want them to love me – I need them to vote me off the island, ASAP... and yet, I don't know, part of me does want people to like me. We all want to be liked, right?

I adjust my bikini as I walk. I feel like it's riding up my butt – or maybe it's supposed to be there – and I feel little more than a sneeze away from a nip slip, but it's too late to do anything about it now. Hilariously, the bikinis seemed like they would cover more than the swimsuits – all of them had those cut-outs that look great if your body is perfect, but otherwise could not possibly contain other lumps and bumps. Mine is a simple black two-piece. Modest by reality TV standards – which only makes me feel even more self-conscious, because I know everyone else will be in slivers of neon fabric, gracing their perfectly toned, well-oiled bodies.

And then I notice Arabella – the host – waiting to greet me. Arabella obviously knows that Lockie and I are part of the crew, filling in, but she's a professional so she doesn't let on.

God, she's stunning. She's wearing a slinky bronze dress – there are those cut-outs again – and her hair in her trademark perfect waves that somehow defy the humidity.

'And you must be Cleo!' she announces, her smile brighter than the sun above us. 'Come and join us.'

My legs feel like jelly as I step forward. The sand moves beneath my feet, making me feel unsteady. And here they are, the contestants that Lockie and I spent so long picking out.

Honey. Camilla. Ozzy. Tony. Faces I've looked at more than my own reflection recently because we've been so busy trying to get everything perfect.

Now they're staring at me like I'm one of them. This is so surreal.

Honey twirls a lock of platinum-blonde hair between her fingers, batting her lashes, her head tipped curiously. She's made a name for herself as everyone's favourite airhead since she was on *Roomies*, a reality show where people have to live in an apartment together.

Then there's Camilla. She's beautiful but she rarely smiles. Her face is perfectly symmetrical, perfectly pouty, and she looks perfectly miserable to be outside Knightsbridge – even though we're in paradise. She's from *City Knights*, a fly-on-the-wall show showing the Knightsbridge elite having the time of their lives. I honestly can't imagine her lasting five minutes here – then again, I feel the same way about myself.

Tony is from a similar kind of show, except he's from Essex, and he's a fun-loving geezer. He keeps running a hand through his hair, making sure it's perfectly blown back still. He's got a perfect tan already, and the whitest teeth I've ever seen, and I know manicured eyebrows when I see them.

And then there's Ozzy, a genuine beefcake. He's tall and broad, toned to perfection, mixing golden retriever energy with pure rugged manliness. He wears his longish blonde hair in a man bun, which really works for him, and only adds to his sporty, outdoorsy look. He's from some survival show, I never watched it, but they had to go to the toilet in the wild and eat plants. Whatever he did eat, it looks good on him.

And then, of course, there's Lockie, and seeing him here, in his trunks, his ripped body on display – you know what? He looks just like one of them, like he was made for this show. The only person who doesn't look like they belong here is me.

I know them all – too well – and I'm starting to think pretending I don't is going to be harder than I thought.

'So, Cleo, our final contestant,' Arabella purrs. '*Welcome to Singledom*. You and Lockie are our two civilian contestants, joining our reality TV legends. Are you excited?'

Okay, as cover stories go, it's not the best, but it will have to do. My throat is dry. I can hear the cameras zooming in, I feel like I'm surrounded.

'Yes.'

Wow, one word, I'm just a big bag of charisma, aren't I?

Arabella tilts her head, her eyes sparkling on cue.

'Do you think "the one" might be sitting here, waiting for you?' she asks me.

She will have asked everyone questions, when they came out, but being the last one makes me feel like I'm being put on the spot.

Me? Find the one? Please. None of these guys are 'the one' for me. I can't say that on camera though.

'Who knows?' I say, smiling, shrugging, trying to channel my inner islander. 'I really hope so.'

I really don't.

'I hope you do too,' Arabella says. 'So, islanders, your adventure begins right here. Head to your campsite, on the beach, start building shelters, making fires – whatever you need to do to survive the night. If you feel inclined to couple up, you can, but for now – you're a team. Give yourselves the best chance of surviving together – tomorrow, you divide and conquer.'

Okay, now the show really is on the road.

We all walk together, none of us really knowing what to say just yet, although Honey is squealing with each step. The path is rough sand mixed with patches of dirt, winding through palm groves towards where we camp. My eyes keep darting, clocking every camera watching us as we go, hearing that noise they make as they pan with us. There's nowhere to breathe. Nowhere to get a break from the twenty-four-seven monitoring. Well, except the outhouse, a shed for one with a bucket that has to be routinely emptied. Obviously I knew this was the toilet situation, I've worked on this show for years, and yet I feel like the reality of it has just caught up with me. This is where I'll be 'going' for the foreseeable.

The camp itself is just a clearing where the woods meet the beach. We have some supplies stacked neatly at the edges. Wooden poles, ropes, palm fronds, a flint kit. The illusion of survival, prepped and laid out, ready for us to play, and yet it's all still so real. Like, I don't know what to do with any of that, and I've seen the show, I've seen other people try to survive out here, and yet I've never really taken notes – why would I?

Ozzy claps his hands, raring to go.

'Right! Well, I've done this before, so I'm happy to take the lead,' he begins. 'So let's crack on. Tony, Camilla, you start on the shelter poles. Honey, you and Cleo get the fronds. I'll work on the fire – Lockie, you can help.'

'What's a frond?' Honey giggles.

To be fair, I only know because I've seen the show before.

Ozzy is delighted to be in charge, and I don't mind, because at least someone is taking care of things. If he knows how to make a shelter, that's one less thing for us to worry about.

'I've just had my nails done,' Tony says. We all stare at him. 'What? I like to keep tidy nails, there's nothing wrong with that.'

'You knew where you were coming, bro,' Ozzy tells him.

Camilla narrows her eyes at the poles.

'I'm not touching them if he isn't,' she insists.

'I can do that,' Lockie tells them. 'I'm sure Ozzy doesn't need me to start a fire.'

'Not at all, bro, I just wanted to make sure you felt included,' Ozzy tells him with a pat on the back.

Wow, okay, are the alphas squaring up already?

'I'll help you,' I tell Lockie. 'Camilla, Tony – you can help Honey.'

'Thanks,' Lockie says.

'You're welcome,' I reply.

'So, Cleo, right? First time on a show like this?' Lockie asks.

I can't help but smile.

'Something like that,' I reply.

'I think we're the only two normal people this year,' he says.

'Are you saying that lot aren't normal?' I check.

We look over at them. Camilla, Tony and Honey make a pretty useless trio, with none of them really knowing what they're doing, while Ozzy is the opposite, singing to himself as he starts the fire with ease.

'Are you saying they are?' he replies with a chuckle.

We work side by side, pretending we've never met, chatting

like strangers. It's weirdly... easy. Like we're meeting for the first time all over again. He asks about my 'type', I volley back with banter. It feels almost natural – until I catch a camera glinting from a tree and my stomach drops, that is. Because none of this is natural really, is it? Not the flirting, not the introductions, none of it.

I glance at the others, throwing themselves into the chaos of challenges, or staying true to their reality TV personas, and my throat tightens with respect. They do this every day. They live their lives like this, putting it all out there in front of the cameras, their good sides and their not-so-good sides, shall we say. And now, for one night only, I'm supposed to do the same.

It's just one night, that's what I need to remind myself. Anyone can do anything for one night, right?

Tomorrow the real contestants will arrive. Tomorrow Lockie and I will be 'voted off', sent back to our real jobs, back on the relative safety of the yacht where we belong.

I repeat it to myself in my head like a mantra as the sun dips lower, painting the sky orange. Just one night. Just one night. Just one night.

We'll be back on the yacht, our fifteen minutes firmly over, before we know it. Right...?

13

There's no way I got more than an hour or two of sleep last night – what was I expecting? A good night's rest is about as likely as free Wi-Fi for all guests. We're not here to be comfortable, we're here to be tortured.

I just kept closing my eyes, hoping some degree of unconsciousness would show up out of pity or boredom, but my brain was too active. Plus, for a deserted island, there are so many noises. Greenery moving, critters scurrying around, the sound of the ocean – and, of course, the cameras. Even if you manage to stop looking at them you don't forget that they are here, because as they turn to follow us, that mechanical noise easily gives them away.

Oh, and if it isn't the noise, it's the physical discomfort. The sand feeling too hard, too soft, grains of it working their way into my bikini top and feeling scratchy against my skin. Knowing what I do about the show, I know there's a chance to get beds, at some point soon, but I'm hoping that won't matter. By the end of the day, I should be gone. Back on the yacht. Eating catered food and then sleeping in my nice real bed. Ugh, a real bed. It's only been one night and I'm fantasising about a real bed like it's an ex-boyfriend, the one that got away. Not that I fantasise about missing my ex, if I fantasise about anything, it's ruining his life, but you take my point.

Even just a pillow would help. A pile of dried-up palm leaves is not a pillow, or anything even close to a pillow, and it's not even like I can use my spare clothes to pile up like a pillow because the only clothes we have are teeny-tiny bikinis and barely there swimsuits. I could take everyone's clothing and I still wouldn't be able to feel it under my head.

I have no idea what time it is, the show banks on it, but it has been light for a while so I'm going to call it: it's morning.

The air is already hot and sticky, and the sun is shining bright and relentless. There's no gentle breeze, nothing to take the edge off, just pure humidity. I can feel beads of sweat forming at the back of my neck before I've even sat up, like I'm slowly beginning to melt. The urge to get in the sea is overwhelming – but then again, I remember how warm the water is here, so I doubt it would do much. The only sure-fire way I know to cool off is the waterfall over the lagoon – it's man-made, not that you'd know, and the clean water that flows is what contestants (and me now) use to shower. I've seen it in the editing studio, and on TV, but I've never actually been to it in all the years I've been working on the show. It's going to be weird, seeing it in real life, like visiting the Eiffel Tower or the Golden Gate Bridge for the first time.

I roll over and see Lockie.

Of course he's managed to sleep – and he's still flat out, on his back, starfishing on the sand. I watch his chest rise and fall as he breathes, in and out – it's almost relaxing, trying to match his breathing. Ironic, really, when usually he causes me nothing but stress. It's weird, we've barely spoken about anything apart from work since the masquerade ball. Just small talk here and there – like we've just met. In a way it's helping, we're not acting like people who know each other, there's an awkwardness between us.

He even snores attractively, if you can believe it. A kind of soft, rumbly sound that would be soothing in a different context, like if you were sleeping next to him in bed, not melting into the sand beneath you, trapped on a reality TV show with cameras filming your every move.

I am hyper-aware of the cameras again, Lord knows how many are on me right now. Watching me watch him. Shit. That'll look fantastic in the edit, won't it? Maybe they'll add a slow zoom and some romantic music, making it look like I'm perving over him when really I'm wondering how much sand I could throw at him before it would disturb his pleasant slumber.

Yep, definitely time to get up, to be normal and boring and secure my ticket out of here.

Walking down to the beach, I can see that Ozzy is already moving around by the firepit. He's shirtless – of course he is, all of the men will be shirtless for the duration of the show but, in balance, his trunks cover more skin than my bikini.

He looks like he's cooking something, smoke curling around his large frame as he hovers by the fire. He turns to look at me as I approach him and he lights up.

'Cleo, good morning,' he says. 'Did you sleep well?'

'Ehh,' I reply, smiling back.

'I can help you get more comfortable tonight,' he suggests – he sounds more caring than flirtatious. I suppose survival stuff is his thing though.

'That would be great, thank you,' I reply. 'What are you making?'

'Breakfast,' he replies as I step closer to look. 'Grilled pineapple. Fancy some?'

'I'd love some,' I reply.

They leave us some fruit to get us started but otherwise food has to be found, caught or won – and even then, it's not like a Maccies or made by a Michelin-starred chef, it's islandy-type food.

The smell hits me and my stomach growls before I can stop it.

'Best fuel there is,' he says as he flips a piece with flair. 'Best fuel we've got right now, at least. It would be better with some fish, for protein.'

I pull a face.

'I'm not sure about fish for breakfast,' I reply.

'You will be, in a few days, when your body is demanding to be fed,' he informs me with a knowing grin.

I won't be because I won't be here.

I sit cross-legged beside him, the sand already hot beneath my thighs. I thank him as he hands me my breakfast on a thick, chunky leaf. It's sticky and sweet and burns my tongue, it's so good. I hadn't realised how starving I was.

I chew it slowly, savouring the way it tastes, feeling so lucky that it isn't a chunk of fish.

Ozzy takes a seat next to me and devours his food like a wild animal.

'Steady on,' I joke. 'I'm not going to take it from you.'

'You say that, but I once had to wrestle a goat to get my dinner back,' he replies with a laugh.

'You did not wrestle a goat,' I reply, amused.

'You're right, it wrestled me,' he jokes. 'Maybe. It depends who you ask. I do have a scar on my leg to show for it.'

'I'm not sure if that's badass or not,' I reply.

'One of my scars has to be cool,' he insists jokily. 'There was the time I slept in a hammock during a thunderstorm. It caught the wind like a sail – if I hadn't landed face down on the floor, it probably would have taken me out to sea.'

'You're way into survival stuff, right?' I check – although I know. 'Pretty sure I've seen a TikTok of you eating bugs.'

'Ahh, they weren't that bad,' he replies. 'Crunchy. Sort of like crisps if you don't think too hard about it when you eat them.'

I would think so hard about it – probably for the rest of my life.

'And my scars, I don't know, I sort of like them,' he continues. 'They tell a story – show my resilience. Like, I got this scar here from a machete accident.'

The line stretches diagonally across his torso, pale against his tanned skin. It's clearly not recent, and his abs are puffed up just fine beneath them, but it looks like it was a bad one.

I wince just looking at him.

'Go on, feel it,' he says. 'You can still feel the ridge.'

'Oh, I...'

'Go on,' he says again. 'It doesn't feel like you'll expect it to...'

I can feel the cameras on us – I swear I just heard one move, to get a better angle of the action. The producers are probably foaming at the mouth back on the yacht. If Simon is in there he'll be screaming at me to do it, to touch Ozzy's abs.

My hand is on the way before my brain can have a real say in it.

My fingers brush his warm skin, skimming his scar, running back and forth over it while he watches me.

I suddenly realise how close we're sitting. How intimate this must look. The air feels thicker now. My heart is pounding – I hope the mic can't pick up on it.

This is exactly the kind of moment we live for on the show, the start of what looks like something, a moment...

And that's when a voice behind us says: 'Good morning.'

I yank my hand away like I've just accidentally touched the fire. I hear the cameras moving, trying to find their new angle, waiting to see what happens next.

I turn around and see Lockie standing there, one arm behind his head as he stretches. His hair is a sleepy mess but in a way where he's totally pulling it off. His expression is neutral, but I catch a flicker of something... I'm not sure what. It turns into a smirk soon enough.

Somewhere, a gull screams overhead – sort of mirroring the screaming in my head, but rather than it being an act of solidarity, I think it probably just wants my pineapple.

I open my mouth to say something – anything – but I'm saved by the bell.

Literally. A bell sounds before someone speaks to us over the intercom.

'Islanders! Please gather at the firepit.'

It grabs everyone's attention. Honey runs over, squealing, joining the rest of us. Camilla isn't far behind her. It's Tony who appears last in a pair of skintight budgie smugglers. I feel my eyes widen – there's no way he doesn't have a coconut or something stuffed down there.

'It's time for your first challenge,' the voice of the island tells us. 'A team challenge, so get into pairs.'

Ozzy's eyes light up.

'Yes, finally!' He looks at me. 'Wanna team up?'

'Me?' I blurt.

'Yeah!'

I hesitate. The plan – if you can even call it that – is for me to stick with Lockie. We'll blend into the game together, couple off, and then bow out gracefully when the real cast arrive.

But Ozzy is smiling at me, and the cameras are rolling – they're fixed on us right now. If I refuse him, I don't know, won't it seem fake?

So I nod.

'Yeah, sounds great,' I reply.

Out of the corner of my eye, I see Lockie's face. There's a flicker of surprise, maybe even disappointment? Probably just because I'm not sticking to the plan.

Before anyone can say another word, Honey sidles up to Lockie, twirling a strand of hair.

'We could be partners?' she says, batting her eyes. 'I'm, like, really bad at, like, building things. Or… most things. But I'll try?'

Surely no one could say no to that smile, even if she sounds like she'll be more of a hindrance than a help.

Lockie wraps an arm around her to reassure her.

'Don't worry. You'll do great,' he says.

The voice booms again. 'Today, you'll be building camp beds. The first two couples to finish get to keep their beds. The couple who comes last will return their materials and sleep on the sand.'

'Oh, brilliant,' Tony mutters, rolling his eyes. 'So I'll mess up my hands building, or my back sleeping on the sand again.'

Camilla glares at him – I think she's just realised they're going to have to work together.

'But, if we're a team, and you're going to need to do the work, and you won't…'

Wow, she's so entitled.

'I'll try,' Tony says. 'We both have to try…'

'But they both have an alpha,' she replies. 'It just seems unfair, that I'm the only one who doesn't get an alpha.'

'Who's Ann Alpha?' Honey asks, looking around.

Camilla gives her a look like she's just asked if that big light in the sky was a big lamp. 'No, darling, alpha male,' Camilla tells her. 'Like... the strongest, most dominant male.'

'Ohhh.' Honey's mouth forms a perfect O shape. 'Yeah, 'kay, I don't know what that is.'

Lockie reaches forward to get some water from the pan over the fire and Honey quickly grabs his hand.

'That handle gets hot,' she warns him. 'Be careful.'

Lockie smiles.

'Aww, you've got my back already,' he tells her.

'Okay, well, pineapple and water for everyone,' Ozzy says. 'Then we can get started.'

We have to boil our water, that we get from a nearby stream, before we can drink it. It's weird, if you drink it before it's properly cooled, it feels more drying than hydrating.

Then it's time to take our positions for the challenge. There are three stations on the beach with materials stacked up ready to be used. We're assembling wooden camping beds, but not like IKEA flat-pack; it's just cut wood that you hammer together. At least the part we lie on is a stretchy, elasticated sheet that is held in place – well, if you do a good job. We're making two single beds each and, like I said, all being well, I won't be here later tonight. But... good to bag myself a bed, just in case.

Ozzy instantly takes charge of ours, his muscles flexing as he hits pieces of wood together with a casual expertise. I mostly just hand him things. He barely needs me, to be honest, but we're a team.

Looking over, I can see that Lockie and Honey are floundering, though he's doing his best to take the lead. Honey stands beside him with a hammer, squinting at the wood like she's not sure which end is which.

Meanwhile, Tony has sat down on a pile of planks.

'I don't do manual labour,' he announces.

'For God's sake, do something,' Camilla shrieks at him, but he's too busy inspecting his nails to see if he's dinged his manicure.

I almost feel bad for her. And for him. Almost.

Ozzy is halfway through tying off our second corner when Lockie glances over.

'Looking good, mate,' Lockie calls. 'Especially with that spider on your neck.'

Ozzy freezes.

'What?'

'There.' Lockie points vaguely. 'Oof, it's a big one. Do they bite here?'

Ozzy jerks sideways so fast he nearly topples the whole bed frame. His hammer slips and lands on his toe. I swear I hear the crack.

I wince.

'Are you okay?' I check.

His jaw tightens and his eyes bulge. For a second, I think he's going to explode. But then I watch him visibly shove the pain somewhere deep inside, forcing a smile back on to his face.

'Jokes like that aren't funny in the wild,' he tells Lockie. Then he turns to me. 'I'm all good, barely felt a thing.'

Lockie's smirk falters. Just slightly.

Ozzy gets right back to it, finishing our bed like nothing happened, and sure enough, we're the first couple to finish.

'Congratulations, Ozzy and Cleo! You've won your beds.'

Ozzy takes me by the waist and lifts me clean off the ground with ease, spinning me in a victory twirl. I squeal before I can stop myself, heat rushing to my cheeks.

I notice Lockie's eyes are on us. Unamused.

Second place goes to Lockie and Honey, whose half-crooked beds somehow hold together well enough.

Tony and Camilla... well, they're still sitting on a pile of wood, glaring at each other.

'Sorry, Tony and Camilla,' the booming voice declares. 'You'll be returning your materials to the hatch. No bed for you tonight.'

Camilla looks like she's mulling over the idea of rage-quitting the show. Tony shrugs and mutters something about a combination of sand and sunburn exfoliating his skin.

'Let's try them out,' Ozzy suggests.

Currently the beds are side by side. What usually happens, when people couple off, is that they push their beds together to make a double. Ozzy gives them a nudge closer together, but not quite touching, before we lie down.

'See? We make a good team,' he says. 'We should stick together.'

He's sweet. He's handy, as my gran would say. He's objectively gorgeous. But as he beams at me, all I can think is: I'm not here to take part. I'm not here to find someone. I'm a prop, an understudy drafted into the mix before the real stars arrive.

Still. I can't deny it. That was... fun, for me at least. I'm not sure Lockie is having as much fun, the look on his face speaks volumes. What is it saying, though? I have no idea.

14

We're all gathered around the firepit, eating some food, and trying to relax after a chaotic day on the island.

I say trying to relax because, one, it's hard to relax when you're being filmed, and two, I'm surprised Lockie and I are still here. The real contestants must not have arrived yet. I just need to be patient.

Ozzy spears a piece of fish with a stick he's fashioned into a skewer – because of course he has. Everything he does is so intensely manly.

'Enjoy,' he says. 'Help yourselves. And no complaining, because it's this or nothing.'

'No complaints here,' Tony says, talking through a huge mouthful. 'Swear down, after my old dear's Sunday roast, best thing I've ever had. It's well fresh.'

'It's... edible,' Camilla adds. She nibbles delicately, like a cute little bunny.

Honey's sitting cross-legged, swaying slightly as she eats, looking the happiest she's ever been.

'It's kinda salty,' she says, then beams like that's a compliment.

I can't quite figure Honey out. Something about her vibe is just... off.

Lockie wipes his hands on his shorts – there are no serviettes in paradise – and nods at Ozzy.

'You keep this up, we'll build you a statue out of sand,' he jokes.

'Like I'm like your god?' Ozzy replies, impressed.

'Sure,' Lockie says with a laugh.

'I'm just doing my best, using what's here,' he replies. 'Fish are practically volunteering to jump in the fire. I am looking for a goddess though...'

I pick at my portion, grateful it's stopped my stomach from growling in complaint.

The disembodied voice of the island crackles through the speakers all of a sudden.

'Islanders, there is something in the hatch. The first boy to get there wins a perk.'

There's a beat of stillness. Then they're off – well, Lockie and Ozzy are.

You've never seen true alpha chaos until you've watched two grown men, both part peacock, part toddler, race for a mystery box like it contains the one cure for a disease we all have.

Sand slings everywhere as they run, and they're neck and neck for the most part.

Tony doesn't even flinch. Just bats a lazy hand and keeps chewing.

'I ain't competing with those two in a race,' he says. 'I'd rather keep my dignity.'

'You're not going to run like a good boy?' Camilla asks with a twisted smile.

'You'd go mad if I called you a good girl,' he replies.

'I love being called a good girl,' Honey adds in an overly sexy tone.

Camilla doesn't look impressed – Tony does though.

Honey leans forward, watching Lockie and Ozzy go, tipping her head and biting her lip like it's a Diet Coke break.

'Oh my God. Look at them. They're like... antelopes,' she says. 'But, like... well fit.'

'Honestly, it's embarrassing to watch,' Camilla adds. 'Respect to you, Tony, for not bothering.'

I don't say anything. Mainly because I'm too busy watching them tear across the sand like they've been training for this moment all their lives, but also because I'm still very aware that we're being filmed. I don't want to be caught saying anything I'll regret.

They're neck and neck. Lockie's longer strides eat up the ground, but Ozzy's pure power. Every few seconds one pulls ahead, then the other.

Tony starts commentating, like it's the Grand National.

'Ozzy takes the lead, Lockie is hot on his heels, then Ozzy again, but Lockie's right behind him, then Ozzy...'

They're almost there when Ozzy does something superhuman. He digs deep, shoulders dropping, stride widening. He just... powers forward. Like he's been storing a turbo boost in his calves for exactly this moment. Lockie tries to match him, but it's too late. Ozzy slams a hand down on the hatch, claiming his prize.

'And it's Ozzy who wins,' Tony announces.

Lockie arrives half a second later and bends over, his hands on his knees as he sucks in air like he's been minutes without it.

Ozzy straightens up, catching his breath first, and pulls out an envelope, holding it up like a trophy. He jogs back, a little smug bounce in his step. Lockie trails after him, wiping sweat off his forehead with the back of his hand. He looks beat.

Ozzy stops by the firepit, holding the envelope proudly.

'Well,' he says, grinning, 'that was invigorating. Bit of light exercise.'

Lockie collapses onto the sand with a dramatic groan.

'That took at least a year off my life,' he confesses. Well, there's no point trying to pretend otherwise when you're huffing and puffing and your face is kind of purple.

'Good,' Tony says, not looking up from his fish. 'Much as I like you, mate, it means I might win the next one.'

Ozzy makes a show of opening the envelope. Then he clears his throat, adopting a dramatic TV announcer kind of voice.

'If you're holding this,' he starts, pausing for dramatic effect, 'you've won a prize. But first... everyone gets to play a game.'

A mixture of groans and whoops comes from the group.

Ozzy keeps reading.

'There are cards in the envelope. One at a time, islanders will take a card and complete the challenge written on it – sounds easy enough.'

He pulls out the stack of cards and places them in front of us.

Honey claps like a toddler at a birthday party.

'Oh my gosh, I love it, I love it.'

We circle the firepit, taking our seats, letting Ozzy hand everyone a card.

Honey goes first. She looks at her card and giggles.

'Kiss the islander who is your usual type,' she reads out.

She swivels her head towards Tony. Then Lockie. Then Ozzy. Pretending to deliberate in real time – but then she looks at Lockie and you can tell her mind is made up. She stands, totters over to him, and plants a kiss on his lips. It's slow – romantic even – with lips parted. And I'm... I'm jealous? Surely I'm not. I already dodged that bullet.

Lockie gives a little bow.

'I'm honoured,' he says with a smile.

I notice him glance at me for a second, then quickly look away.

Next is Tony. He grumbles as he reads it, like it personally offends him.

'Fuck sake – do a sexy dance for the islander you fancy the most,' he reads.

He looks at Camilla for a split second. She scowls back at him.

'Don't you dare,' she warns him.

He chooses Honey instead. His 'dance' involves two hip thrusts, a dab, and what I think is supposed to be the worm, but he can't get off the floor so he's just sort of humping the sand. It's a dance – it's not sexy.

Camilla's turn.

'Whisper something flirty to the person you think would be the worst kisser,' she reads.

Poor Tony – her eyes go straight to him. She doesn't hesitate. She walks over, leans in, and says something in his ear that makes the colour drain from his face. I don't know if he looks turned on or terrified.

Ozzy goes next.

'Shake hands with the islander you think would steal your partner,' he reads.

He glances over at Lockie.

'Just because you're competitive, mate,' he tells him, offering him his hand to shake.

'Fair enough,' Lockie replies, taking it in good spirits.

My turn – I'm dreading it.

'Oh!' I say, seeing that it's not that bad. 'Give a hug to the person who you think will look after everyone. Well, that's easy... Ozzy?'

'Aww, you babe,' he says as he comes to take his hug.

'Well, you're pretty much our daddy,' I tell him, not thinking about the words I'm using.

'Daddy?' he jokes. 'I'll take it.'

Love finding new and awkward ways to embarrass myself. That better not get clipped and go viral.

Then it's Lockie's turn.

He takes a card, flips it over, and reads aloud: 'Kiss the neck of the girl you could see yourself settling down with.'

'Oof, that's a heavy one,' Honey blurts.

My mouth goes dry.

Honey immediately tosses her hair and angles her body toward him, as if to say she's ready. Well, she did already kiss him, so she looks like she reckons he's going to return the favour.

Lockie surveys the group calmly. It feels like it takes him ages to decide.

Then he walks straight to me and every part of me freezes.

He stops in front of where I'm sitting by the fire. He doesn't say a word. Just reaches down, takes my hand, and gently pulls me to my feet, like this is a rehearsal and I forgot my cue to stand.

I can feel every pair of eyes locked on us. The cameras too. I can imagine Simon bouncing in and out of his seat in the control room, jumping for joy, thinking he's going to get some action.

Lockie steps closer. So close I can smell sun cream on his skin and, God, he smells good. Kind of like he's wearing after-shave, but we don't have anything like that here. It's just him.

His fingers brush my hair aside, clearing a way to my neck,

slowly and gently enough to make my pulse throb in every part of my body. Then his lips touch my neck.

Not a quick peck. Not a jokey tap-and-go. It's slow. Warm. Deliberate. It goes on...

He lingers, breath teasing my skin, lips grazing in a way that makes my knees want to give way. For a second or two – maybe even longer – I forget the cameras watching us. I forget why we're here. I forget my name!

I... melt. Fully. Like ice cream in the sun. My hands wrap around his arms, like I'm holding him in place.

And then he stops.

I snap back too. The world around us comes back into view – the fire's crackle, the camera's whir, oh, and everyone watching.

I step back, slowly, like I'm stepping away from danger, getting myself to safety. I pull my long hair forwards again, covering the scene of the crime, trying to act like it never happened.

Oh. Acting – that's it. Lockie is just putting on a show. He has to be, right? Oh, God, and I enjoyed it. I melted into his arms, forgot where I was, loved every second of it. I'll just have to say I was acting too. No one could torture the truth out of me. Because the truth is... I was way, way into it.

I don't think anyone knows what to say now.

The anonymous voice of the island booms out, smug as ever: 'Islanders, it's time to couple off. As the winner of today's race, Ozzy will choose first.'

My heart does this weird hiccup thing. Oh, God. I know this is fake, I know we're only meant to be here for a short stint, but still, standing in front of people and waiting to see if someone picks you? I'm getting PE flashbacks.

Ozzy stands, brushing sand from his shorts, taking the

moment so seriously. He looks around the circle with a blank expression, giving nothing away.

'Well,' he says, puffing air from his cheeks, 'I just think, like, you've gotta go with your gut, yeah? And connection is important. Real connection – and I think I've made one.' He glances at me for a second, then away. 'So... the girl I'm choosing is someone I've already bonded with, someone who gives as good as she gets, someone I trust.'

My ribcage tightens. Don't be ridiculous, I tell myself. He'll pick Honey – who wouldn't pick Honey? Or Camilla. Christ, even Tony, literally anyone who isn't a crew member undercover.

'I pick... Cleo.'

For a second, I don't move. I don't breathe. I genuinely think I've misheard him.

Me?

Honey's eyebrows hit her hairline. Camilla looks faintly insulted too.

Ozzy just smiles at me, open and easy, like this is the most normal thing in the world.

I stand, my legs wobbly with surprise, and move to stand by his side. He puts a warm hand on my back in that casually possessive way that producers love. Someone in the control room – probably Simon – is probably fizzing with delight. Almost as much as the champagne will be fizzing. Even I can tell this is great TV from here. I might get a slo-mo walking shot out of this, which is equal parts horrifying and hilarious.

And then the voice speaks again.

'Lockie, your turn.'

I don't know why I'm holding my breath still.

Lockie scans the girls, eyes unreadable behind the firelight. But then he smiles.

'The girl I'm choosing is the one I've had the most fun with so far – our beds may be shaky, but we're solid. Honey,' he announces.

She squeals like she's just won a holiday and launches herself into his arms. He catches her, shooting me a glance that I try to ignore.

Then Tony, who looks like he'd rather be anywhere else, sighs.

'Well, that leaves me and you, Camilla,' he tells her.

'Stunning to be chosen last, thanks, guys,' she says sarcastically.

And... it's done. The first coupling. Tony and Camilla, Lockie and Honey, and me and... me and Ozzy!

There's this odd buzzing in my chest – part nerves, part disbelief, part... pride? Being chosen first shouldn't matter. I'm not here to 'find love' or win airtime or make a showreel. I'm here to fill a gap, to play along, and then get out. But still, I feel a little like I've won something – a game I didn't know I was playing.

Lockie gives me a look across the fire that I can't quite read. Maybe it's annoyance. Maybe it's because he thinks I'm getting too into it. It's not jealousy... is it? Either way, it makes my insides feel like jelly.

Let me have my moment though. Ozzy chose me. Me! Over two influencers. We've been styling it out like Lockie and I are the two normal people they've thrown into the Z-list mix, so to be chosen... wow.

Not that I'll let it go to my head. Not that I care – not really. None of this is real – I'm not here as a contestant, I'm here as a glorified prop. A stage marker until the real deal arrives.

Still... it is kind of an ego boost, right?

15

I wake up to the gentle sound of the waves, the beautiful tweeting of the birds – and Ozzy, staring straight at me.

I sit up in bed, quickly, because for a second my brain can't make sense of the world. Then I remember where I am, what's going on – that I'm on a reality show, sleeping on the beach, in a bikini that – oh, thank God, it's still covering all my bits and pieces.

I can just hear the voiceover now – *Day three on the island, and Ozzy is watching Cleo snore.*

'Good morning,' he says, flashing me that winning smile.

'Morning,' I reply, desperately trying to smooth out my hair. 'Have you been awake long?'

'A couple of hours,' he says casually. 'I like a morning run, so I did a few lengths of the beach. This place really is deserted, you know?'

Oh, I know.

He looks annoyingly fresh for someone who has been sweating back and forth across the sand. He just looks so... alive!

I don't know how I'm going to achieve that without a coffee and a shower.

'Yikes,' I say. 'At least we have the cameras looking out for us.'

'Yeah, seems kind of odd, that they've moved production off the island,' he replies. 'I saw the old studio building. That's where the luxury suite is, right? I hope they still have that.'

I know that they do.

'I hope so too,' I say with a smile.

'We've had a delivery for breakfast,' he says. 'Grapes, bananas, pineapple...'

'Sounds great,' I say – but it sounds like fruit. Just fruit. A waffle and some Nutella to go with it would be spot on.

Before I can move, the loudspeaker crackles to life – the voice of the island that always makes me jump. I wonder if I'll get used to it, or if I'll be back off dry land by then... which feels like a weird thing to say.

'Good morning, islanders!' it booms. 'Just a quick update – weather conditions may not be ideal later today. If the wind picks up, you are permitted entry to the storm shelter. Please follow safety instructions if required.'

I tense up.

'Do they have a sponsorship deal with an insurance company?' Ozzy jokes.

I laugh but I'm worried. They're not going to let the storm get to us, are they? Not that they can stop it but they have a duty of care to us, to protect us...

'Here's hoping it's a luxury shelter,' I say, knowing full well it isn't.

'Morning,' Lockie says, placing a hand on my shoulder. 'Are you worried about the storm?'

'We were just having a joke about it,' Ozzy tells him. 'We're good.'

Ozzy gives him a look. Not quite aggressive, but enough to say *hands off my partner*.

Lockie catches it, smirks, and moves the convo along.

'I'm sure we'll all weather the storm together,' Lockie says.

'I saw the shelter, on my run,' Ozzy replies. 'It's basically a hole in the floor with a hatch. Not big. But I reckon it'll do the job, if push comes to shove.'

'Guns like that, you could punch it away, surely?' Lockie jokes. 'But I'm sure we'll be fine. How bad can the weather be? We're in paradise.'

I glance down the beach, where the sea glitters under the sun. It's hard to believe anything bad could happen here – but there's something about the stillness, the heavy air, it feels... off. It's the kind of quiet that, on TV, is always followed by a jump scare or, on a show like this, a surprise recoupling.

'I really hope you're right,' I say quietly.

Lockie grins.

'I'm always right.'

I give him a look that says *you wish*.

He laughs and heads off, probably to get some water. I know I could do with a gallon.

'He doesn't know what he's talking about,' Ozzy says when he's gone. 'I've participated in enough survival shows to know you never underestimate Mother Nature.'

'We're lucky to have you,' I tell him. Well, we are. It's rare someone takes part who is into this sort of survival stuff.

'I've got your back,' he reassures me. 'We're a couple.'

It's weird, to be in a couple – with Ozzy, who chose me, not Lockie, who was under orders to pick me. I'm not here to take part, am I, so it's not like I wanted to be chosen... and yet, I don't know, it's hard not to feel something – some kind of way, as the contestants would say – about being picked first.

I'm only human, so somewhere, deep inside, I do think about what it would be like if I were actually participating, what I'd do, and if I could win. But then I remember that I wouldn't win, how could I, up against reality stars. I'm no one – and I'd rather leave than stick around and win...

Although I do have insider info, I know how the show works, what viewers like... but I'm not here to win, I'm here to lose. And the sooner the better.

16

Where. The. Hell. Are. The. Real. Bloody. Contestants?

I'm starting to worry that Simon has forgotten about me and Lockie. We're still here, in the middle of our second full day, and we're keeping up the act but I don't know how much longer I've got in me.

'Cleo,' Lockie calls out.

I turn to look at him. He's dripping wet from his swim in the sea. Water is rolling down his body, droplets weaving in and out of the contours of his muscles, and I'm trying to ignore that his swim shorts look much clingier when they're wet.

'Yeah?' I reply.

'Can I borrow you?' he asks.

'Erm... yeah,' I say cautiously.

Ozzy, who is doing push-ups next to me, eyeballs me as I go.

'This way,' Lockie says, leading me towards the sea. 'I have something to show you – you're going to love it.'

I hesitate – part of me doesn't want to give him the satisfaction of dragging me away from Ozzy – but curiosity gets the better of me. I brush the sand off my legs and follow him down the narrow strip of beach until the voices of the others fade into background noise.

The tide is coming in – or going out, I haven't been paying attention – so we have to walk a little to get to the water.

'You look stressed,' Lockie points out.

'Oh, I'm fine,' I insist, very much for the audience's sake, well aware that our mics are obviously still on, and the cameras can see down here (even if it's not as closely).

'I know this relaxation tip,' he says. 'I thought you might like to try it with me.'

I look at him and notice something subtle, him pleading with me with his eyes, letting me know not everything is as it seems.

'Sounds great!' I say with faux enthusiasm. 'I could always be less stressed.'

Ain't that the truth.

We stop just before we reach the water. The sea doesn't seem as calm today, waves breaking and foamy on the sand, crashing against any rocks that dare to stand in its way. Still, it seems like paradise. On the surface. If you forget that we're taking it in turns to empty the outhouse, and I haven't had my turn yet. I'm hoping I'll be voted off before my turn comes around, if I'm being honest with you.

'Okay, so how do I relax?' I ask, sounding like I really need it. The breeze whips my hair into my mouth, which only makes me feel more stressed.

'Try to relax,' he says, taking deep breaths in and out.

Is he just trying to wind me up?

He gestures to the horizon.

'I read something once that said if you sit quietly and stare out to sea, while holding hands, it's supposed to be... good for you. Calming. Resets your head. You only have to do it for a minute. Want to give it a go?' he asks.

I really, really don't – but I don't think all is as it seems. I think this is for the cameras.

'You want me to hold your hand?' I check.

'It'll relax you,' he says with a smile.

I roll my eyes for a split second, so only he can see, but fine, I'll do it. I place my hand in his. His palm is warm, his grip steady. It feels... No, I'm not doing that, I'm not thinking about how it feels. It feels like a hand.

His thumb brushes against mine, slow and deliberate, like he knows exactly what he's doing. I guess he does. He's probably held a hundred hands on a hundred beaches. Convinced a hundred girls to make the biggest mistake of their lives by thinking they were special to him.

So we're sitting, looking out over the bluey-green water, holding hands. The sunlight reflects on the water, sparkling like glitter. I take a deep breath of the salty air and, he's right, this does feel better. I could almost forget the cameras, the competition, the fact I feel like I'm trapped here... but not quite. Lockie doesn't say anything, but I can feel him watching me out of the corner of his eye.

'And now we face one another,' he says. 'Holding both our hands.'

I humour him, because I've come this far, but I'm still so confused.

And then he moves, quick, precise as he plunges our hands into the sand, letting it cover them up and above our wrists. It doesn't do much to ease my confusion.

'What are you doing?' I ask.

'Shh. We've got one minute before the tamper alarm goes

off,' he says. 'The sand muffles the mics. Talk fast. No one will be able to hear us.'

There's a real urgency in his voice. He must want to talk exit strategy.

'You and Ozzy,' he begins. 'You seem close.'

My mouth falls open.

'Are you actually... are you jealous?' I blurt in disbelief.

His jaw tenses.

'No. I'm not jealous – of course I'm not,' he insists. 'I'm smart. We're supposed to get voted off together, remember? As a couple. If you're with Ozzy and I'm with Honey, we can't both go, can we? Most likely, you'll end up staying longer. But if not you, then me. Maybe both of us.'

Shit, he's right. I knew that was the plan, I guess I just got a little carried away. I'm not actually enjoying myself, am I? I didn't want to be here, or doing any of this, I guess I just got... temporarily caught up in it all.

His fingers squeeze mine under the sand.

'Right, yeah, I didn't think of that,' I reply.

His eyes dart from side to side, his usual level of confidence not quite there. Silly of me to think he was jealous. He's right, we go together, or at least one of us ends up staying. Plus, Ozzy is popular with the public, so if I'm with him I'll be collateral damage, I'll end up staying, and I cannot stress how much I want to get off this island.

'So, what do we do?' I ask.

'We need to end up together,' he says quickly. 'We need to flirt, to seem inseparable. The next vote will probably be the public pairing people off – we want them to choose us.'

'But we don't even like each other,' I point out.

His eyes widen, his head tips.

'Well, we pretend we do,' he replies. 'Failing that, if they think it will piss Ozzy off, they'll put us together. Either reason will do.'

'Fine,' I mutter. 'Fine. We can pretend – it's probably just for a day, right?'

Time must be up. Lockie pulls our hands out, shaking the sand off before he lets go. He was clever, I think, making sure the camera didn't see our hands (it's not the crew we need to hide from, it's the twenty-four-seven live feed the public can tune into), so maybe it just seemed like technical problems.

Thankfully the tamper alarm didn't go off. I exhale, my heart racing faster than it should for something so small.

My hands are shaking a little, which I try to disguise by pretending to brush sand off my legs. I'm not sure who I'm trying to fool – Lockie? The cameras? Myself? All of the above, probably.

He's right, of course – annoyingly. Pretending to be into him is smart. We need to end up together, if we're going to get out of here as soon as possible.

As we walk back toward camp his hand brushes mine again – casual, almost accidental, but then he hooks his finger with mine.

It's a move, I'll give him that. He's setting out his stall, showing that he's interested in me, letting Ozzy know too.

But it's all for the cameras, right?

17

The voice of the island booms out through the speakers, scaring the life out of me – so still not used to it then.

'Islanders! Time for your next challenge. Teamwork makes the dream work – and today, you'll need it! You must build a raft sturdy enough to support your whole team for two minutes. This is a team effort so, if you succeed, everyone's a winner. A prize will be delivered to the hatch. Good luck.'

I hope the prize is new contestants – real ones – because then I get to leave.

Ozzy cracks on, like he was born to do this.

'Right,' he says, instantly stepping up to take the lead – not that I can think of anyone who could do a better job. 'We'll need logs, rope – or vines, something buoyant. Bamboo maybe. I'm happy to dish out jobs.'

Of course he is.

The rest of us are happy to be told what to do. We shuffle toward the beach. The tide's out, the sand is hot – it's not the kind of day for doing a task. Lockie's carrying an armful of bamboo in a way that is just... so sexy, like he's advertising aftershave for a luxury brand. I could swear he's angling his muscles towards the camera, so they don't miss a second of his flexing.

Camilla takes a seat on the sand, legs crossed, palms up like she's trying to relax.

'I'm not getting splinters,' she says flatly. 'Or dirty. Or wet.'

'Camilla, come on,' Ozzy says, trying to razz her up. 'It's a group challenge. This is to win something for all of us. Be a team player.'

'Okay, I will,' she replies. 'I'll provide the moral support.'

Honey, meanwhile, is tying vines around two bits of driftwood.

'Do you know what you're doing?' Tony asks her.

'If you criss-cross the tension points, you'll... erm... No, not really, I just made that up to sound smart,' she says with a giggle.

I glance at her as she does a comically bad job. Tony takes it from her and has a go instead. There's something about Honey that I can't figure out. Something in her tone, in her ditziness...

She smiles at me, big and blank. I give her a wave. At least she's trying, unlike Camilla.

Lockie wanders over to me, all smiles.

'Need a hand?' he asks. He squats so close I can see the golden flecks in his green eyes. 'I've done my bit – it was easy.'

'I've got it,' I say.

He stays crouched beside me anyway, close enough that I can feel the heat from his skin. His arm brushes against mine, just for a second, I hold my breath.

'I don't know, I think you need me to help,' he says, his tone flirtatious. 'I think you need my hands.'

'I'm perfectly capable of—'

I pull the vine too hard, lose my balance and crash into him. He's only crouching, so I knock him over with ease, and of course, I land right on top of him. Trying to steady myself, to use my limbs to my advantage, only makes me spread them wider and wrap myself around even more thoroughly. Our landing position is Lockie lying on his back, me straddling him.

If Simon is watching this, he'll be buying himself a new sports car to add to his collection.

For a second, it feels like the world has stopped turning. Lockie is holding me steady, his hands on my waist holding me securely in place on top of him. I'm resting my hands on his chest, to keep myself upright, and I could swear I just heard a camera zooming in.

Then someone coughs.

I snap to my senses and scramble to my feet.

'Easy, girl,' he tells me – I must have hopped off a little too fast.

'Are you okay, Cleo?' Ozzy asks me, taking me by the hand, pulling me away from Lockie.

'I'm fine,' I tell him. 'Just… clumsy.'

'Don't blame yourself, Lockie was distracting you,' he reassures me.

'I was offering to help,' Lockie tells him. 'It's not that deep.'

'Let's just get this done,' Ozzy tells us. 'We're almost there and I want to win.'

My cheeks go hot. I focus hard on the vine, but my fingers keep fumbling the knot. Honey comes over and helps me – between us, we crack it.

'Love triangle alert,' she sings at me under her breath.

'Oh, no, it's not a triangle,' I insist.

'Ooh, a square?' she says excitedly. 'Who else is in the mix?'

'No one,' I say with a soft laugh.

I pretend not to notice anything is amiss, focusing on tying the vines, but the air feels thicker suddenly. Ozzy's jaw looks tighter than usual, and when Lockie laughs it just seems to make Ozzy tense up more.

I wonder if the producers are placing bets on how soon someone snaps. That's what they usually do. They take bets on all sorts. First kisses, who will quit, who will have the first row. It feels like any one of those things could happen any minute.

It's a relief, when our raft is done, and even more so when we all get on it and it stays afloat.

'Islanders, all of you must board the raft.'

No prizes for guessing which one of us isn't on it.

'Do I really need to?' Camilla whines. 'Look – it looks fine.'

'Then it's fine to get on it,' Ozzy says, his patience a little thinner than usual.

'We'll make room,' Lockie tells her. 'Cleo, move up to me.'

He opens up his arms so I can back into him, almost. Then he wraps them around me.

'Fine, fine,' Camilla says. 'But if I fall in, I will kill you all.'

Not an overreaction at all. And speaking of overreactions...

'Lockie,' Ozzy says once we're back on dry land. 'Can I pull you for a chat?'

'Uh-oh,' Honey whispers to me. 'Drama tiiime.'

'Sure, mate,' Lockie replies.

Lockie flashes me a wink, then follows Ozzy toward the firepit. I try to focus on my conversation with Honey, which is now about whether or not the island has materials for a pillow fight, but I can't. I'm trying to read their body language.

'I thought they'd be fighting over me, you know,' she says, following my gaze. 'Disappointing, really.'

'Oh, they are not fighting over me,' I insist.

'Please,' Camilla says with a huff. 'They're more likely to be fighting over airtime.'

Charmed.

Ozzy's body language is pure tension – tight shoulders, arms folded, and he's clearly ranting. Lockie looks like he's trying not to laugh, but his foot taps restlessly on the sand.

I can't hear what's said, but I can tell the tone. The clipped words, the defensive smirk, the final head shake. Then Lockie turns and walks back over, looking far too pleased with himself for someone who looked like they were having an argument – so presumably he won.

'What was that about?' I ask.

'I've just been warned off "his girl",' he says with a smirk, wrapping the word 'girl' in air quotes. 'He cited the bro code and everything.'

'His girl?' I reply. 'What, me?'

'His words, not mine.' He laughs. 'Don't worry, he only means because you're coupled off. And I don't take orders from jealous men who need to loosen their man bun a little, I think it's tugging on his brain.'

'Just don't try to wind him up,' I say.

'Cleo, I'm not trying to do anything to him,' he replies. 'You, on the other hand... that's another story.'

And with that, he walks off.

At first I feel my cheeks flush, then pressure building in my forehead, then my palms sweating... but then I remember, he doesn't mean that, it's for the cameras. He's flirting with me so that the public puts us together, so we can get the boot together, so we can go back to working on the show rather than starring in it.

God, I'm tired. Tired of pretending. Tired of acting for cameras. Tired of trying to manage who's playing what part in a script that doesn't really exist. I guess this is Lockie's thing, his speciality, scripted reality. This whole thing is a set-up. None of it's real – not for us, at least. And Ozzy, I'm sure he doesn't care about me, he's just playing the game. Viewers love this, it's how you stay in.

I just need to remind myself of the plan: stay calm, stay dull, get voted off. The only way home is by being boring. Lockie too. Sadly it doesn't seem to come naturally to us. It's like the more I try to be boring, the more I end up as the accidental highlight reel.

I need to do better... or worse, I guess – because the next vote will put us into new couples (the public always decides the second pairing on the show), and I need to be lumped with Lockie. Perhaps I don't need to try so hard. If Ozzy seems jealous, people might just make the call to put me with Lockie just to piss Ozzy off. That could work. That would keep things interesting. Then we can start being boring or making the others seem more interesting, and then, boom, we're gone.

The sooner we do this, the sooner I can get back to the yacht – and to the real world.

I just hope no one I love has tuned in to see this disaster unfold. Because if they have, I might never live it down.

Thankfully none of them watch it, and with flagging views it's not like it will make the news. Just so long as I don't do anything interesting.

Usually, that's not a problem for me.

18

Watching reality TV might make it seem like contestants are always sitting around having dull chats. But when you're actually involved in reality TV – whether working behind the scenes or starring in it – you realise that those conversations about nothing are actually a big part of the day. It can't all be challenges, and you definitely can't just nap your way through it; it's all about keeping things entertaining. Now that I'm here, I truly understand how genuinely, genuinely boring most of those conversations can be.

'I just don't see the point of learning to do things myself,' Camilla says, brushing sand from her forearm. 'I have a lash girl, a brow girl, a hair girl, two spray tan girls, and a cleaner. My PA does all the annoying bits like paying my parking tickets, knowing my passwords and remembering people's birthdays. I have everything covered.'

'You don't remember people's birthdays?' Tony checks.

'Well, some,' she says. 'I know when my own is, obviously. But others, yeah, I have a girl for that.'

'Even, like… your mum's birthday?' he replies.

'Obviously, I know my mum's birthday, darling,' Camilla says, offended that he even asked. 'But my assistant sends her a card. I don't do post offices. Or licking envelopes – who knows where they've been?'

'Everywhere,' Tony jokes. 'Does your assistant wipe your arse for you?'

I shouldn't laugh.

'Funny you should talk about hygiene, because I used the outhouse after you, and it was foul,' she announces for everyone to hear.

Tony places his hands on his chest like she's shot him.

'I'll have you know I'm a very clean boy,' he informs her with a smile.

'I also heard you got your downstairs waxed on TV,' she says. It's like the words taste dirty in her mouth.

He bursts out laughing.

'It was part of the show! It's fly-on-the-wall,' he says in his defence.

'Poor fly,' she says with a smirk.

Honey lets out a little giggle, then tries to hide it behind her hand.

'You lads ever had anything waxed?' Tony asks Ozzy and Lockie.

'Yeah, didn't hurt a bit,' Ozzy insists.

The sky rumbles, distant and low. It makes me glance up. The light is... off. Not dramatic yet, but dulled, like a filter has been laid over everything – or taken away, I guess, because the weather is usually so perfect it looks fake. It's giving less Bahamas, more Blackpool. I squint at the horizon, half-expecting the apocalypse to roll in with a laugh track. Even the birds have shut up. When the island goes quiet, you know something's about to go wrong.

I wish I knew what Simon's weather guy was saying about all of this.

Although I guess there's no need. The heavens have ripped open. No warning rumbles. No polite drizzle. Just a sudden, violent wall of rain, battering us. The storm is officially here, then.

Squeals, swear words, scrambling to our feet – we all head to our shelter, only for the top to blow right off it the second we get there. The wind is really kicking up, bending the palm trees, taking what few things we have and sending them hurtling down the beach. Even if we chased after them, where would we put them?

Then the voice of the island crackles over the nearest speaker, but it's not playful, or dramatic, or full of innuendo like usual. It's urgent. Panicked even.

'Islanders. Proceed to the storm shelter immediately,' it says. 'Stay calm and move quickly. I repeat – proceed to the shelter now.'

Not one person stays calm. We go nought to stampede right away.

Tony's already halfway across the sand (so he can actually run) before the voice finishes speaking. Camilla bolts after him (so I guess she doesn't have anyone who runs for her). Honey squeals and pelts after them. Lockie and Ozzy turn at the same moment, their instincts kicking in at the same time.

I sprint as fast as my feet will let me, but the wet sand has turned into a slip 'n' slide and my left foot goes out from under me without warning. I hit the ground with a splat, right as I reach the trees, meaning – just my luck – I land in the mud. For a second, I contemplate just lying there and letting the elements do their worst. I know, I'm paranoid about going viral, but one fall is a fall. What if I keep getting up and falling down, again and again – I'm not ready to become a meme. Probably not worth dying for, though.

'Shit!' I blurt.

I try to scramble up but the mud just keeps slipping, giving me nothing to grip, no way to get back on my feet.

I look up in time to see Ozzy turn back. He hesitates, just for a fraction of a second. His eyes flick to the treeline, the storm, the others sprinting ahead. It's a moment of calculation, pure survival brain.

Lockie doesn't hesitate at all. He doubles back immediately, skidding in the mud, practically sliding into me.

'I've got you, it's okay,' he says.

He scoops me up, one arm under my knees, the other around my back, and runs with me in his arms.

The raindrops are so big they almost hurt, pounding my skin, getting in my eyes, making it almost impossible to see.

Tony stands by the shelter hatch, waving frantically.

'Quick, quick,' he calls out.

We reach the hatch just as a gust almost rips the door from his hands. We all pile inside, squashing up tight like we're playing sardines, so that Tony can close the door.

Instant darkness, then dim emergency lights buzz to life. It's so cramped – shoulders touching shoulders, knees overlapping, someone's elbow in someone else's ribs.

It smells like the apocalypse in here, and it sounds like it outside. Wind roaring, rain thrashing against everything, the sound of palm trees snapping like twigs.

Honey wipes at her face, trying to flick the water from her eyes.

'I've watched every series of *Welcome to Singledom* and I've never seen weather before. Like, bad weather. Not ever.'

'It is *Survival of the Fittest*,' Ozzy reminds her.

'I thought that meant, like, hotness,' she replies.

Obviously it's a pun.

'I guess the show is closer to storm season this year,' Lockie points out, still catching his breath.

I give him a sideways look. He's the reason we're filming this late – all his new ideas, which are working out just wonderfully for us, by the way. I'd say something, but he did just carry me to safety, so I'll hold my tongue... for now.

Camilla's hugging her knees, horrified.

'Everything is going to be filthy,' she says.

Because that's our biggest problem.

'The rain will clean it all, love, don't worry,' Tony jokes.

Ozzy squeezes water out of his hair before re-securing his man bun. He seems relatively calm.

'These storms come in big and ugly and then leave like nothing happened,' he tells us. 'We'll be back to paradise before you know it.'

I don't know about that. I've worked on this show for multiple seasons and I've never seen weather like this. It's hard to imagine what we'll be going back out to.

'Right!' Tony claps his hands once. 'Alphabet game. Foods. A to Z. Let's go.'

'Are you a child?' Camilla asks him.

'We've nothing better to do, 'ave we?' he reminds her. 'Come on, we'll go mad.'

'I'll go mad regardless,' she says.

'I believe that,' he replies. 'Come on, Honey, you can go first.'

'A... apple,' she says proudly.

'Good one,' Tony replies. 'Who wants B?'

Camilla sighs and rolls her eyes dramatically.

'What about when we get to X?'

'Extra apples,' Honey says, beaming like she's solved all our problems.

I lean my head back against the wall. This is going to feel much longer than it is – however long it is. I try to count the seconds by the sound of rain but lose the will before I even get to fifty. It's an interesting feeling, experiencing both boredom and mortal danger at the same time. It doesn't make for a very good headspace.

Ozzy closes his eyes.

'Perhaps we should sit quietly for a bit,' he suggests. 'Sometimes the sound of a storm can be relaxing.'

A fresh crash of thunder rattles the hatch roof. I think it's safe to say no one is relaxed, not even him.

Lockie shifts in his seat, then casually drapes an arm around my shoulders. I stiffen for half a second, then force myself to stay neutral. I have to remember it's for the cameras, even in here. I can see just the one, up in the corner.

Still... for half a moment, with the world falling to pieces outside, his arm feels warm and solid around me. It makes me feel better, even if it isn't real.

The storm doesn't sound like weather, it sounds like war.

It feels like hours of the wind howling, the rain hammering the tin roof like it's trying to break in, thunder rumbling so loudly I feel it physically rattle me. Conversation dried up after the third round of the alphabet game (J is for 'Japan', K is for 'Kyrgyzstan', L is for 'Let's never play this again'). The storm shelter is barely big enough for six people to crouch in, let alone lie down. It's a glorified hole with a hatch, dug into the ground and lined with rusty metal. It barely seems fit for purpose, but we're still here (in both respects).

We're crammed shoulder to shoulder along the curved wall, squashing one another, getting on each other's nerves.

Honey's curled up against one corner, twisting her damp hair into curls. Camilla keeps flinching every time water drips from somewhere overhead, as though getting any wetter will suddenly make her hair look worse. Tony is just staring up – I'd love to know what goes through that man's mind. Ozzy is sitting cross-legged, eyes closed like he's meditating, like he's mentally somewhere else. And I'm still with Lockie, his arm still around me, still taking comfort from the warmth of his body.

No one's spoken in maybe twenty minutes. I think we're all a bit sick of each other's company, to be honest.

Eventually the weather lets up, the noises calm, the shelter doesn't feel like it's shaking. The air feels different, all of a sudden, like the island can breathe again.

Lockie runs a hand through his hair.

'It sounds like it's over,' Lockie says.

Ozzy cocks his head and listens to the nothingness.

'Yeah, it'll be out to sea by now,' he adds.

Nobody moves at first. It's like we're all waiting for someone else to be the idiot who opens the door first and gets struck by flying debris or blown out to sea.

'I'm not sitting in here with you lot any longer,' Tony says, heading for the door. 'If I die, I die outside, not in here from boredom.'

The hatch door creaks open and... yep, the storm has passed. We can go back outside.

One by one, we crawl out and... oh, it's bad.

Palm trees bent like snapped straws. Fruits and branches and God-knows-what scattered everywhere. The storm has ploughed through the island and taken no prisoners.

That's not the worst part though. There's something so, so much scarier than our camp being trashed. It's as we're walking through the trees, back to the beach. You know that unnerving sound of the cameras following us, panning as someone in the control room remotely stalks us? The only thing more unnerving than hearing them, it turns out, is not hearing them. They're not moving. No one is controlling them. I don't think anyone is watching...

The others don't notice. Perhaps they're not as sensitive to them as I am, or they're too busy taking in the aftermath.

Our shelters are gone. Flattened and/or scattered like confetti. The beds we built seem to have survived but they're not where we left them and they're soaked like everything else is.

Camilla hugs herself.

'Well, we can't sleep here,' she says. 'Not now.'

She looks around for a camera to complain to.

'Do you hear me? I said we can't sleep here,' she shouts when she finds one.

'She's got a point,' Tony says. 'I'm surprised no one has come to get us, to take us to safety. They must be on their way... right?'

Honey wipes her nose and looks up at one of the cameras above our camp.

'They wouldn't let us stay here if it wasn't safe,' she says, voice wobbling. Then, louder, to the lens: 'Right? You wouldn't leave us here if it wasn't safe?'

This is normally where the camera would switch from looking at Camilla to looking at Honey but it doesn't move an inch.

Lockie catches my eye. He's noticed it too. That the cameras aren't moving any more.

'They'll reply soon,' Ozzy says. 'For now, let's start Operation: Clean-up. Even if they are coming, we can't leave the beach like this. It's not good for the wildlife. We might as well put every-thing back.'

Tony nods. 'Yeah, come on. It will be easy if we all do it.'

'If we all do it?' Camilla repeats back to him. 'I've been through a lot.'

'We've all been through a lot, princess,' Tony claps back.

Honey instinctively wraps an arm around Camilla to comfort her... only for Camilla to wrinkle her nose every time Honey sniffs hard.

'Perhaps the speakers here got too wet,' Lockie suggests. 'Maybe the crew are trying to speak to us. I'll go for a walk, check the others.'

'Good idea,' Ozzy says.

'Be careful,' I say instinctively.

'Of course,' Lockie replies.

I smile, but my stomach is in knots.

If the speakers aren't responding, if the cameras aren't moving... that means no one's watching – I daren't even think about why not.

'Okay, let's move the beds back up the beach,' Ozzy suggests. 'If they dry out in the sun, we can at least sit. And if it rains again...'

'Let's not even think about that,' Tony suggests.

No one argues. Everyone wants a task – anything to make this feel temporary, like we're past the problem and at the solution.

We carry materials back to where we had them, trying to make things right again. The silence between us is brittle. Every few minutes I look at the cameras, to see if they're moving again, if there are any signs of life, but no such luck.

Something's wrong. Something is definitely very, very wrong. I don't know if it's with the island, the yacht or both, but it's bad.

It's not just the storm, or the mess, or the way the vibe has changed. It's the feeling that we really are well and truly deserted now. We're off-grid, off-brand for the most part, and off the rails. For the first time since this started, I think we might actually be on our own. I know Lockie wanted to raise the stakes – I guess he got his wish. Although even Lockie wouldn't have wanted things to pan out like this. We're alone, with no idea what's going on, and no director to tell us what to do.

Reality TV just got real.

19

No matter how much dried mud flakes off my skin, I never feel any cleaner for it.

Everything feels kind of mucky. The air smells earthy, rather than beachy, and the ground feels wet and sloppy underneath my feet. The last thing I need is to fall again (although if I'm going to, better to do it now, before I get cleaned up).

I'm walking with Lockie to the lagoon so that we can get cleaned up. I'm muddy from when I fell and he got covered in second-hand mud when he carried me.

Without really saying as much, I guess we've decided to keep up the act – well, imagine if our new friends knew we were show plants now – but also, we don't really know what's going on, so best to stick to the script. Still, that doesn't mean we can't troubleshoot things together. Or shower together.

'It doesn't seem like the cameras are working here either,' he says as we reach the lagoon.

Wow, it's so beautiful. It looks perfect – the beauty of it being man-made, with crystal-clear water falling from the waterfall.

'That's what I was worried about,' I say with a sigh. 'I've noticed they're not following us. It's a dead giveaway.'

'So no camera feed, no audio – nothing,' he continues, rubbing his chin thoughtfully.

'But they wouldn't just abandon us here,' I insist. 'They would send help, send someone to get us, get the show back on the road – something. Anything!'

'But no one meant to do this, it was the storm,' he reminds me. 'It's probably fried half the tech. If the rig's down or the signal is blocked, they could be cut off from us completely. Big boats can't get close, it might not be safe for small boats yet.'

My heart pounds so hard if this were a cartoon you would see it jumping out of my chest.

'So we're actually stranded?' I say, although I know the answer. 'And all alone?'

I half-expect him to laugh at how silly and dramatic I'm being but he doesn't. This isn't some manufactured-for-TV twist, Mother Nature is the showrunner now, and she's even worse than Simon.

'Not forever,' he says, like that will do anything to soothe me right now. 'They'll come for us when they can. We just need to keep calm and take care of each other.'

'You can't just tell me to "keep calm" and expect me to feel better,' I insist.

'Think about the flight here, when the turbulence hit,' he reminds me. 'I was there then and I'm here now. Okay?'

I nod reluctantly. He has a point.

'The good news is that I don't think the whole island is without power because, look, the waterfall is still running,' he points out. 'So not only can we still shower, but it's a sign of life. Perhaps it's just the transmitters, for the audio and video that are down, which is why they can't see or hear us, and we can't hear them, but they'll be working on it.'

'I really hope you're right,' I reply. 'But the show can't go on, not with everything broken, and the island trashed. They'll have to send help.'

'I'm sure they will,' Lockie replies.

I step under the waterfall, letting the freezing cold water crash over me for the first time, and it's as shocking as it is invigorating. I can't help but scream.

Lockie steps under too, to wash the mud away. I try to focus on the feeling of the water, the sound of it crashing, of the pump that carries it to the top so that it can crash down over us. And then I feel Lockie, behind me, his hands finding their way to my shoulders, rubbing them, trying to massage out some of my tension. I let out a little moan. My God, that's good. For all the bravado and excessive manliness, his touch is actually quite gentle, but firm where it needs to be.

I lean back into him before my brain can object, my spine pressing against his chest, my bum practically clicking into place against his shorts as the water pours over us.

I turn my head slightly so I can look at him and as I stare into his eyes he gives me a smile that says—

'Am I interrupting something?' Ozzy calls out.

His voice practically barges between us, separating us suddenly.

'I'm just – we're just washing the mud off,' I say, probably too loudly, like someone caught in the act.

'Find anything out, mate?' he asks Lockie.

'The cameras look dead,' he replies. 'I think we're offline. We'll just have to hole up until the crew sends a rescue.'

Ozzy's reaction is very on-brand: no meltdown, no worries, he just practically embraces the potential end of the world.

'Okay,' he replies. 'Then I'll manage the emergency protocols. We'll be back up and running in no time.'

Of course we will. Ozzy lives for stuff like this.

'The shelters are half up,' he tells us. 'We've still got the beds. I can get a fire going with the dry stuff I found under the tarps. There's driftwood everywhere. The weather has levelled out. We'll handle it, so... let's go.'

I'm so glad he's here – our island daddy. Well, with no producers pulling the strings, no supply drops, no hatch giving us just enough stuff to keep us going, we really are surviving on our own.

Ozzy walks off into the trees.

'We'd better follow him,' Lockie says, running his hands through his wet hair.

I can't help but let out a little laugh.

'What?' he asks.

'Be careful what you wish for,' I tell him. 'Next time you're thinking about raising the stakes.'

He half smiles, half sighs.

Well, it's all good and fine saying you want the islanders to feel deserted, until you are one, and you're actually cut off from civilisation.

All we can do is our best now. It really will be survival of the fittest – or whoever is coupled off with the fittest, at least.

20

By the time we make it back to camp, the adrenaline has worn off, and all that's left is silence – the uneasy, stunned kind of silence that settles around everyone like a fog.

The wind moves through the trees – nothing like it was doing earlier – with a gentle sound, the waves are crashing gently again, it's like the island is done being chaotic. I wish I could say the same for the rest of us.

We're all waiting for the same thing: that familiar, bossy, ominous voice to come through the speakers. The one that usually tells us what to do, what not to do, when to do it and so on. We need our instructions.

But it doesn't come. I don't know how long we wait, but the quiet in the group feels more unbearable as time ticks by.

Camilla's the first to break the silence. She smooths her hair, regaining her composure – or trying to at least.

'So... what now?' she asks. Her voice trembles, but she covers it well enough with her usual snootiness.

No one answers immediately. Everyone's eyes flick around camp, looking at each other, or the treeline, or the sea – looking for whoever is going to come and save the day. Still, no one appears. Not even a voice through the speaker to tell us to hang in there.

Lockie rubs a hand over his jaw, his brow furrowed in a way I don't think I've ever seen before – well, he's usually so chilled out.

'I think we're off-air,' he mutters, more to himself than anyone. 'We would have heard something by now, if we were still connected.'

He looks up, meets my eyes for a fraction too long. For just a second, I see the real Lockie – and he looks scared.

The thing is, it's a sensible decision for anyone to make, but coming from Lockie – someone who works in TV – you know it's probably true. We're probably screwed.

'Well, that's it then,' Tony says. 'Show's over. We go home.'

'How?' Camilla asks. 'How do we get home? Because I want to go home right now. This isn't fun any more. I'm not sure it was fun to begin with – but it paid enough to clear my tax bill.'

'You're getting paid in money?' Honey blurts.

'You guys are getting paid?' Tony adds.

Oh boy, oh boy.

Normally, contestants are paid a flat fee for each week they're on the show, but these guys are reality TV stars, so each one negotiated something different with the production company. Or nothing at all, in Tony's case. I have nothing to do with that side of things.

Tony stares into the crate where we keep our fruit.

'Is this it? We're meant to survive on cocktail garnish?'

'I'm happy to keep fishing,' Ozzy says.

'I appreciate that, mate, but I'd murder you for a bag of crisps,' Tony replies.

'You'd try,' Ozzy corrects him, deadly serious.

'Even if we just had, like, some sauces or something,' Tony continues pointlessly. 'Bit of ketchup, spot of hollandaise.'

'Yes, brunch would fix everything,' Camilla says with a roll of her eyes.

Tensions are building. I can't believe we're scrapping over food already.

'All right, let's play a game, break the tension,' Lockie suggests. 'If you could eat anything right now, what would it be?'

'Pizza,' I answer immediately. 'And I wouldn't say no to a bit of the island pineapple on it.'

'I'm with you there,' Lockie says. 'Maybe a bit of pepperoni too. A fancy Hawaiian.'

'I'd have pasta,' Honey says. 'The round one, from—'

'From a tin?' Camilla chimes in. We all shoot her a look. 'Come on, we all know she's talking about spaghetti hoops and not orecchiette puttanesca.'

'It all sounds good right now,' Honey says with a shrug, either not detecting or not caring that Camilla is making fun of her.

'I miss protein,' Ozzy says, with all the sadness you'd reserve for a dead relative. 'I'd do anything for a protein shake.'

Words I never thought I'd hear, and words I'd absolutely never say. You ever hear me say that and you need to call someone, because it's a covert cry for help.

'Vanilla whey with peanut butter, banana, oats...' Ozzy fantasies out loud.

'Blended beige slop,' Camilla says, turning up her nose.

'I want a full roast,' Tony says, cutting to the chase. 'Roast beef, horseradish, mash and roasts, Yorkshire puddings the size of your head. And gravy so thick you could slice it.'

Well, that does sound good. Apart from the choppable gravy, maybe.

'I could go for a Greggs,' Lockie says. 'That's all I need, to be happy.'

'Well, while you're all drinking brown paste, lumpy gravy and sausage rolls, I'd like to be dining on steak tartare and truffle fries with a nice, crisp glass of champagne,' Camilla says with a dreamy sigh.

'The only part of that I fancy is the "crisp",' Tony jokes.

We all laugh.

'I'd love some fresh oysters,' Honey says. 'With a side of saffron risotto... or, just, like, I don't know, cheesy chips?'

'Cheesy chips, now we're chatting,' Tony says. 'Anything but fruit.'

'Didn't I see you eat five bananas yesterday?' Camilla reminds Tony. 'And you're whining about not wanting fruit. Who eats five bananas?'

'Mini bananas,' Tony insists. 'And I was hungry.'

'Well, you can't be eating five bananas now, when we're going to have to ration the food,' Camilla informs him.

'Look, we can make it all last, and we can top it up,' Honey reminds us. 'Like, we'll take turns, to gather supplies.'

'Well, I don't fancy that,' Camilla snaps.

'You'll learn to love it, if you like to eat,' Tony replies.

Bloody hell, we're only just starting to talk about food rations and we're ready to kill each other. Or maybe these guys are always like this.

'We just need a good system,' Lockie says finally. 'Food, water, tasks. No one hoards, no one slacks.'

'This is getting a bit *Lord of the Flies* for my liking,' Camilla replies.

Is it?

'You know you're going to have to empty the outhouse at some point,' Tony reminds her.

'Erm, I don't think so, darling,' she replies.

Ozzy steps in. 'Look, I'll take outhouse duties, it doesn't bother me.'

'You don't have to take the worst job every time, you know,' Honey reminds him.

'Someone has to do the stuff no one else will, and it doesn't bother me,' he replies. 'I'll do what I can, to keep us safe, but I need you all to work with me.'

'You're so good in a crisis,' I tell him with a smile. 'We're lucky to have you.'

I notice Lockie turn to look at me but I don't meet his gaze.

'I'll... manage morale,' Camilla suggests.

I can't even say 'nice try' to that. Terrible, terrible try.

'That's not a job,' Tony informs her. 'And you're terrible for morale.'

'I like doing the water,' Honey says. 'I can keep on it, doing trips, boiling it – maybe Camilla can help with that.'

'And we'll have to do this for how long?' Camilla asks, not satisfied to be dodging toilet duties.

'Maybe not that long,' Honey says softly. 'Maybe they're just... delayed. Like, technical problems. Because of the storm.'

'Well, fuck eating fruit and sleeping on the floor,' Tony says. 'If this isn't being filmed any more then I want off, right now. I'm sleeping in a proper bed and eating something that didn't come off a tree.'

Ozzy exhales, long and slow, his calm voice cutting through the tension.

'There are four single beds,' he says, thinking aloud, 'so... two doubles if we push them together. We could fit three to a bed if we had to.'

'Yeah, I've made that work before,' Honey offers up innocently.

Camilla crosses her arms, one hip cocked, clearly beyond irritated now.

'Well, presumably you guys want to sleep together,' she says, looking pointedly between me, Lockie and Ozzy. I'm not sure if she means me and Ozzy, me and Lockie or all three of us. No one asks for clarity, her words just hang in the air.

Ozzy clears his throat uncomfortably. Lockie looks at me, telling me to take the lead.

My cheeks flush. I wish I could bury myself in the sand.

I open my mouth to speak but Camilla carries on first.

'So Honey and I will share,' Camilla continues.

'Erm, I'm here too, you know,' Tony reminds her. 'Or have you forgotten?'

'I'm trying to,' she claps back. 'I suppose you're in with us then.'

It really is hard to know who has the short straw. All of us, I think.

'It'll be cosy!' Honey says, trying to stay positive.

'Claustrophobic is more like it,' Camilla replies.

I glance toward Lockie and Ozzy – my bedmates for the foreseeable. Lockie's biting his lip, clearly trying not to laugh. He catches my eye, and for a moment it's like we're the only two people on the island – well, the only two in on the joke, maybe.

'We'll be okay,' I tell everyone. In a way, I feel responsible for us all being in this situation, but there's nothing I could have done.

'Yeah, everything is calm now,' Lockie adds. 'It won't be much different to yesterday.'

Camilla screams, loud and unbelievably high-pitched. 'Ugh! What is that?' she shrieks, pointing at something on the floor next to us.

On the sand just a few feet away from where we're sitting, there's a pale starfish, limp and still, half-buried in the sand.

'Oh, no,' Honey says, rushing over. 'Don't touch it!'

'Why not?' Tony asks, squinting. 'It's dead. We should just bury it.'

'I'm not having a funeral for a creature,' Camilla protests.

'It might not be dead,' Honey says, crouching beside it like a tiny marine biologist in a bikini. 'See, its limbs are curled, but not rigid. And those tiny dots there? Sometimes they just shut down when they're stressed.'

'You're telling me it's having a panic attack?' Camilla says in disbelief.

'Someone definitely is,' Tony says under his breath.

Honey ignores their bickering. She gently scoops up the starfish in both hands and heads for the sea. 'If it's still alive, it needs seawater. Fast.'

We all follow her to the shoreline, weirdly invested in this little starfish, and if it's going to make it. She kneels down, lowers the starfish into the shallow water, and holds her breath.

For a moment, nothing happens. The waves roll in and out, washing over her hands. Then one of the starfish's arms (are they arms?) twitches. Then another. Slowly, it starts to move. The little ripples of life running through it give me more hope than I expected.

'See? It just needed help,' Honey says brightly. 'I saw that on TV once.'

'Thank God you did,' Ozzy replies. 'I know how to survive – not how to help other creatures survive.'

'You're doing a great job with us,' I joke, smiling at him.

He laughs. Then Lockie joins in. Then Honey, then Tony – even Camilla cracks her face.

'Well, that's one good thing today,' Lockie says, standing next to me.

His fingers brush mine, just barely. Just enough to make a connection.

'Yeah, not everything here is dead in the water,' I reply.

Lockie bumps my shoulder with his, acknowledging my terrible pun. I bump him back, and then our eyes meet.

As silly as it sounds, I'm glad he's here. I'm glad I'm not doing this alone.

We stand there, all of us, watching the starfish until it disappears beneath the waves. We're still silent, but it's not as suffocating now.

I feel daft, getting a lump in my throat over a starfish, but somehow it feels like a sign. Everything could be okay.

I'm just not sure how exactly yet.

21

We're under strict instructions from Ozzy today. Find things to help us survive, don't get into any scrapes that might kill us. Easier said than done.

He pretty much gave us a TED Talk, on all things survival, imparting so much information it inadvertently went in one ear and out of the other.

My two main takeaways, and I think they'll serve me well, are this: don't eat anything without getting him to check it first (he mentioned various toxic fruits) and watch out for eels. I will most definitely be watching out for eels.

So it's just me and Lockie, walking through the jungle, looking for anything that might be useful. It doesn't seem like there's anything useful out here, least of all us.

Lockie walks ahead, using a big stick to push things out of the way.

'In a dream world,' he begins, pausing to swipe leaves out the way, 'I want to find a stone pizza oven, and all the ingredients to make pizza. What about you?'

'An M&S Simply Food,' I say with a sigh. Now this is my kind of fantasising. 'A Colin the Caterpillar would really take the edge off right now.'

'I miss food,' he replies. 'Even just, like, the rush of getting a Tesco Meal Deal, getting £9 worth of stuff for like half the price.'

'I'm so hungry for bread, I'd pay the £9,' I say with a laugh.

'I'd even settle for a PlayStation,' he replies. 'Just, something to do. I could play *Red Dead Redemption 2* for days without moving, that would pass the time.'

I laugh at him.

'You're sort of living it,' I remind him.

'It's not the same,' he reassures me. 'Plus, I don't have a horse, and if I did, Ozzy would probably try to eat it for the protein.'

He probably would. That's not a joke.

'How long before he starts trying to work out which one of us has the most meat on us?' I reply.

'I've definitely seen him eyeing you up,' Lockie replies.

Hmm, I wonder what he means by that, there's a tone I can't quite put my finger on.

'There's higher ground up near the ridge,' Lockie says. 'If we climb it, who knows, maybe we'll be able to see something, or start a fire so that someone can see us? It's worth a try, right?'

'And if we fall to our deaths?' I reply.

'I mean, you seem more likely to fall than me, but I'll keep you safe,' he tells me. 'So I'm up for it if you are.'

'I've nothing better to do,' I reply.

The deeper you head into the jungle, the more it feels like it's swallowing you whole.

Lockie leads the way, his big stick still in his hand, chopping through the vines like he's done this before. Then again, we've been walking for ages now. At least it feels that way.

We reach a clearing halfway up the ridge. There's an old

metal mast, half-rusted, sticking out of the ground like some relic from a different era.

'What's that?' I ask.

'It could be a relay tower,' Lockie says. 'I don't know if they use it... Either way, it looks fried. Like it's been hit by lightning.'

'Can we fix it?' I ask optimistically – I'm not usually an optimist, so I don't know why I'm starting now.

'Even if we have the skills, we don't have the tools,' he says. 'But we could follow the cable, see where it goes? Maybe a control room or something.'

'It's worth a try, right?' I reply, unsure of myself. That optimism didn't last long.

We follow the line of cable down a narrow slope, ducking under branches and clambering over roots, until the ground levels out into a small clearing. And there, right in the middle, is a hatch. The metal hinges look corroded but intact.

Lockie crouches and brushes dirt away. 'This could lead somewhere,' he says.

'This isn't *Lost*,' I remind him. 'There's no one down there.'

'I know,' he says with a sigh. 'I thought there might be power, but I can't get it open. There's power somewhere, we just need to find it. I suppose we can keep looking, but we should probably head back to camp. I think this might be a lost cause.'

'I think that about almost everything, all of the time,' I half-joke.

'You're an overthinker?' he replies.

I nod. 'Isn't everyone these days?'

'Sounds difficult,' he says, silently confirming that he doesn't have this issue. He can't be that easy-breezy, can he?

'Well, when you're going about your day, what do you think about all day?' I ask.

'Nothing,' he replies. 'Just... whatever the task at hand is. What do you think about?'

'Everything,' I say, deadpan. 'Anything. All day.'

He laughs a little at my delivery, rather than my – y'know – overwhelming anxiety.

We push through another patch of trees and find running water – a stream.

It's maybe ten feet across, the water seeming like it's rushing fast enough to take you with it, whether you want to go or not.

'I'm not crossing that,' I tell him.

'Why not?' he replies.

'Eels,' I tell him.

'Do you even know what an eel looks like?' he replies.

'No, which is why I'm not chancing it,' I insist.

It's his turn to laugh at me.

'It's just water,' he says.

'It's fast and it's mysterious and I just can't bring myself to do it,' I reply. 'You can go, if you like, I'll head back...'

'Yes, because I can just let you walk back alone, without worrying about you,' he chuckles sarcastically. 'Come on.'

He bends next to me, hooks an arm under my knees and another around my back, and scoops me up – again.

I shriek and cling to his neck.

'Lockie, oh my God,' I squeak.

'If this is the only way, it's the only way,' he says.

He strides through the water with me in his arms, steady as anything, and if he does feel an eel then he keeps it to himself.

'That okay?' he asks as we reach the other side.

'No, not really,' I reply. 'You'll probably have to carry me all the way back to camp too.'

'In your dreams,' he says with a smile as he sets me down.

'Worth a try,' I reply.

It's nice to be able to have a laugh, in the middle of all of this. Well, if you don't laugh, you cry, and none of us can afford to give up the fluids.

22

I have never lain so flat, so still, or so awkwardly in my entire life.

Then again, I've never shared a bed with two men. Two incredibly hot, attractive, muscular men. I know, it should be a dream, but it's kind of a nightmare.

The air is thick and humid. It's dark, apart from the light of the moon and the dim glow of the nearby firepit. Somehow it all just makes this seem so much more... intimate.

The two single beds click together nicely – entirely intentional by show bosses, so that people can share beds – and somehow I've ended up in the middle.

It's not exactly big enough for three. Having Ozzy on one side and Lockie on the other is like lying between two boulders. It's just generally uncomfortable in every way. My spine is flat against the wood – there's no way I can sleep like this.

I wiggle my legs to wake them up.

'I think we all need to be on our sides,' Ozzy suggests. 'We'll have more space that way.'

'Yeah, I think that might help,' Lockie replies.

I freeze for a moment. Ozzy shuffles, causing the bed to creak beneath us.

'Lockie, probably best if we both face out – give Cleo some space,' Ozzy adds.

'Got it,' Lockie replies.

Oh, this is all just so awkward and stilted and I can't stop cringing.

I can feel Lockie shifting on the other side of me, turning his back so he's facing outward. Ozzy does the same. Now I need to pick a side to lie on – literally, I need to pick a side. Who should I face? Ozzy or Lockie? I guess it has to be Lockie, right? I've known him the longest – I've been tolerating him for like six months now. That's got to count for something.

So I do, I roll to him, my face resting just behind his back.

Lockie shifts a little closer – or maybe I imagine it. I take a sharp breath. Does he know what he's doing? Or is he just that oblivious?

'Is that okay?' I ask them both.

'All good,' Lockie replies.

'Yeah, fine,' Ozzy adds after a few seconds.

Can he tell which way I rolled? He must be able to, right? He doesn't know I've known Lockie for months, but I can't exactly tell him, can I?

'I hope that's your knee in my back,' Lockie jokes.

I think he's trying to lighten the mood but I feel my cheeks flush.

'Can we just try to sleep, please?' Ozzy asks, clearly not amused.

'Yeah, sorry,' I reply.

The hard part was fitting the three of us in the bed. Now for the impossible part: actually sleeping like this.

Lockie shifts again, a slow, maybe deliberate move that

brings his feet up to mine, our toes touching. It's the dumbest, smallest thing, but it feels like electricity. I stare at the back of his head, willing my heart to quiet down and hoping Ozzy can't hear it from behind me.

With Ozzy's warmth at my back and Lockie in front of me playing footsie and just, you know, the threat of a tropical storm returning at some point, while we're stranded on an island, surely anyone would struggle to sleep, right?

Scratch that. Lockie's breathing evens out, slow and steady, and I'm pretty sure he's sleeping already.

There, see, it's easy. I just need to do the same.

And then I feel Ozzy reach around, place his hand on my hip, and give me a brief, reassuring squeeze. And then he leaves me to sleep.

Yep, this is awkward. I think the only way this is not awkward is in a porno, and *Welcome to Singledom* is really not that sort of show (except according to some snooty reviewers, at least).

I just need to sleep, I just need to sleep. And do everything I can tomorrow to avoid spending another night on this island. I just have no idea what that is yet.

23

Unsurprisingly, I can't really sleep.

I think I have slept, a bit, on and off, but I'm awake again. I think it's going to be like this all night.

It's only as I come around a little more that I realise I'm on Lockie's side of the bed – and he's not here.

I sit up quickly, the feeling of uncertainty compelling me to get out of bed. Luckily I spot him right away, sitting by the firepit, poking at the embers with a stick.

'Hi,' I say quietly as I approach him.

'Hi,' he replies. 'Can't sleep?'

'Not really. You?'

He shakes his head. 'I thought I'd give you a bit of space,' he replies.

'That's a shame, I thought you'd keep me warm,' I reply with a smile.

He laughs.

'I was worried the storm might come back, but I think it's blown over,' he tells me.

'The weather or the drama?' I check.

'Both,' he says with a smirk.

For a moment, we just sit there, watching the sparks drift up into the darkness.

'I knew this was going to be strange, being on the show,' he starts, pausing briefly to gather his thoughts. 'But I didn't think it was going to be this strange.'

'Yeah, winding up stranded and deserted on a tropical island isn't all that common, is it?' I reply. 'But, if movies and TV have taught me anything, then we're probably doing it all wrong. Aren't we supposed to, like, sculpt a big SOS into the sand, or stick a message in a bottle and send it out to sea?'

'You can try those tomorrow, if you like,' he replies with a laugh. 'We're lucky we have Ozzy, he knows all about survival. Survival takes priority over rescue, right?'

'It makes sense,' I agree. 'My instinct would have been so focused on getting rescued, I probably would have neglected eating, drinking, shelter. You're right, we're lucky to have him.'

'Your island partner,' he reminds me. 'Are you still coupled off?'

'I think that went out of the window when the show went off-air, don't you?' I reply.

'Yeah, perhaps,' he says.

'You ever think,' I say finally, 'how weird this all is? That we're sitting here, like... strangers, pretending to be on a dating show, and now we're basically a survival group?'

Lockie chuckles. 'Yeah. I didn't exactly picture this when I signed up for TV work.'

We listen to the fire crackle for a little longer. Then...

'You're good at this, you know,' Lockie says.

'At, what, not being able to sleep? Yeah, I'm great,' I joke. 'Years of experience.'

He laughs. 'No, at keeping everyone together, in order, making sure we're all doing what needs to be done,' he replies.

'I think we're all doing great, given the circumstances. I'm panicking on the inside.'

'You're hiding it well then,' he replies. 'The first step towards being brave is pretending that you are. Eventually it comes naturally.'

I look at him for a moment – and I mean really look. I try to read him, to figure out what's going on in that brain of his. Whatever it is, it always looks so peaceful. Even here, now, with all that's going on, he seems so calm.

'Why aren't you scared?' I ask.

He doesn't answer right away.

'Who says I'm not?' he replies.

The honesty in his voice surprises me. He looks away, out toward the sea for a few seconds.

'I just learned a long time ago that fear doesn't help,' he replies. 'It's there, of course it is. You feel it, you move through it, and then you do what needs doing anyway.'

'Just like that?' I reply.

'I wouldn't say "just like that" but... yeah,' he says. 'You do what you need to do, if not for yourself, then for the people you care about. I have people on this island I care about a lot. That's my motivation, that's what keeps me pushing forward, trying...'

'That makes sense,' I say with a smile.

I think that might be what's motivating me, too. If I were alone, I don't know. I think I'd probably just lie on the sand and wait to be rescued or washed out to sea. But our weird little family feels worth fighting for.

'You should try to get some sleep,' he tells me. 'Who knows what tomorrow will bring?'

I shake my head. 'I'll stay up with you a bit longer,' I tell him.

'Thanks,' he replies.

Looking out to sea, I can just about make out the flash of lightning in the distance.

'Don't worry, that's far away,' Lockie tells me. 'We'll be fine.'

'Are you always this optimistic?' I ask.

'Only when you're watching,' he says, glancing at me.

I roll my eyes, but I can't help smiling.

I shiver, just a little – I don't know if it's from being cold, tired, stressed or all of the above. Lockie reaches out and wraps an arm around me.

'Better?' he asks.

'Yeah. Thanks.'

For a moment, I think about leaning in, about resting my head on his shoulder. But I don't. I'm not brave enough yet – or willing to pretend I am either.

'We can go back to bed soon,' he says. 'I'll be your own personal hot-water bottle.'

'My hero,' I reply.

And for one strange, fleeting moment, it almost feels like everything might be okay.

It does make a difference, having him here, in the same boat (or not, as the case may be) with me. It almost makes me feel like it's all going to be okay.

Almost.

24

Waking up between Ozzy and Lockie is like waking up between two sexy radiators.

Of course, it takes me a second to remember why my face is full of someone's shoulder blade and why my legs appear to be wrapped around his.

I, walking cringe-fest that I am, have decided in my sleep that I should choose a man to attach myself to and I've done just that, I've picked a side and I've latched on to whoever was there.

For better or worse, it's Lockie.

He's in front of me, fast asleep, back pressed against my front like we've been together for ten years and sleep like this most nights. Behind me, Ozzy has done similar, he's right up behind me, his body pressed against mine, his arm draped over me. And of course, my arm is over Lockie, resting against his abs.

It's light but quiet – and thank God. This would look so, so bad if anyone were looking. Not only that, but if either of these two wake up, if they realise the position we're in... oh God. How do I get myself out of this without waking either of them?

Okay. Okay. I need to not panic, for starters. There must be a way out of this. I just need the two of them to get up before they really realise the compromising position we're in. Where's the bloody storm when you need it?

I'll try to move slowly, see if I can get either of them to stir, to naturally roll over without waking up. I only need one to budge, then I can edge away from the other.

Maybe I can escape one limb at a time, if I just...

Lockie shifts, not fully awake, just a sleepy stretch, and in the process his hand slides down and finds mine.

And now we're holding hands – I couldn't be more frozen in place if I tried. There is absolutely no getting out of this one, unless I opt for some kind of *127 Hours*-type manoeuvre – cutting off a limb, that is. Nothing else.

A blood-curdling scream rips through the air. Everyone bolts upright at once. We're all on our feet before we know it, ready to run to the rescue.

Well, that did the trick.

Camilla shrieks again. We all hurry over to see what's wrong. Honey and Tony are already trying to console her.

'My lucky crystal!' Camilla wails. 'It's gone.'

Tony squints at her.

'Are you sure it was all that lucky?' he asks sleepily, trying to lighten the mood. 'Because, no offence, but we are all stranded on a deserted island.'

She shoots him a filthy look, but otherwise ignores him.

'Someone took it while I was sleeping,' she says. 'I fell asleep holding it, and it's gone. Someone must have taken it.'

'Yeah, that's definitely what happened,' Tony says sarcastically. 'They probably took it to the pawn shop on the other side of the island.'

'Oh, do get lost,' she snaps at him. 'I know one of you has taken it.'

'Babe, I don't think anyone has,' Honey reassures her.

'Like, I'd say check our pockets, but we don't have pockets,' Ozzy adds. 'But we can help you look for it...'

'Oh, yeah, right, so whoever took it can pretend to find it?' she replies.

I did wonder which one of us would crack up first and, yeah, I did think it would be Camilla, to be fair.

'Okay, well, we're all up now, so what's the plan?' Ozzy asks. 'I think some of us need off this island ASAP.'

'Right, what shall we try?' Lockie says.

'That building, where the hatch is...' Ozzy starts.

'I think it's the old production building,' Lockie says. 'But there's no one there this year, right? They said they were opening the hatch remotely.'

He knows it is.

'I say we break in,' Ozzy says. 'If everything's set up to run remote, there'll be tech in there. Supplies. Tools. Maybe a radio.'

Lockie rubs the back of his neck. 'I checked it yesterday. Everything's pretty locked down,' he replies.

'We'll try again, together,' Ozzy says.

'Breaking and entering, a plan I understand,' Tony jokes. 'I'm in.'

'Can we, like, get arrested for that?' Honey asks.

'If the police can find us, let them,' Tony says. 'Then we'll be saved.'

'We should eat first,' Ozzy tells us. 'Even if it's just fruit, everyone grab a piece from the basket.'

Tony gets there first – as usual.

'Oh, mate, that is rank,' he says, peering in. 'Cor, it stinks.'

The fruit basket, the one that is supposed to keep our precious food safe, is tipped over, the contents spilled out. It's covered in sand and bugs, it's gone squishy under the hot sun. It is, without a doubt, ruined.

Honey claps a hand over her mouth.

'Oh my God.'

'Okay, that's actually vile,' Camilla says, not keeping eyes on it for more than a few seconds. 'Someone needs to fix that.'

'You can't fix rotting food,' Tony informs her.

'But you can replace it,' she tells him. 'So chop-chop.'

'Chop-chop?' he blurts back to her in disbelief. 'Chop-chop? I'm not the woman who does your bikini line.'

'Oh, you're vile too,' she replies. 'I bet the person who does mine has a nicer job than the poor person who does yours.'

Ozzy crouches beside the basket and examines the scene.

'They're in everything,' he says. 'This belongs to the bugs now. They've eaten half of it. Who left it open?'

We all go silent, looking each other up and down.

'It was fine last night,' I say slowly, looking around at everyone. 'Has anyone been to it today? Could the wind have done it?'

'There's no way this weather did this,' Ozzy says. 'The storm, yeah, but it's been calm since. Someone messed up.'

'Well, don't look at me,' Tony says.

'I'm looking at you,' Camilla tells him. 'You were probably in there, trying to sneak another five bananas, and you left it open or you knocked it over – or both.'

'Or you did it, to make me look bad,' he replies. 'Let's not rule that out. You've clearly got it in for me. That or you fancy me, that's why you're always negging me.'

'Oh, in your dreams, you horrible little man,' she snaps back.

That clearly touched a nerve.

'I took *one* banana,' he clarifies. 'One! Last night. And I closed the basket, without a doubt.'

'Clearly not properly,' she claps back.

This isn't getting us anywhere.

Ozzy huffs as he paces back and forth across the potential crime scene.

'Enough,' he snaps. His voice is louder than usual, and you can hear the frustration creeping in. Well, you don't mess with Ozzy's food, it's what he feeds his muscles. 'It's like someone doesn't want us to succeed,' he says. 'Do I think it was intentional? No. Do I think it was one of us who dropped the ball? Yes.'

'This is what I'm saying,' Camilla tells him. 'It wasn't sabotage, it was stupidity. Probably Tony's stupidity. Or perhaps...'

She turns to Honey, probably to accuse her, then thinks better of it.

Ozzy kicks at the sand, still simmering.

'We can't afford slip-ups like this. The food's not going to last forever.'

He's right. We all know it. If we run out we won't just be annoyed. We'll be screwed.

My stomach feels heavy, and Lord knows it's not because it's full, but because of the situation. It's not about the fruit, not on its own, but more about the supply chain generally. Ozzy's right. There's only so much fruit on this island, isn't there? I know, it will keep growing, but surely the trees and plants can only produce so much so quickly, and if we plough through it, well, how long does it take to grow back? How long can we last like that? And the same goes for fishing – the fish can't be infinite, can they? My anxious brain is starting to wonder whether or not the fish get wise to the fact they're actively being fished every day, and all take off together, to find somewhere new to live?

I suddenly feel very aware of how alive our food is, how precious it is too. How we're all going to need to step up our game, if we're going to make it last.

'Okay, look, it doesn't matter whose fault it is,' Lockie says. 'If it's anyone's. All that matters is that we don't let it happen again. So we come up with better safety measures, or we perform routine checks. We can replace the fruit, no problem at all, but if we keep bickering and turning on each other, well, we're just not going to survive. As a team, we're strong. On our own, we're weak. Except maybe Ozzy.'

I love that he adds a little joke to the end of his empowering and motivating speech. And he's right about all of it (even Ozzy). We do need to stick to our plan; we're strongest as a team. All we can do is replace the fruit – there's plenty out there for now – and focus on our plan. Survival first, rescue second.

'He's right,' Ozzy says, exhaling pure stress like he's trying to expel it from his body. He does actually seem a lot calmer by the end of it.

'I know it sucks, and that we're all hungry now,' Lockie continues. 'But it's done. We'll clean it up, throw away the bad stuff, and replace it. I'm always happy to go off and find food.'

'And I'm happy to help,' I add. 'And we know Ozzy is great at fishing. We're going to be okay.'

I'm doing my best to join in on the motivational chat, but I think I'm trying to remind myself more than I'm trying to convince anyone else.

It seems like Lockie has done the trick, he's eased the tension yet again, brought peace to the camp, calmed us all down, given us one shared goal to focus on, and it's realistic, like getting food for the day, not wild, like hoping the production building has a helicopter outside with the keys in the ignition.

I watch him for a second, the way he smooths things over without making anyone feel small. He's good in a crisis – and this really, really is a crisis.

'Let's just head to the old production building,' Ozzy says. 'If the answer to our problems is there, then none of this matters, does it?'

Lockie glances at me but I daren't look back. It could be that he's giving me a look about what's going on, or he could have realised I was spooning him and holding his hand when he woke up. I don't want to risk it.

'Okay, let's all go,' I suggest. 'Let's stick together.'

'Did you sleep okay?' Lockie asks me as we set off.

'I've had better,' I tell him plainly.

And now... time to try breaking into a building that I know for a fact is super secure. This ought to be fun.

25

I'm not sure if the old production building looks bigger or smaller than I remember. Smaller, I think, compared to how much space we had on the yacht, but bigger because, you know, I live outside now.

Lockie takes charge, approaching the purpose-built structure, looking for somewhere to get in. The hatch – the one that auto-opens for us – is locked, and the only way to override it is with the keypad. We're real contestants, at the end of the day, so we don't have the code.

'There must be a way to get the hatch open?' Tony says. 'Can we guess the code?'

'There must be hundreds of potential codes,' Camilla says.

'Thousands,' Honey adds.

Lockie kneels beside it and gives the lock a determined pull. Then he tries a code.

'Well, it's not 1234,' he says with a laugh.

'Try 0000,' Honey suggests.

I think we all know that's a waste of time.

It's tamper-proof, like everything else, I know that for a fact.

'So what now?' Camilla practically groans. 'We just die here?'

Christ, we're not there yet, are we?

'We eat,' Ozzy says, nodding his head slowly. 'Survival comes first. We'll worry about rescue after we're fed.'

I think we all know by now that there is a fate worse than death, and it's Ozzy not getting his protein. Well, what would we all do without Island Daddy?

'We need to be proactive,' he says. 'I'll catch us some fish – Cleo, fancy being my assistant?'

'Sure,' I reply.

'I'll gather some coconuts,' Tony says. 'This is, like, the home of coconuts. We'll always have them.'

'Coconuts aren't actually from here,' Honey muses.

'What are you talking about?' Tony says with a laugh. 'Of course coconuts are from here. They're everywhere.'

'Oh yeah, duh,' Honey says with a chuckle. She knocks herself on the head with her knuckles.

'Right then, I'll collect coconuts,' Tony says. 'You two are on fishing duty. What else?'

'Honey, Camilla, you two boil water – I've already been to the stream to collect some,' Ozzy says. 'We'll all be thirsty when we're done. And Lockie...'

'I'm staying here,' Lockie tells him, running a hand over one of the walls. 'I'll keep trying to find a way in. There has to be a weakness somewhere.'

Ozzy frowns. 'Sounds like a waste of energy, but it's yours to waste,' he replies.

Lockie's eyes don't move from the wall.

'Maybe,' he replies. 'Worth a shot though, right? If you guys have everything else covered.'

Is it weird that I feel uneasy, leaving Lockie here alone? I know he'll be fine but, I don't know, it sort of feels like we should stick together. No man – or woman – should be out here alone. We all need someone watching our backs. I suppose the cameras were good for that...

'Okay, Cleo, are you ready for a fishing lesson?' Ozzy asks me.

'No?' I say with a laugh.

I follow Ozzy, glancing back at Lockie. He's a man on a mission, determined to get inside. I'm sure he'll be fine, so long as he doesn't hurt himself.

Let's be real, I'm more likely to hurt myself fishing. I'm amazed that so far the only injury we've had was Ozzy dropping a hammer on his toe – but I don't want to tempt fate. She's already on the rampage.

26

I'm ankle-deep in the sea, holding a sharp stick, waiting for a fish. Has it really come to this?

Ozzy presses himself up behind me, holding my arms, guiding me. You know, in the movies, that sexy way guys teach girls how to play pool by essentially dry-humping them? Well, we're doing that, just, you know, to stab a fish. What could be sexier?

He slides his hands over mine to reposition them on the spear.

'Get a nice, firm grip on the shaft,' he tells me.

That had to have been on purpose.

'Okay,' I say, pretending I didn't notice.

'It's all about the way you move,' he continues. 'It's in the stance, the hips – bend forward, just a little.'

He's either making this sexy or I've had too much sun.

I narrow my eyes, scanning the water for fish, trying to play it cool, but my heart is pounding.

'You don't have to teach me, you know,' I say. 'I'm happy to just watch you. You're so good at it.'

'Ah, but what if I wasn't here?' he replies. 'What would you do for food?'

'A good point, but I don't plan on ever getting into a situation like this again,' I counter.

'And here's me thinking I could invite you on my next adventure,' he says. I can hear him grinning.

'Oh, absolutely,' I say sarcastically. 'We could do *Naked and Afraid* together. I'm already afraid.'

'It wouldn't take us long to get naked,' he whispers into my ear.

'Ew, what are you two doing?' Camilla asks, joining us.

'What does it look like?' I call back. 'We're fishing.'

'Not that,' she replies. 'Anyway, Honey is doing my head in. She's boiling water, but I want to look for my crystal, but she won't help – will you guys help?'

'We're catching dinner,' Ozzy tells her. 'You know, so we can eat. Seeing as though most of the fruit we had to hand got infested, and fish are pretty much the only form of protein we have.'

'Really? Because it looks more like you're getting it on in the sea,' she replies.

'I wish,' Ozzy jokes quietly. I give him a playful nudge with my elbow.

He really is teaching me to fish – but I don't suppose it needed to involve us getting so up close and personal.

'Ow,' he says. 'Ow, ow, ow – oh God, oh God. Shit!'

'Oh my gosh, have I hurt you?' I blurt. I didn't do it that hard, and the man is carved from stone, for crying out loud.

'Shit, shit, shit,' he continues. 'Fuck!'

Whatever has happened to him, it's really hurt him, and it only seems like the pain is getting worse.

He hurries out of the water and drops onto the sand. He rolls around on his back – it looks like he's trying to grab his foot.

'Jellyfish...' he says, although it sounds more like he's using his breath than his voice. 'Stung... jellyfish...'

He can hardly get his words out. His face is bright red, the veins are bulging in his neck, looking like they might explode. I have no idea how painful a jellyfish sting is but, if it can take down a man mountain like Ozzy, it must be really bad.

'Shit, what do we do?' I ask Camilla. Not that I'm expecting her to know. She probably has someone on her team who takes care of jellyfish for her, so it never comes up, never ruins her picture-perfect, mega-expensive holidays – the ones, if her Instagram is anything to go by, she goes on about twenty-five times a year.

'Okay, I think I know what to do,' she says – and she sounds like she means it. 'In that movie with that woman... You know the one, she's got red hair, I think she was married to, oh, what's his name, from... it doesn't matter. Anyway, what I saw them do, and it worked... you're supposed to... ugh, I can't believe I'm saying this... you're supposed to urinate on it.'

Oh. Oh, no. She wants one of us to... oh boy. Oh, shit... Now that I think about it, I think I've heard that before too. Actually, I think I saw it in an episode of *Friends*. You can't take medical advice from *Friends*, can you? It's not like it's... *Scrubs*... or like you should take advice from sitcoms at all. Camilla says she saw it in a movie – is that more or less reliable than a TV show?

Ozzy groans dramatically.

'Help...' he says weakly. 'Heeeelp... heeeelp...'

His voice loses strength with each word he calls out.

'Aren't you going to do it?' Camilla says. 'The man needs help.'

'Heeelp...' Ozzy moans right on cue.

'I literally went to the outhouse just before we started fishing,' I tell her quietly. 'I couldn't do it if I wanted to.'

And I really don't want to, I'm sure that goes without saying.

'Well, I'm not doing it,' Camilla announces. 'Absolutely not. Not a chance.'

'Help...' Ozzy says again. His body is stiff, his eyes bulging, the veins on his neck throbbing even faster than they were before. He really does need someone to do something, and fast. I wish Lockie were here, perhaps he'd know what to do – I'm sure, logistically, he'd find it a lot easier to pee on Ozzy's foot too.

'Absolutely not,' Camilla doubles down. 'The therapy I'd need...'

Just as I'm wondering whether it's worth me trying, at least, seeing if I can get anything going – although how much do you need? A little isn't going to cut it, is it? – Honey comes running down the beach, to see what all the commotion is.

'What's happened?' she asks genuinely. 'Can I help at all?'

'Oh, this is your girl right here,' Camilla insists. 'I'll hazard a guess it's not her first time doing this... so... I'll leave you all to it.'

'Jellyfish,' Ozzy pants at Honey. 'Stung... foot... help...'

'Right, okay, I know what to do,' Honey says calmly.

'I cannot watch this,' Camilla declares, before heading back to camp. 'I'm sure some people would pay to, but not me...'

Her rant fades to silence as she walks off. She wasn't being much help anyway.

Honey empties out one of our water flasks and then fills it with seawater. She's quick but calm, a woman on a mission. She pours it over Ozzy's foot before filling it again, pouring again, filling again – always with seawater. I'm yet to see her even think about peeing on him. Then she examines the sting on his foot, using a shell to flick off any bits that might be on it, and then rinsing it again.

'Okay, there's nothing there now,' she tells him, giving his leg a reassuring squeeze. 'You got away clean. No bits stuck to you. You're going to be all right.'

Whatever she did must have helped, because Ozzy is breathing more normally, and his face is slowly fading back to its usual colour. He can form whole sentences too.

'Oh my God, thank you so much, Honey,' he tells her. 'You... you saved the day.'

'You're lucky she came,' I tell him. 'Camilla wanted us to pee on you – well, she wanted me to. I'd be making a mental note, of who did and didn't want to pee on me in a crisis. That girl is just not a team player.'

Ozzy manages a laugh and I feel relieved. I mean, come on, we've all been relying on him for so much. What would we do without him? My fishing lesson was more about dry-humping than it was actually fishing, I'm not ready to take responsibility for those duties yet.

'That actually makes it worse,' Honey says immediately. 'You're supposed to rinse with seawater, then soak in warm water. It breaks down the venom. I think I picked it up from some boring nature documentary my ex used to watch.'

'Thank God you did,' I reply. Then I notice something. 'Do jellyfish stings make your toes go blue?'

'Oh, no, that's from when I dropped the hammer on them,' Ozzy says. 'It's the same foot.'

I don't know if it being the same foot makes it better or worse.

'Ouch,' I reply, wincing. 'I don't know how you didn't cry then, and I don't know how you're not crying now. I'm almost in tears just from spectating.'

'Well, it's not good for men to cry, is it?' he says as we help him limp up the beach, back to camp. 'Especially not in tough times.'

'It absolutely is good for men to cry,' I insist.

I'm surprised he said that but, then again, other than anger and frustration, he hasn't been all that emotional.

'Why wouldn't it be good for a man to cry?' Honey asks. 'It's normal.'

'It shows weakness,' Ozzy tells us. 'You guys need me strong, not soft.'

'No, we just need you,' I tell him.

'It's good for everyone to cry,' Honey insists. 'Boys, girls, whatever. If you bottle it up then you explode eventually. And it doesn't always come at the most opportune times. You need that slow release, not catastrophic malfunction.'

'I'll risk it,' he replies with a chuckle.

I smile, but we're not wrong. He would do well to let it all out, now and then, just to regulate his brain.

'Hey, Cleo, thanks for not peeing on me, by the way,' Ozzy tells me.

'Ah, there's always next time,' I joke. 'But, yeah, you're welcome. Thanks for not needing peeing on.'

He laughs. This is definitely a conversation I don't think either of us ever imagined having.

Back at the firepit, Tony and Camilla are piling up coconuts.

'I thought we could cut some open, drink them, like we're on a fancy holiday,' Tony suggests.

'Sounds great,' I reply.

Honey takes a pot of water from over the fire and adds cooler water to bring the temp down.

'Sit with your foot in here for a bit,' she tells Ozzy.

He lowers his foot in and exhales.

'That feels loads better already,' he tells her.

'Helloooo,' Lockie calls excitedly as he emerges from the jungle carrying a large wooden crate.

Ozzy perks up.

'Please tell me it's survival gear,' he says.

'Even better,' Lockie says with a grin.

He crouches by the firepit and sets the crate down with a thud. Then he pops the lid off.

Bottles. Dozens of them. Dark glass, dusty, with chunky corks and battered labels.

'Rum!' Lockie announces proudly.

Without missing a beat, Ozzy grabs a bottle, rips the cork out with his teeth and takes three big gulps, like it's water.

'It's a natural painkiller,' he says when he finally breathes again.

'What pain are you in?' Lockie asks.

'Long story,' I say. 'I'll tell you later.'

Lockie wipes his hands on his shorts.

'I got the hatch door open. Looks like the next delivery was booze – probably a reward for some challenge we never got to.'

Tony picks up a bottle and examines it.

'May as well drink it then,' he says. 'Make a night of it.'

'The show must go on, right?' Lockie replies.

'Great idea,' Honey says. 'Let's eat and drink and, I dunno, play some island games or something.'

Lockie takes the open bottle from Ozzy and raises it.

'To surviving,' he says. 'And to whatever happens next.'

We all toast.

I look around the fire, at our weird little group, and smile. It's about time we had some fun, somewhere, in all this stress.

What's one night off from the end of the world?

27

As the night draws in and we all gather around the firepit, things seem a lot calmer. Maybe it's because we feel like we have a plan for survival, maybe it's just a healthy dose of optimism – probably, though, it's the rum. We've all had a lot of rum.

Well, if the cameras are off, if no one's watching, if the show's gone dark... what's the point in pretending any more? We may as well let our hair down.

'If we're stuck here, we may as well have fun,' Honey suggests.

'I thought we were having fun?' I reply with a laugh.

'More fun,' she adds. 'Let's play some games. We do what the show would make us do. Only we get to make up our own rules.'

'Sounds good to me,' Tony says. 'Let's 'ave a laugh.'

Well, she's got a point. If we were on-air, show bosses would have us playing games like this. It will be more fun without the cameras, everyone can be themselves.

So that's what we do. We feed the firepit with wood before taking our seats around it, each of us with our own cocktail. Turns out all those coconuts came in handy, we're drinking a mixture of rum and coconut water – like we're on a fancy holiday – and it's glorious.

This is the closest we've come to feeling like we're at a resort rather than in a nightmare. The air smells like salt and smoke and booze, and when the breeze shifts, I catch the scent of Lockie's skin. It must be the sun cream he's wearing – thankfully we still have our bottles of factor fifty – it smells delicious.

'They always have contestants play something meaningful, and something horny,' Honey muses.

'Meaningful?' Tony repeats. 'Can't we skip to horny?'

'Let's build up to that,' Lockie says with a laugh.

Yeah, I think we might need a few more drinks before we tackle anything horny.

'What about: two lies and a truth – I prefer to play it that way,' Honey suggests. 'Losers have to drink.'

'He'll be sloshed then,' Camilla says, nodding towards Tony.

'Erm, I'm great at games,' Tony protests.

'Whatever, I just mean you're a loser,' Camilla says.

He scowls at her. It's hard to tell for sure but these two either despise each other, or they're madly in love. Sometimes the two aren't that dissimilar.

We start with Tony, he's raring to go. He's used to living his life on the small screen, so he thrives when the spotlight is on him.

He rubs his jaw thoughtfully.

'All right, here are mine,' he begins. 'One: I once dated Dua Lipa. Two: I can speak fluent Portuguese. Three: I cried during *Fast and Furious 7*.'

Camilla doesn't even blink.

'The last one. Obviously,' she says. 'The other two are impressive, the last one is pathetic.'

'That film was emotional,' Tony claps back.

'So I'm right?' Camilla confirms.

'Let's just move on,' Tony says.

So she is right.

Camilla's turn is next. Hers are so on-brand.

'I once had dinner with a duke, I was expelled from school for fighting, and I don't like champagne,' she offers up.

'The first one is the truth,' I say. 'Because I cannot imagine you fighting.'

'And everyone likes champagne,' she replies. 'Correct.'

Then Honey goes.

'I have two degrees. I still sleep with a night light. And I think you're all amazing.'

'Aww, you're so sweet,' Ozzy says. 'We love you too.'

'Bit much,' Camilla adds. 'But, yes, okay. Lockie, what about you? Your turn.'

I take a sip of rum and feel the heat in my mouth, and the booze surge through my veins.

'Okay, okay,' he says, draining another coconut. 'One: I always seem to get in trouble. Two: I lied on my application form for the show. Three: I've never been in love.'

'You totally lied on your form. Everyone does,' Honey says.

'Oh yeah, what was the lie on yours?' he replies.

She pretends to zip her lips closed and looks away.

'Maybe it's the last one,' Camilla says. 'Lockie, have you ever been in love?'

'I kinda want everyone to answer that question,' Honey adds.

Tony scoffs. 'This is actually boring,' he says. 'Can't we play the horny games now?'

I think I would probably rather take my chances with that than open up about love – or hear Lockie talk about his loves, for that matter.

'Yeah, we could play something else,' I say.

'I know,' Tony replies, grabbing one of the empty rum bottles. 'Spin the bottle, truth or dare edition. I've seen the show before, that's a popular one.'

Tony looks like a kid on Christmas morning, eyes wide, practically vibrating with excitement. Camilla sighs like she's too posh for this but doesn't move from her seat. Ozzy's lounging back on his elbows.

'Go on then,' he says.

'Yeah, I'm game,' Honey adds.

Everyone looks over at me and Lockie.

'I'm in if you are,' he tells me. 'We can't be the only holdouts.'

'Yeah, okay, let's do it,' I reply, emboldened by the rum.

Lockie lifts his coconut cup in a silent toast. I hold mine up too before taking another big gulp.

The first few rounds are harmless, silly and fun.

Honey is dared to drink from her coconut without using her hands, which she somehow manages by clamping it between her lips and throwing it back.

'And that's how you do it, babes,' she announces proudly. 'I'm here all week.'

'We're all here all week,' Lockie replies. Everyone cracks up.

Tony gets a dare too – to fake the slo-mo walks the show often shows. He struts around, ever so slowly, absolutely nailing it. Even Camilla allows herself to be amused by him.

Everyone must be a bit sick of telling the truth – or we're just so bored and drunk that we're all choosing dare.

'Ozzy, truth or dare?' Tony says.

'Dare,' Ozzy replies. 'Obviously.'

'I dare you to give someone a sexy dance,' Tony says. 'You can choose who.'

I feel myself tense up a little. He's not going to choose me, is he? I guess we were coupled up, when the show was still on-air, but it feels like a lot has changed since then.

'Okay then, I choose... you!'

As Ozzy chooses his victim he points at them – and it's Tony!

Tony laughs and protests and screams.

'Ten out of ten for enthusiasm, mate!' Tony says when Ozzy is done. 'But you're not my type.'

Eventually the bottle lands on Lockie.

'Lockie, truth or dare,' Honey says.

'It has to be dare, doesn't it?' he says, grinning, far too confident for his own good.

Honey taps her finger on her chin, thinking.

'Okay... I dare you to kiss my neck,' she says. 'Like you did Cleo's.'

The laughter hushes off into something more serious.

My heart is pounding all of a sudden. Maybe it's the rum, maybe it's the way Lockie glances at me, like he's looking for permission, or apologising or... I don't know.

'I'm waiting...' she sings.

Lockie glances at me, eyes searching. It's quick, but it's there, like a silent question.

I shrug, pretending I don't care. My stomach, however, is twisting itself into knots. And this time I don't think the rum is to blame.

He leans toward her. Honey tilts her head, hair spilling over one shoulder. The firelight glows against her skin. Somehow this moment seems much more romantic – perfect even. He does it, he kisses her neck, slowly but confidently, for long enough that even Camilla lets out a whistle. I hate that I notice how good he is at it. Even watching it looks good. Oh, God, I'm jealous. I'm actually jealous.

Honey giggles, but her eyes dart to me, watching my reaction. I take another swig of my rum, trying to play it cool, but I'm jealous.

'Okay,' Honey says with a sigh. 'Just as good as it looked when you did it to Cleo.'

Everyone laughs. Everyone except me.

I take another drink, hoping it will flush the feeling away.

Tony grabs the bottle next, spins it. It slows… and… it lands on me.

'You're up, Cleo,' he says, smirking. 'Truth or dare?'

'If everyone else is choosing dare then: dare,' I reply – also, if I choose truth, someone might ask me if that made me jealous, so I guess I'm choosing dare for the foreseeable.

Tony leans back, a grin spreading across his face.

'I dare you and Lockie to kiss,' he says. 'Properly kiss.'

Lockie looks at me, serious now.

'You don't have to,' he tells me. 'I'll do your forfeit.'

'If Cleo won't kiss you, then you have to kiss Honey,' Tony replies.

The problem is, I want to kiss Lockie. I really want to. And I definitely don't want to watch him kiss Honey.

I know, we've got a past, and it's hard to imagine a future – not just together, but at all. We're all stuck here so… what's to lose? If kissing him, just to see how it feels, makes me feel a tiny bit better, then why not?

'Okay,' I say, trying for casual. 'It's just a game.'

Lockie moves closer, slow enough that my heart starts hammering. The fire crackles next to us, the heat warming my skin – well, it's that or the anticipation. He pauses, inches away, giving me a chance to back out.

I don't.

When his lips touch mine, everything else just… fades. I can forget we're on the island, that we're stuck here, that we have a crowd of people watching us. His hand cups my jaw with a tenderness that melts me and his lips taste so good, like rum and coconut. I can't resist meeting his tongue with mine. I think I make a sound – something between a sigh and a laugh, and Lockie smiles against my mouth. Like it's another one of our jokes.

It's not a TV kiss. It's not for the cameras. It's real. Too real.

When we finally pull apart, no one breathes for a second.

'Okay, my next dare better be to do that,' Honey jokes as she fans herself with both hands.

Ozzy laughs, but there's an edge to it. I try to laugh too, but my hands are shaking almost as much as my knees are. Lockie sits back down next to me, his thigh pressing against mine, and I'm terrified he's going to feel it. How much that got to me.

The game goes on – because of course it does – but I can't quite think straight. The bottle spins, the dares get bolder, and the laughter gets louder. No one else kisses but, through it all, Lockie and I keep finding ways to brush against each other. It's a knee, a shoulder, a glance that lingers just long enough. The tension between us is undeniable now.

Ozzy has to strip down and run into the sea yelling, 'I'm the king of the island!' – which he does, and loves. If we did have a king of the island, it would most definitely be him. I'm not sure who the queen would be though.

Eventually Lockie gets dared to whisper something into my ear that would make me blush. He leans in, his breath hot against my skin, and says: 'If we didn't have an audience, that kiss wouldn't have stopped there.'

My skin feels like it's on fire.

'Oh my God, what did you say?' Honey squeaks. 'It worked!'

'I'll never tell,' Lockie says.

I don't think I could if I wanted to.

Finally the game starts wrapping up. I think we're all drunk, tired, and there's something about when your stress levels dip, that makes you feel like you're ready for bed.

When I sneak a glance at Lockie, he's already looking at me, smiling like he always does, flashing his dimples, but something feels different this time. It feels dangerous but... I don't know. Real? God, I hope it's real. Or maybe it's the rum, the isolation, the threat to our lives. That's what I try to tell myself, but I know I'm lying.

Because I don't just fancy him. I like him. And here, on this island, with no escape, and no cameras to keep me in check, I don't know if it's a terrible idea or a great one.

28

Rum-tinted glasses go a long way to making everything look just great. If you're ever going to end up stranded in a potentially life-threatening situation, I highly recommend rum – although I'm sure there are exceptions to the rule, like if you're the pilot of a crashing plane, or a doctor performing surgery. Maybe it's not a good idea in any situation but ours.

The best thing to do on a deserted island late at night, when you're drunk and have a sort of situationship with your colleague, is to stay in camp, sit still and wait for the rescue mission to turn up.

And yet... and yet... I find myself walking through the jungle with Lockie. He's holding my hand, leading me somewhere – he says he's got something to show me.

I catch my toe on a tree root or something and stumble forward. He turns around, his reflexes barely affected by the rum, and catches me.

'So graceful,' he teases.

'Shut up,' I reply, but I'm kinda drunk, so everything is funny.

'We're almost there,' he tells me. 'Can you stay upright just a little longer?'

'Where are we even going?' I ask, ignoring his sarcasm.

I try to peer ahead, but it's dark and all the trees look like all the other trees.

'Have you brought me out here to murder me?' I ask plainly.

'If I wanted you dead I'd just stop saving you,' he replies. 'We're almost there.'

The jungle is dark and humid at night, and every noise sounds like the thing that's going to kill me. I trip at least two or three more times before we reach our destination.

Lockie laughs every time.

'You're enjoying this,' I accuse him as I stumble over a rock.

'I just don't understand how you're falling over everything you can find,' he says with a chuckle.

We finally reach the old production building, where we were earlier. He circles around the back as he drags me behind him.

'We're here!' he announces proudly.

'Yay!' I cheer sarcastically.

'Up you go then,' he says, clasping his hands together to give me a leg-up.

'You're kidding,' I reply.

'I never kid,' he says seriously. 'Come on, up you pop.'

It goes against every survival instinct I have but I step into his palms and let him boost me up toward the terrace above us. I scramble over, then lean back and help to pull him up – not that he needs my help.

Lockie lands beside me, less graceful than he probably intended, and we both burst out laughing.

'Nine out of ten,' I tell him. 'The dismount let you down.'

'Surely I get bonus points for lifting you up in one piece,' he replies.

I roll onto my hands and knees and stand up. This building gets reconfigured each year, so we could be anywhere. Hopefully it's the room where they keep the biscuits.

'Oh my God.' I twirl on the spot. 'We're on the private terrace. The luxury suite terrace.'

He nods, proud of himself.

'Ta-da!'

'If the cameras were still rolling, this would be the part where we get a dramatic close-up and romantic music,' I point out.

He smiles softly as he approaches me.

'Music or not, it's pretty romantic,' he says. 'Plus, we don't need music and a montage to dance.'

Before I can reply, he takes my hand and pulls me gently into the middle of the terrace. His other hand finds my waist.

'Really?' I laugh in disbelief.

'Just dance with me,' he replies.

So I do. We sway, slowly, my arms around his neck, his hands on my hips. The breeze blows through my hair, keeping me cool, and honestly, I don't think the moment could get any more perfect... until Lockie starts singing 'Can't Help Falling in Love' by Elvis Presley – our song – although his impression is terrible.

I snort, bury my face in his shoulder, helpless with laughter.

'No one would ever get clearance to air that,' I point out.

'Thank you – thank you very much,' he jokes.

He's singing louder now – well, it's not like anyone is going to hear, is it? Somewhere between him dipping me and the fits of giggles, I feel myself melting into his arms. I literally cannot help falling for this man; the song is hypnotising me.

'So, can we get inside?' I ask, remembering why we're here. 'Do they have supplies? A radio?'

'We can't actually get inside,' he says. 'However... they must have been in the middle of setting up, because there is one thing that they must have accidentally left outside...'

'Oh?'

Lockie pushes the box towards me.

I plonk down next to it. Lockie joins me, to watch the unboxing.

'Is it life-saving supplies?' I ask.

'Erm, not exactly life-saving,' he replies. 'More like... morale-boosting.'

I peep inside and start laughing. It's the box we opened back in London. The adults-only box of promotional stuff sent to us to promote on the show.

I pull out the giant dildo and cradle it to my chest.

'My emotional support dildo,' I coo.

'See, there's that smile,' he says with a laugh. 'That thing will outlive us all.'

'Aww, I hope so,' I joke.

I dig a little deeper in the box.

'Ooh, coconut-flavoured lubricant,' I say, reading the bottle. 'Why does it have to be coconut? We have loads of coconuts here. Why couldn't it be pizza flavour?'

'I don't think there's much – if any – call for pizza-flavoured lube,' he replies.

'Erm, did you not just hear me request it?' I remind him.

We both stare at the bottle.

'Are you thinking about trying it?' I ask him.

He looks at me, his eyes wide.

'Oh, God, not... sorry – I mean tasting it,' I babble.

'I will if you will,' he replies.

We unscrew the cap and both dab the tiniest bit onto our fingers. Oh, it doesn't smell good at all.

'To island life,' I say, raising my finger like it's a glass of champagne.

'To island life,' he replies.

We clink our fingers then suck them and...

'Oh, God,' I blurt.

'Not nice,' he says. 'Not nice at all.'

'Yeah, I'll stick to real coconuts, I think,' I say, putting the bottle back in the box.

'Maybe pizza flavour really would have been better,' he replies.

We lie back on the deck, close enough that our arms are touching, and look up at the stars. There are a hundred things I could say – most of them stupid, some of them brave. Things I don't have the coconuts to say.

He sighs.

'I'm glad we got stuck together, you know,' he says softly.

I glance at him. He looks like he means it.

'Yeah,' I admit. 'Me too – I would have preferred it to be on the luxury yacht, but I'll take what I can get.'

Lockie just laughs.

A beat passes. Then another.

'You know,' I whisper, 'if this were televised, this would be the part where you kiss me.'

'Is that so?' he replies.

'Yep,' I say, rolling onto my side, propping myself up on my arm.

Maybe I'm drunk. Maybe it's because we feel doomed. Maybe it's because we kissed in the game, but suddenly all I can think about is kissing him again. Just... because. Because why shouldn't I? Why shouldn't we just do what feels right when the world has gone to shit?

I inch a little closer, ever so slowly, giving him the chance to meet me in the middle.

But instead of closing the gap, he just keeps looking up at the stars. He doesn't move. Doesn't look at me. Doesn't do anything except keep staring upward.

I laugh, like maybe he's doing a bit, but... nope. Nothing.

Okay then.

Maybe I imagined it. Maybe the kiss in the game was just a kiss in the game, and it would have been the same for him whether it was me, Honey, Camilla – or even Ozzy.

I flop back onto my back and glare at the sky too. What's so special up there, that's better than a kiss with me, eh? What question is he looking for the answer for?

I've got one of my own – an answer, that is. I now know for sure that I will never, ever, ever understand this man.

29

Waking up to the birds singing and the warm sunshine on my face makes me feel like I'm on an all-inclusive holiday somewhere. Except the only thing inclusive here is fear and stress – and you can always go back for seconds.

I roll over and look at Lockie on the floor next to me. My movement must wake him up.

'Good morning,' he says, all smiles.

'Morning,' I reply.

Falling asleep on the terrace was never part of the plan. Sleeping is all we did, though – I can't seem to push out of my mind that he wouldn't even kiss me. Not that I'm irresistible but, come on, it was the perfect moment.

'Nice to get away for a night, wasn't it?' he jokes.

I laugh.

'We probably shouldn't have slept here, should we?' I say. 'The others will wonder where we are.'

He yawns, stretching his limbs, sending a ripple through his muscles.

'It'll be fine,' he reassures me. 'We'll head back now. If

anyone asks, we'll just say we fell asleep trying to break into the old production building. We kind of did...'

'Kind of being exactly the right term,' I reply.

I try to stretch my back, but it feels nowhere near as satisfying as it looked when Lockie did it. My muscles don't ripple, but my spine does click.

As we gather ourselves to head back to camp, I glance over at the box of sex toys we rifled through last night. My emotional support dildo peeks out of the top, its glitter catching the sun kind of like the ocean does.

'I should probably leave that here,' I say, nodding in its direction.

'Probably for the best,' Lockie says with a laugh.

'Although, to be fair, it could come in useful for stunning fish or knocking down trees,' I point out.

'I don't think I ever saw Bear Grylls with one,' he jokes. 'But we know where it is, if we need it.'

We head to the edge of the terrace and Lockie offers me his hand to climb back down. I go slowly, because I quite like not dying, and I've already survived so much. This would be a stupid way to go.

It's sort of weird, climbing off a terrace together in the daylight, sneaking back to camp – it really is like we actually spent the night together... not that I'm dwelling on it (I am).

As we walk through the jungle, I'm rehearsing my story in my head, what we'll say, how we'll spin it. It's believable enough, that we were trying to break into the building, right?

Thankfully it doesn't matter. When we arrive back, Camilla is already up and she's on the rampage.

'He put faeces in my bed!' Camilla screeches at us.

'And good morning to you too,' Lockie says with a smile, trying to ease the tension.

'Human. Faeces. In my. Bed.'

Oh boy, she's really on one today.

'Who did?'

'I'm sure it wasn't, like, on purpose, babe,' Honey says as she rubs Camilla's back, trying to soothe her.

Accidental or not, it sounds like a horrible thing to wake up to.

'He said it was a present! The sick freak,' Camilla goes on. 'Then he disappeared into the jungle. Probably knew I'd go mad – probably off collecting more. Ew!'

Lockie and I exchange a look.

'Who are we talking about?' I ask her.

'Tony, obviously,' she snaps.

Ozzy is already in the water, fishing, which means Lockie is the 'man of the house'. I look at him and smile, letting him know it's him who needs to investigate.

'I'll have a look then, shall I?' he says reluctantly.

He crouches beside the bed and takes a look. Then he prods it with a finger.

'Oh my God, ew, don't touch it!' Camilla says before gagging dramatically.

Lockie laughs as he picks it up.

'Well, it's not faeces,' he tells her. 'Look – it's a fossil. A really fancy one, actually. See...'

'Oh,' Camilla says simply.

We all lean in to look. He's right. It's a little spiral-shaped stone – probably from some prehistoric sea creature. It really is beautiful.

'He probably found it to replace your crystal,' I say. 'So you'd have something to hold. Something pretty from the earth, you were saying how much you missed it, for grounding you...'

She chews her lip and, and for the first time since we met, she looks like she feels genuinely guilty.

'I... may have screamed at him,' she says. 'I called him a freak and told him to get lost and never come back. I thought he was pranking me.'

'Don't worry, Cleo and I will go find him, we'll talk to him,' Lockie reassures her. 'We'll get him to come back, to talk to you, and it will all be okay.'

'He doesn't have a bad bone in his body,' I tell her. 'He'll forgive you.'

'Yeah, okay, thanks,' she says, her voice much softer than usual.

'Come on then,' Lockie says. 'Let's go find our boy.'

We call Tony's name down the winding jungle path. It doesn't take long before we find him – sort of like when a kid runs away from home, but hides out in the tree house in the garden. Then again, we're on a small island, so how far can he run?

Eventually, a voice calls back. 'Stay away!'

'Mate, we just want to talk to you,' Lockie calls back.

'Fine. But don't come too close,' Tony replies.

Odd.

We follow his voice and find him sitting on a fallen tree, probably taken out by the storm. He's hunched over, like a sad garden gnome, and... oh, God.

His face is tomato red and covered in angry-looking little bites.

'Mate, what happened to you?' Lockie asks.

Tony doesn't look up.

'I was trying to find something nice for Camilla,' he says. 'Something to replace her crystal she keeps banging on about. I found something, but I also found a bunch of bugs. I've been using coconut water on my face, to hydrate my skin, and I guess they like the taste so... eaten alive.'

'You were getting her a gift?' I say with a smile. 'We've seen it, it's beautiful. She's seen it too now, she really likes it.'

'Really?' he replies. 'Because she just started screaming at me, and I didn't want her to see my face, so I just bolted. I can't go back like this. What will she think, if she sees me?'

'No one will care,' Lockie tells him. 'They're just bites. Annoying, but they heal.'

'They will care,' he replies. 'I'm known for being a pretty boy. That's literally my only thing. Why would anyone like me like this? Camilla definitely won't. And I sort of... like her. I like our banter, our bickering. But if she sees my face like this, it'll give her the ick, won't it?'

'She loves the fossil,' Lockie replies. 'And she really likes you too, we can all tell. And she feels bad for shouting. Just come back and talk to her.'

Tony shakes his head.

'It's embarrassing,' he says with a sigh.

I crouch down to look him in the eye.

'You think that's embarrassing?' I start. 'Two nights ago I woke up to realise I'd spooned Lockie in my sleep. And, if that's not bad enough, Ozzy had done the same, and spooned up to me. We were like a sandwich.'

Tony laughs.

'Okay, yeah, that is worse,' he replies. 'Okay, fine, I'll talk to her.'

'Don't mention what I just told you,' I warn him playfully.

'Come on then,' Lockie says, offering him a hand to pull him up.

Tony hesitates, then takes it. We head back along the beach, Lockie and me falling just a couple of paces behind him.

'So you spooned me in your sleep, huh?' he teases me.

'You think that's embarrassing?' I replied. 'You held my hand in your sleep.'

'Who said I was sleeping?' he replies with a wink.

'Ouch!' Tony cries out as he steps on something sharp. It looks like a broken shell. 'Shit, fuck, ow!'

Camilla, hearing the noise and spotting us from camp, comes charging down the beach to help, just like a *Baywatch* babe.

'Are you stung? Do you need me to pee on it?' she shouts as she pulls her hair from her mouth.

Okay, so not *just* like a *Baywatch* babe.

I can't help but smile though. She must think it's another jellyfish attack. She must also like him a lot, to be willing to pee on him.

'I'm not, like, into that,' Tony offers up.

'Oh, no, your face, are you okay?' Camilla asks with genuine concern.

'Just bites,' he replies.

'Well, let me bathe them for you,' she says. 'Because I want to talk to you, to thank you for my present – I love it.'

'Bathe them in water, yeah?' he checks.

'Yes, of course,' she says, not picking up on the implication. 'Come on.'

'Our work here is done,' Lockie says as we follow them back up the beach to camp.

'Looks like she still fancies him,' I point out.

'Erm, she just offered to pee on him,' Lockie reminds me. 'I'd say she loves him.'

I laugh. Maybe he's right.

'Well, if that's *amore*, I'm glad I can't seem to find it,' I reply.

'You'll find someone who wants to pee on you, one day,' he

jokes, giving me a playful shove. 'Come on, let's grab some food. Pineapple or coconut, decisions, decisions...'

I smile, but jokes aside, I feel like he just ushered me to the friend zone. No, I don't want him to pee on me, but he didn't want to kiss me, and this just feels like a playful reminder.

Anyway, I need to forget about it for now. I'm not looking for love, I'm looking for rescue. There's plenty more fish back home, it's only here where the dating pool is limited.

I just need to make sure I get there, then I can worry about the rest.

30

A watched pot of water never boils, it's true, because Tony and I have been watching this one for what feels like forever.

'Can I borrow you, Cleo?' Lockie asks, rocking up next to us.

I look at Tony. He just shrugs.

'Yeah, take her,' he says. 'The water's not going to boil faster with two of us looking at it.'

Lockie jerks his head for me to follow him.

'What's up?' I ask as soon as we're out of earshot.

'I've been talking to Honey,' he says quietly. 'And something isn't right, but I've got a plan to get to the bottom of it.'

'Okaaaay...' I say. 'Do I need to know anything?'

'Just watch,' he tells me.

He grabs a piece of weird spiky fruit in one hand and a bottle of water in the other, then marches over to where Honey is sunbathing.

'What are you doing?' I ask.

'I'm going to eat it in front of her,' he tells me. 'Or try to, at least.'

'Have you had too much sun?' I ask him.

'Just watch,' he replies. 'Hi, Honey!'

'Hi, sugar,' she replies playfully. 'What have you got there?'

'I found this fruit,' he says, sitting down next to her. 'So I'm going to eat it. And apparently, if you eat fruit after, you can drink seawater without dehydrating. I read it on the internet. The internet is never wrong.'

'Have you had some already?' she asks.

'No,' he says cheerfully. 'But I thought we could share. So, down the hatch...'

He puts the bottle of seawater to his lips to drink it, taking a big old swig. He really has lost his mind.

Honey slaps the bottle out of his hand.

'Don't drink that!' she snaps. 'It's idiotic to think you can! And that fruit is ackee – you can't eat it raw, it's toxic! How can you be so dumb?'

Lockie tilts his head curiously, a smug grin spreading across his face.

'How can *you* be so dumb when you're so smart?' he replies.

Honey freezes.

'Honey... are you hiding your intelligence?' I ask.

She groans as she throws her hands up in submission.

'Yes, okay. Fine. It was for the show,' she says and, oh my God, it's like her voice has changed. It's actually much lower and slower. 'People don't like their bimbos smart, and men like me way more if I'm ditzy and I don't challenge them or threaten them in any way.'

'No man who likes you more for pretending to be anything other than yourself is worth liking back,' Lockie tells her. 'I like smart women. Plenty of men do. If you let yourself actually be yourself, you'll see that.'

Honey's face softens.

'I know you're right,' she replies. 'I guess I could tone down the act, start bringing a little more of myself to my character.'

I shrug.

'I like this version of you the most,' I say. 'She's been here all along, keeping us safe...'

'It's idiotic not to research where you're going, what the danger is, what to do in certain situations. I wish I'd read up more on being marooned.'

We both laugh.

'Well, I might not be dumb, but I do still like a tan, and you're blocking my light,' she tells Lockie.

'We'll leave you to it,' he says with a laugh.

'You have a real thing for fixing people, you know that?' I say as we walk away. 'First Camilla and her hostility, Tony and his self-consciousness, now Honey. What are you going to do about Ozzy?'

Lockie laughs.

'Isn't Ozzy perfect?' he replies.

'Not really,' I say. 'Almost, but he can't cry. He says it shows weakness.'

Lockie nods once, very seriously.

'Then we make him cry,' he says.

'I'm sorry, what?'

'I'm serious,' he replies. 'If you see me trying something, follow my lead. We need to show him that it's okay. And, as for your issues, I'm working on it.'

'My issues?' I echo. 'What about yours?'

'What issues?' he says innocently.

I roll my eyes.

'You do have a way of getting through to people,' I admit. 'Making them feel better. Maybe that's why everyone likes you.'

I don't mention that that's probably also his problem. There's a little bit of Lockie for everyone. Which is why he can never really be all mine.

I glance up at the sky. It's not looking so good again.

Lockie catches me staring.

'I'm sure help will arrive before anything kicks off again,' he reassures me.

'I hope so,' I reply. 'Because this feels like the calm before the storm... again.'

'Oi oi,' Ozzy calls out.

He barrels across the sand like a golden retriever who just found a big stick.

'I've saved the day,' he declares proudly.

Lockie raises an eyebrow.

'Have you?' he replies.

'Yep, I found a boat,' he announces.

That gets everyone's attention. Camilla sprints over.

'A boat? You beautiful, beautiful man!' she says. 'What kind?'

'It's a motorboat,' Ozzy says. 'It was in one of the old outbuildings. And it works. The fuel tank is more than half full. Should get us pretty far – far enough to find civilisation.'

'Oh my God, no way,' Honey says.

'We have you to thank,' he tells her.

'Me?' she replies.

'Yeah, it had another one of those number keypad thingies, for security, and I remembered what you said, about trying 0000, so I did, and it worked,' he says, cackling victoriously.

We all look at Honey.

'Just a trick of the IT trade,' she says. 'One of my degrees is in computer science, and 0000 is often used by default – it's the first one we try. That and "password" for alphabetic passwords.'

Wow, so she really does have two degrees.

I look over at Lockie – I wonder if he remembers, back in

London, when we were planning the show, telling me that if we ever needed an IT expert on the show, he would eat his hand. I won't mention it, just in case he doesn't remember, because I'm not sure we can rule out eating limbs for survival just yet. What Ozzy is saying does sound positive, but you know me, always the pessimist.

'So not only do we have a boat,' Ozzy starts, basking in our awe, 'I know how to steer one. So we're almost golden.'

Camilla squeals, clinging to his arm. 'Okay, let's go. Right now. Goodbye island, hello civilisation and electricity and baths, and—'

'Wait,' I interrupt. 'You said almost golden.'

'There is some bad news,' Ozzy replies.

Of course there is.

'The boat can only fit four people safely,' he informs us.

The silence is heavy.

'So four of us go and two stay?' Camilla says. 'I don't think that's a good idea. Like, it's first come, first saved? Like on the *Titanic*? That's not fair. It's all of us, or none of us.'

Well, I wasn't expecting that from Camilla.

'Or,' he says quickly, 'we tow the raft. Secure it with vines, attach it to the back, pull it along to the mainland.'

Tony winces.

'Can't we all just squeeze into the boat?' he checks.

Honey shakes her head immediately.

'No. If it's rated for four people and two of our people are muscly gym bros, it will buckle before we even get out to sea,' she says, now she's happy being smart.

'None taken,' Tony says, pretending to be offended that he's not muscular enough to be a problem.

Camilla's face goes pale. 'Okay, but I can't swim,' she says. 'So I don't think it would be a good idea for me to go on the raft.'

'I can't either,' Tony admits quietly.

Camilla doesn't even mock him. She just wraps an arm around him in solidarity.

'I probably could,' Honey says. 'But I'm not the strongest swimmer.'

'I'll go on the raft,' Lockie says immediately. 'I'm a great swimmer.'

Every eye turns to me, to see what I've got. To be fair, I am a strong swimmer, so it probably should be me too.

'I'll go on the raft too,' I say before I can overthink it.

'All right. I steer the boat. Camilla, Tony and Honey join me. And we secure Lockie and Cleo on the raft,' Ozzy confirms. 'We might actually be getting off this rock.'

'Now?' Camilla asks. 'It's getting dark...'

'It is, so here's the plan: we get everything tied and secured tonight. Fix the raft to the boat, test it, and make sure it's secure. We sleep on it. At first light tomorrow, before any more storms roll in, we set off.'

Camilla exhales, long and slow.

'One more night. I can do one more night,' she chants.

'We might as well make the most of it,' Tony adds, eyeing up the leftover rum. 'Throw ourselves a bit of a goodbye party.'

Just one more night. Food, fire, booze, and a plan for morning. I can do that too. Camilla is right, it's just one more night.

Tomorrow we gamble our lives on a motorboat and a raft held together with vines. What could possibly go wrong? A lot. Absolutely loads. So all the more reason to make tonight count, right?

31

It feels strange, this calm – and you know what they say about calm.

Honestly though, this is the most organised and together we've felt since we got here, but we have a plan, and an understanding, and it's given us this weird sense of normality. We're just a group of friends, sitting down to have dinner together, having a lovely time.

I mean, yeah, we're dirty, and hungry for carbs, and my God do I need some caffeine, but we're eating fish, and roasted fruit, and polishing off the last of the rum. It's nice. Like we're all on holiday together.

The firelight flickers between us, making us all feel warm and cosy, and for once no one's bickering or plotting, and it feels like a million years since the rules of the show felt like they mattered. Even the ever-present sound of the sea seems gentle tonight, like the island is giving us a little bit of a break ahead of tomorrow.

It really has felt oddly normal tonight. Honey laid out our food on big leaves, like we're in a fancy restaurant. And Tony made us more coconut and rum cocktails – they might be the things I miss the most, when we're back home.

'To tomorrow,' Tony says, raising his coconut. 'Because tomorrow, we might actually make it off this godforsaken island.'

'Hear, hear,' Camilla adds.

I smile as I glance around the fire. Somehow, after everything that's happened – the storms, the scares, the bickering – I feel... grateful? Like maybe this weird, broken little group is exactly what I needed. I thought I was trapped with a bunch of reality TV dummies but, nope, they're all great. Each one of them has depth and skills and a lot of love.

Lockie catches my gaze and smiles.

'Don't start getting emotional, guys,' Honey says. 'You'll make me cry.'

'I could shed a tear,' Tony tells her. 'For good and bad – mostly because I'm desperate for one of my mum's Sunday roasts.'

'Aww, that's so lovely,' Camilla says.

'You'll be back with your mum soon,' Lockie reminds him. 'And, whatever day it is, I'm sure she'll make you a roast.'

Ozzy sits opposite me, shaking his head with a grin.

'You're all crazy,' Ozzy says. 'We should be punching the air.'

'I'll do it when we're back on different dry land,' I joke.

'I might say a few words, if you don't mind,' Lockie says, standing up.

'Ooh, speech, speech,' Honey shouts.

'Okay,' Lockie starts, pausing to take a breath. 'Since this might be our last night here—'

'No, it will be,' Camilla practically heckles. 'Be positive, be positive.'

'In that case then, before we go...' he corrects himself with a smile. 'I just want to say... You're all great, and I wouldn't have wanted to share this experience with anyone else, and I don't think it would have been so easy with anyone else. You've all brought something to the island, something we needed, but Ozzy, mate, you're one of the main reasons we've made it this far.'

Ozzy laughs.

'What, because I can catch a fish?' he replies.

'Because you've held it together,' Lockie continues. 'You've looked after everyone. You've been the leader we didn't even realise we needed. And a great leader at that.'

Ozzy smiles.

'Thanks, mate,' he replies.

I know what Lockie is doing, he's trying to tap into Ozzy's emotions, to get him to actually show some. I think he needs my help.

'And,' I add, standing too, hooking my arm with Lockie's, 'you've been our anchor. Literally and metaphorically. You kept us grounded. You made us feel safe.'

Ozzy chuckles awkwardly, rubbing his neck. 'All right, all right, that's enough,' he says modestly.

'You built half this camp with your bare hands. You made sure we had food. You were the first one to fish for supplies, even when the waves were insane. You didn't complain once.'

'And you took on outhouse duties,' Honey adds.

'And you didn't make a big deal of it,' Camilla adds.

'You really are our island daddy,' I say with a little laugh.

'Yeah, mate, we love you,' Tony tells him.

'I think we all owe Ozzy a toast,' Lockie says. 'Come on – to Ozzy!'

'Guys...' Ozzy's voice sounds tight, his eyes are blinking, are we finally getting through to him?

'You've got the biggest muscles out of all of us,' I tell him. 'And you've got the biggest heart too.'

Ozzy wipes away the happy tear that escapes his eye.

'Give over, you're making me fill up,' he tells us. 'I get it, I get it, I'm amazing. I'm just glad this didn't happen on camera.'

'We've taken a mental picture,' Honey teases him.

Tomorrow's going to be hard. Maybe even dangerous. But right now? Right now, it feels like we could do anything, as long as we do it together – as cringe as it sounds.

I can't resist resting my head on Lockie's shoulder. I just feel so comfortable – which is ironic, given how uncomfortable this island is.

'Okay, okay, if Ozzy's getting a speech, we're all getting one,' Honey declares.

Tony groans.

'Oh, God.'

'Go on, Honey, we'd love to hear it,' Lockie encourages her.

Honey shifts on her seat and tucks her hair behind her ears.

'Right,' she starts, suddenly shy, 'before all this, I thought the biggest thing I'd ever do was... I dunno, bag myself a job on breakfast telly, or be the ditzy one on a panel show. But I haven't been scared here. Not really. 'Cause I knew you lot wouldn't let anything happen to me. And I've done things I never thought I could – but I've also found out that the best thing for me is to be myself. That people will like me for me.'

'We love you, Honey,' I call out, like I'm a diehard fan at a footie match.

'Well, I didn't think I'd last a day,' Camilla says, taking to her feet. 'I thought I'd be useless. Or worse – I'd die.'

To be fair, that is worse.

'I know I can be...' She pauses. 'A lot.'

'You're a lot of wonderful,' Tony tells her. 'An absolute diamond.'

Camilla blows him a kiss.

'You've all put up with me. And I've – weirdly – enjoyed roughing it with you on this island. This is roughing it, right?' she checks, not wanting to be offensive.

'It is,' Ozzy reassures her.

'Phew,' she replies.

'My turn next,' Tony announces. 'I've never gone this long without a mirror. Or decent clothes. Or just the essentials like moisturiser.' We laugh, but he's serious beneath it. 'But I think... I think I needed it. It turns out people don't actually hate me when I'm not trying so hard. And I kinda like not worrying about whether my eyebrows are doing that weird thing – you've all been too polite to point it out.'

I don't think any of us has a clue what weird eyebrow thing he's referring to, but that's being self-conscious, isn't it? You worry about things that other people don't even clock.

'Your eyebrows look banging, mate,' Lockie tells him.

Tony smiles.

'I'll worry about my pores when I'm back home, but here – who cares?' he adds.

'I'll drink to that,' Ozzy tells him. 'And to being your island daddy. Honestly, it's been an honour. You say I've taken care of you – it's been my pleasure. And you've been a joy to take care of.'

Suddenly all eyes are on me, like I'm the only one who hasn't been yet. I got in on Lockie's – does that not count? I guess not.

'Your turn,' Camilla prompts me. 'Don't think you're getting out of it.'

I open my mouth, then close it again. What can I say that hasn't been said already?

'I suppose...' I start slowly, staring at my emotional support coconut. 'I didn't think I'd cope this well. Or at all. I've never been... brave.' I laugh softly. 'Not like this. I thought I'd crumble. And if I could have boarded the first plane home, I probably would have.'

'No, you wouldn't,' Ozzy calls out. 'We wouldn't have let you.'

He couldn't have stopped me.

'But a very wise man told me that the first step toward being brave is pretending that you're brave,' I continue, giving Lockie a wink. 'I've been pretending this whole time but, I don't know, maybe now it feels real. I feel brave because I know you've all got my back. So... thanks.'

Everyone claps and cheers. It's a proper love-in, but we need it. It's giving penultimate episode edit, but it's natural.

What I want to say, but can't, is that one of the things I'm most grateful for is him. Lockie. That he's here with me. That he's alive. That I'm not going into tomorrow without him. That it will be me and him on the raft, clinging on for dear life together. But I can't say that here, now, in front of everyone, because it's something that leads to a different conversation, and I don't think we're ready to have that yet.

So I smile instead and raise my cup.

'To us,' I say. 'The islanders who survived the storm.'

'We'll be famous when we get home, if we make it,' Tony says.

'When we make it,' Camilla corrects him. 'And I'm already famous, darling.'

Lockie taps his coconut against mine. 'To tomorrow,' he says.

'To getting off this bloody island,' Honey adds.

'To Island Daddy,' Ozzy jokes.

We drink and, do you know what, that might be the last of the rum. Perfect timing, in that case.

'You know what, I don't even care that you've got me blubbing,' Ozzy says. 'It feels good to cry, actually. I feel... comfortable. With you lot. We've been through hell, and we're still here.'

'Like a family,' Honey says softly. 'The best family! The family you choose, not the one you're born into.'

'Yeah,' Tony agrees. 'A weird, dysfunctional, half-naked family. But family all the same.'

'I'll raise a coconut to that,' Lockie jokes.

'Me too,' I reply.

'And me,' Honey says.

'I'll drink to that too,' Camilla says. 'Why not, hey?'

Do you know what, if this is our last night here, then at least we'll all go out together.

I should probably be terrified, but I'm not. We've survived this long because we've stuck together, so if we stick together tomorrow, then why shouldn't it work out?

Anyway, it's a problem for tomorrow. Tonight it's just about having fun together, and being a family. And that clearly means so much to us all.

32

Dinner fades into background noise – the sound of everyone laughing, drinking, having a good time. It's been fun, hanging out together, enjoying ourselves like it might be our last night on earth. Well, when it might, why not, right?

Every so often, I've caught Lockie looking at me across the firepit. Not in his usual way though, I don't know, it's like his cogs are turning. I'm not quite sure what they're telling him.

It makes my stomach twist up, like I'm about to board a rollercoaster with a name like 'Skull Destroyer' or 'Death Trap', or like I'm walking along the edge of a cliff hoping I don't fall.

And, of course, how do I notice that he keeps glancing at me, unless I keep catching myself glancing at him too?

When he finally stands, brushing sand from his shorts, I know before he says a word that he's going somewhere, and I'm going with him. My heart thuds, loud enough I'm convinced Honey can hear it next to me. For a second I panic – should I say something? Should I act chill? But Lockie just tilts his head, a silent invitation, and it's like my feet move without consulting my brain.

'Come on,' he says. 'I fancy a walk.'

I arch a brow.

'Why do I feel like you're about to get me killed?' I ask as I follow him.

He just gives that maddening, gorgeous half-smile.

'Come find out.'

The others barely notice us slip away: Tony's arguing with Camilla about who drank the last of the rum – he says she has a guilty look on her face, she says it's just good genetics – and Ozzy is letting Honey pull his hair into cute little plaits, which makes me think he might be the one who polished off the rum. It's the first time I've felt invisible in weeks, and it's delicious. No eyes on us. No cameras. No producers. Just dark, warm air and the thud of my own pulse in my ears as I follow Lockie into the trees.

The jungle swallows the light quickly. The further we walk, the more the night wraps around us.

He doesn't say anything for a while, just glances back every so often to check I'm still behind him, still following him. I pretend not to stare at the muscles shifting in his back, the way his shoulders move as he pushes through vines, but it's captivating.

'This better not end with me falling into a volcano,' I say. 'Or being snatched up by a net, like you see in the movies.'

'No promises,' he says. 'But I'm pretty sure we'd know if there was a volcano – knowing our luck, probably via it erupting – and if you do get caught up in a net, it won't be mine.'

I'm not so sure about that.

'I feel like we know every inch of this island,' I remind him. 'So I don't know where you could be taking me, unless you got that hatch open, and there really is a man with a bunch of food in there.'

He laughs, softly.

'You'll just have to trust me.'

'Yeah, that's famously one of my weaknesses,' I reply.

The sound reaches me before the sight: water. Oh, we're at the waterfall. I've been here before – not at night though, and it really is something.

The waterfall is silver in the moonlight, crashing into a pool of black glass below.

The rocks feel slick beneath my feet and the roar of water is so loud I have to lean closer to hear Lockie's voice.

'It's better at night,' he says, watching me instead of the view.

'I can see that,' I reply. 'It's beautiful.'

'Come on,' he says.

'What, have you brought me here for a wash?' I joke. 'Do I smell that bad?'

'If you do, we all do,' he jokes. 'But that's not why, just trust me.'

He takes my hand – properly takes it, his fingers sliding between mine, gripping me firmly – and leads me towards the curtain of falling water.

'We're going under it?' I check. 'Because that is just the shower – are you trying to get me wet?'

I regret my choice of word the second he starts grinning.

'Don't say a word,' I warn him.

'I'm not trying to trick you into showering,' he replies. 'And we're not going under it, we're going through it.'

I cock my head curiously.

'Through it?' I check. 'What's through it?'

'Wait and see,' he replies.

He just smirks and steps through first, tugging me gently after him. The waterfall crashes over my shoulders, cold and wild, stealing my breath. And then it fades.

We're behind it, in a hidden alcove behind the water. The

only light comes filtered through the wall of falling water, turning everything silver-blue. It's small, but it feels... safe. Untouchable.

'I had no idea this was here,' I whisper.

'It's where you get into the control room, for the waterfall,' he explains. 'The door is locked, because of course it is, but this might just be the most private spot on the island.'

'I love it,' I blurt.

We sit on a flat rock, close enough that our legs brush. Lockie runs his thumb over my knuckles, absent-mindedly, like he's done it a hundred times. I tuck my wet hair behind my ears and try very hard to act normal, but my breath catches, and I hope he doesn't notice.

We don't say anything, or look at each other, for a while – we just watch the water.

When he finally speaks, his voice is softer than I've ever heard it before.

'I meant what I said before, you know. About not getting through this without you,' he tells me.

'You too,' I reply. 'You wouldn't have been my first choice for the end of the world but next time, if we're unlucky enough to have a next time, you'll make the top five.'

He laughs but doesn't look away after, he just stares at me, and there's something in his eyes...

'You've kept me sane,' he says.

I swallow.

'Right back at you.'

A beat passes – one of those long ones that lasts a lifetime, that feels impossible to breathe normally through.

'At least us being off-air gets you off the hook,' I say lightly, looking back at the water. 'You don't have to pretend to fancy me any more.'

Silence.

'Who says I was pretending?' he eventually replies.

My heart punches my chest. I force a laugh.

'Oh, shut up.'

He doesn't. And he shifts closer too.

'If I didn't fancy you,' he starts, his voice barely audible over the sound of the water, 'could I do this?'

His lips brush my neck – slow, deliberate and, unlike when he did it in the challenge, it feels hungrier. Like he's not going to stop.

'You did that to Honey too,' I manage to remind him, though my voice comes out weak and breathy.

'That was for a dare.' His breath tickles my damp skin. 'And I wished it was you.'

I don't move. I don't blink. I don't even breathe again until he pulls back enough to look at me.

'I don't want to spend the rest of my life wishing it was you, whenever I kiss someone,' he continues. 'So, for the avoidance of doubt, in case you're overthinking things. Cleo – I want you.'

'I want you too,' I manage to blurt back with a smile.

Lockie grins back at me, leaning in so close his nose almost brushes mine.

'So... what do we do about it?' I ask, hoping he comes to the same conclusion as me.

He searches my face, like he's making sure we're on the same page.

'It could be our last night on earth,' he points out.

'It really could,' I reply. 'How do you want to spend it?'

I can't help but bite my lip. That's the only signal he needs.

He gently cups my face with one hand, his thumb tracing my cheek for a few seconds, like this is my chance to retreat, but there's no turning back now.

Then he kisses me. It's not like in the silly challenges or anything we'd do for the cameras; it's slow, real, and frankly terrifying. I melt into him, wrapping my arms around him, snaking one up his back, into his hair where I can't resist grabbing it, just a little.

And suddenly everything – and I mean everything – goes quiet inside my head.

No racing thoughts. No panic. No noise at all. All I care about are his lips on mine, and where this might be going next.

I kiss him like I've wanted to ever since we met – and all the while I've been telling myself I didn't want to.

Lockie scoops me up and presses me against the cool stone. I wrap my arms and legs around him, like I'm unwilling to let him go. Now that we're tangled up, I don't want us to come undone again.

Maybe it's where we are, or what we've been through, or all of it together, but it's wild. We can't get enough of each other, our hands and lips everywhere, things getting more frantic by the second. The two of us finally getting together feels like the missing piece of the puzzle. Like I've finally found just what I needed.

Eventually, Lockie lies back and exhales deeply. I lie with my head on his chest and listen to his heart thumping in his chest. I swear, it's louder than the waterfall.

He runs a hand lazily through my hair.

'If I do die tomorrow, I can't be too mad,' he jokes. 'I went out on a high.'

'Yeah, I'd rather not die, but I don't mind that being the last thing I did,' I reply.

His chest shakes with a quiet laugh. He kisses the top of my head, like it's the most natural thing in the world.

'We'd better get back,' I say, much as I don't want to. 'They'll be wondering where we are – we don't want them to come looking for us.'

'It would buy us a little time, to do that again,' he jokes. 'But yeah, you're right.'

Sneaking back to camp feels like being teenagers again, creeping in the moonlight, trying not to make a sound. It's much easier on sand than it was on my parents' creaky staircase. The others are already asleep, tucked up in their beds together, looking more comfortable for having a few drinks in them.

We slip in beside Ozzy, trying not to make the bed creak. Lockie stifles a laugh against his arm when I lie down with much less grace than I intended.

Settled, we try to sleep, but in the dark his hand finds mine. He squeezes me tightly before relaxing into something comfortable. And then he doesn't let go.

Who knows what tomorrow will bring? Maybe it will go well, or maybe it will go disastrously. Either way, I don't know, but I feel happy – happier than I should for someone who is going to take her chances on a raft tomorrow.

I don't know if we'll make it off the island, or if we'll even make it at all, but right now, in this bed, in this moment, with his hand holding mine, I'm not scared.

I'm happy.

Really, properly happy.

And I'm not faking it any more.

33

When I wake up, for a blissful half-second, I don't know where I am, or what's going on, but then I feel the two large men lying each side of me, and I hear the roar of the ocean, and remember where I am.

That's not all I remember though. I remember the waterfall. Lockie's hands in my hair. His mouth on mine. The way we'd stumbled back to camp in the dark like teenagers sneaking home past curfew. The way he'd found my hand under the blanket and held it like it meant something. He's still holding it now.

Today isn't going to be easy for a lot of reasons so it's easy to stay in the memory of last night.

I feel Lockie squeeze my hand before he speaks.

'Morning,' he says.

'Morning,' I reply.

Ozzy lets out a little snore, inadvertently letting us know he's still sleeping.

Careful not to wake him, I roll over to face Lockie. His hair's a mess, his eyes are still heavy with sleep, and I've never been more attracted to him. He looks at me like he's still not sure last night actually happened.

'You doing okay?' he asks.

'Yeah,' I reply, keeping my voice down. 'You?'

He nods as he brushes hair from my eyes, gently tucking it behind my ear.

'Good morning, campers,' Tony calls out.

Lockie and I give each other some space as the gang head over. Ozzy wakes up and climbs out of bed, leaving the two of us in bed together.

Lockie gives my hand one last squeeze under the blanket before letting go. Then we get up too. I suppose we have to face the day eventually. Before we know it we'll be clinging on to our sea vessels for dear life, hoping for the best, probably expecting the worst.

I know it's going to sound crazy, not only because I didn't want to come here in the first place, but also because I'm not exactly cut out for desert island life, but I actually, kind of – and I can't believe I'm saying this – don't want to leave. The thing is, I'm happy. I'm actually happy. I have Lockie, I have my friends, we have our simple island life. Would I like a Starbucks and a manicure? Yes. But am I worried about what's going to happen between me and Lockie when we go back to real life? Absolutely.

But we've all jumped to action, we're sticking with the plan, and we're doing it.

Lockie stands beside me, watching the others gather supplies.

'Are you ready?' he asks me.

'To send ourselves adrift?' I check. 'Born ready.'

Lockie laughs.

But I wish we could go back to the waterfall, just the two of us, and stay there.

Do you know what though? As scared as I am – about the raft, and letting Lockie hold my heart in his hands – for the first time in a long time, I have hope. Yeah, some things have been shit (on and off the island) but there's hope for getting rescued, and there's hope for me and Lockie. If I just let myself be an optimist for once.

Yes, I've woken up with my usual island backache, but I almost don't mind it, probably because I know it's my last one. Well, when I'm back home, I know I'll look back at this whole experience and remember the good things because there have been some.

'I might use the outhouse, one last time, for old time's sake,' Lockie says.

I laugh.

'Make the most of it,' I tell him.

Lockie heads off, back up the beach, and I don't know why I turn to look at him – probably just because he's nice to look at – but he doesn't go to the outhouse, he disappears into the trees, moving like... I don't know, like he doesn't want to be seen. What on earth is he up to? I suppose there's only one way to know for sure.

So I follow him, creeping barefoot, keeping a few paces back, ducking every time he glances around. He heads deeper into the jungle, behind the old production building – somewhere no one ever bothers going.

My heart is pounding. I guess it's scary, following someone, but there's just something about his body language, like he's up to no good.

I give him a few seconds to get a little further ahead of me, just to see what he's doing because – if it's bad, then I need to catch him in the act.

Except I'm scared to look. What if it is something bad? I don't know what, but I don't know what good it could be either. I just feel like things are so good and, if I look around that corner, and I don't like what I see, then that's it.

I have to look, don't I? I'll always wonder if I don't.

'Yeah. We should be on the boat in under an hour, keep on camera forty-two when we set off,' he says into a walkie-talkie. He's standing in front of an open hatch, one I've never seen before. 'Use the GPS in the wristbands to get a location pin on us. You can intercept as soon as we're—'

'Are you fucking serious?' I snap.

He spins around, his eyes wide. He definitely wasn't expecting me to catch him mid-whatever this is.

'Lockie? What's going on? Over.' I hear Simon's voice over the walkie.

'Cleo—' Lockie starts.

'You absolute arsehole,' I cut him off.

'I can explain,' he tells me.

Ha! Can he? Does he even need to? It looks pretty fucking self-explanatory to me.

'Oh, really,' I say as I approach him. 'Because it kind of looks like you've been sneaking off to talk to Simon? All this time? Were you in on it from the start?'

'No,' he says firmly. 'No, it wasn't like that—'

'Get this stupid wristband off me right now,' I snap, shoving my arm at him.

Suddenly, the microphone on my wrist feels like it's burning my skin.

'Just let me—'

'Now!' I demand.

He hesitates for a split second before crouching in front of the hatch and dragging out a first aid kit. He takes out a knife and cuts through the plastic of my wristband, freeing me from it.

'Cleo, please—'

'I'm not talking to you while you're still wearing yours,' I reply.

He holds my stare, then, without breaking it, cuts off his own wristband. He drops it on the floor next to mine.

'There,' he says quietly. 'No mics. No trackers. There aren't any cameras in this area. Simon can't hear us on the walkie unless I push the button. Can we please talk?'

'You've been filming us this whole time?' I blurt. My voice shakes with anger. 'This entire fucking time? Has it been airing?'

His shoulders drop guiltily.

'Yes. But we didn't plan for it to go like this,' he replies. 'The walkie was just a backup for Simon, in case something went wrong. The storm was real though—'

'I know the storm was real!' I snap. 'It's not the wanking *Truman Show*.'

He swallows hard, trying to find the words that won't piss me off more – good luck to him.

'When it hit, everything did go dark. But then, when the feed came back... I spoke to Simon. He said the viewing figures were through the roof. He said if we stayed put, just a little longer, it would be the best story they've ever had.'

'It's not a story,' I clap back. 'It's our lives. You took our choice away. Our free will!'

'Everyone is going to come out of this looking great,' he reassures me, stepping closer. 'The show is a smash. We kept it alive. Simon loves us for it—'

'Well, I hate him. And I hate you too,' I blurt.

It's not at all elegant, but at least it's honest.

'Cleo, all we have to do is get on the boat, and then the island feed cuts off,' he says. 'You know what the contracts are like, they say if we interfere with the show, they can sue us for damages. So we just play along. They'll switch to rescue footage. There's going to be this big send-off, they're going to have the final today. We did it. Shortest season ever and the most viewers.'

'I don't care,' I say, backing away. 'I don't care about viewers, or Simon, or...'

My voice trails off as something hits me like a slap across the face.

'You knew we were being filmed,' I whisper. 'Last night. When we...'

My face burns with fury and humiliation in equal measure.

'You knew they were watching. And you let me. You let me...'

'Cleo—'

'You bastard.'

'Just let me—'

'Don't say another word,' I insist, backing away from him. 'I'm going back to camp. Out in the open. In front of the cameras where you can't give me your lame excuses. We'll be off this island soon enough, then you and I are done.'

I don't wait for his reply. I run. Branches whip my arms but I don't stop. It's funny, I hated the cameras being on me, they made me feel uneasy. Now they're my safety net. My protection.

I thought the cameras were the danger. Turns out it was Lockie all along.

34

I don't want to talk about it, I just want to get on the raft, and get home to safety. Well, we don't need to talk about it, do we? Because it's on me, I fucked up, I trusted Lockie when I knew what he was like – that's on me. I throw up my hands. Now get me the fuck home.

We're doing final checks on the raft. The tide's coming in stronger today, wind beating the water hard enough to spray us from the shore. Everyone's tense but focused, and bizarrely incredibly upbeat, because we're getting off this rock.

But we wouldn't be us if we didn't have a bit of last-minute drama. It all happens so fast. Tony missteps, getting on the boat, and falls backwards. Ozzy dives in to save him, but lands on his arm.

'Arrrgh,' he calls out.

Oh no, poor Ozzy.

I drop the flasks of water and hurtle over to him. Lockie's already there, helping him up from the water.

'Are you okay?' I ask him.

He stretches out his arm, extending his fingers one at a time, rotating his wrist.

'It's not broken,' he says. 'But it hurts. I can still drive the boat, but...'

'But if we need someone to punch a shark, we'll have to ask someone else?' I joke.

'Lockie can do it,' Ozzy says through a pained smile.

'My money would be on Camilla,' I reply.

'Sorry, mate,' Tony replied. 'But thanks for catching me.'

'We'd all have done the same for each other,' he replies. 'And it could have been worse – one of us could have been really hurt.'

My heart sinks. One of us was.

'You're so strong,' I tell him, squeezing his shoulder.

Honestly, I've done way less, and acted like I was hurt way more. He really has been great for us. I don't know how happy I'd be going out to sea without him.

I go back to retrieve the water.

Lockie is hot on my heels.

'Oh, Ozzy, you're so strong,' Lockie says, mocking what I'm guessing is supposed to be my voice.

'Oh, grow up,' I tell him. 'At least he's honest and decent and...'

My voice trails off as I notice Lockie subtly glance at the camera, then back to me.

Oh, right, because they're going to keep filming us until we set off. Honestly, he's lucky, because I'd be chewing him out if I could. However, when we're off this island, and back to safety, I've decided I have nothing to say to him. This whole thing has been a disaster; everything has gone downhill since he speed-dated his way into my life. Now, I just want to move on, I want to forget about him, to forget that I let myself get caught up in his charm when I really should have known better. It's not like he didn't show me who he was, before we left. But I'm not going to beat myself up, it was the island that ushered me into making bad choices. The dating pool here is small and he was just the easiest option – but the one that has caused me the most heartache.

Ozzy roars like a lion when he gets the motorboat engine going – seemingly one-handed too, what a babe.

'We're doing it,' he says. 'We're fucking doing it!'

The ladies board the boat first, then Tony, then all that's left is for me and Lockie to board the raft.

'After you,' he says.

I'm hoping for a *Titanic*-type situation, where the raft can only hold me, and we have to leave him here. Wouldn't that be sad, if he has to stay here, on this island? I bet he'd love it.

I don't even look at him. I climb aboard and get balanced in the middle. Then he gets on and scoots up next to me. I suppose it makes sense, we want the weight to be as even as possible.

We've tested it a few times and it's holding – Ozzy broke out all of his survival training to find the right kind of vines, to tether the two together. All that's really left to do now is set off.

'Right, let's do it. Say bye-bye, island,' he tells us all.

'Bye-bye, island,' we all call out.

It's odd, knowing what I know now. I thought that this season was a write-off, that the storm hitting right away would mean time, money and resources wasted. In a way, if I have my professional hat on, I'm glad that it wasn't. I just really, really wish I had known. I wish Lockie had told me. Maybe I would have done things differently… maybe. I definitely wouldn't have done *him*.

I grip the side of the raft so hard my knuckles ache. I just need to hang on, just a little longer, and we'll reach the rescue boat. I'm sure the others will be so happy that they won't even question the timing of it, and everyone will be so proud that our plan worked, I'm not going to ruin it for them. Sure, they'll find out that everything has been aired, but that's what they signed up for, right? They're used to living their lives on screen, and they all came across so well. I hope they're happy, and I'm sure they will be. I'm not used to it though, this isn't my life. I stepped in as a favour and, yeah, okay, if I had known, maybe I would have insisted we pulled the plug, so maybe that's why they didn't tell me but... ugh. I hate that Lockie kept it from me, for views, even if it was what we both wanted. I just wanted the choice.

I allow myself a quick glance Lockie's way. He's not looking at me. He's got his eyes on the horizon, probably looking out for Simon and co. Waiting for his big moment, his pat on the back. He got his storyline, that's for sure. A reality TV show gone wrong, survivors trapped on an island, fending for themselves. And I couldn't sue them if I wanted to, I know the contract, I know how flexible it is. Not only does it say showrunners can do, and film, whatever they want, but it says that they can sue any contestant who gets in the way of production. At the end of the day, I signed that contract, I'm a contestant, not an employee, and there's nothing I can do.

I'm pulled from my thoughts by one of the vines snapping. Then another one. Lockie and I stare at one another. Well, what can we do?

Ozzy turns around.

'Just keep going,' Lockie tells him.

'They're going to snap,' Ozzy replies.

'It's okay,' Lockie insists. 'Go, get help, we can swim back to shore. Send someone for us.'

'We can't leave you,' Camilla calls out.

'We'll be okay,' I reply.

They're right. It's not like we can board the boat, or reattach the raft out at sea. We're not that far from the shore, and we do have the luxury of knowing that help is actually, definitely on the way.

Then another one snaps. Then another. Then the final one.

'We'll be back for you,' Ozzy calls out as they speed off, his voice growing quieter and quieter by the split second.

We watch in silence as they speed off. I just need to remind myself that help is coming, help is coming – Lockie made sure of it. It's scripted, at this point. I just need to hang in there.

The raft's already taking on water, now that we're not moving. Lockie looks it over for a second and then turns to me.

'Come on. We need to swim back,' he says.

I laugh.

'After you.'

'I'm serious,' he replies. 'This will start sinking and even in warm water you can get hypothermia. We have to get back to land ASAP.'

I glance overboard and I've never been so close to water that looked so deep – I've certainly never swum in it.

'Come on,' he says softly. 'We'll do it together. I won't let anything bad happen to you.'

A bit rich but, as the corner of the raft starts going under, it's hardly the time or the place.

And without a second more to think about it, we jump in.

The water swallows me whole. I go deep under – deeper than I was expecting – but just as the panic starts rising in my chest I feel Lockie's arms around my body, pulling me up to the surface.

I take a deep breath as soon as I can, filling my lungs with the sweet, sweet oxygen I thought I'd never taste again. My God, it's glorious. I'll never take it for granted again.

'Are you okay to swim?' Lockie asks me. 'It's not far.'

'Yeah,' I manage to reply.

'I'll be right behind you,' he tells me.

We start swimming. It doesn't look all that far but my God it feels it.

We finally reach the sand and I crawl onto it like some kind of swamp monster. I don't even make it to the dry sand before I flop onto my back.

Lockie lies beside me. Even he seems knackered.

'We did it,' he says victoriously. 'You did great.'

'Yeah, well, you would have been gutted if I'd died off camera, wouldn't you?' I say, never too knackered to be spiky with someone who deserves it.

'Can I please explain?' he replies.

'You've got until the rescue team arrives,' I tell him – now I know that there is one, and it's headed our way. Let him try to explain, it's not going to change the way I feel.

'By the time I got in touch with Simon, after the storm, the show was a hit,' he explains. 'Everyone was glued, watching to see if we all survived – but we were never actually in danger.'

'But we thought we were,' I remind him.

'And I regret that,' he replies. 'I just wanted to make the show a hit, and I did – we did. And it just got out of control. But that's why I didn't kiss you on the terrace. The only reason. Believe me, I wanted to.'

I actually laugh in his face.

'Which would be awfully gallant of you, except you had sex with me behind the waterfall,' I remind him. 'Do you think I'd have done that if I'd known we were on TV? I'm beyond mortified.'

'There are no cameras behind there,' he says quickly. 'And no cameras that can see inside, and it blocks the signal, so no microphones either. That's why I took you there. It's private.'

'For a cheeky shag?' I snap.

'No, for a moment, just the two of us, where we could be ourselves,' he replies. 'Look, I know your ex cheated on you, and I get that, I really do, but I like you, I really do, and I won't betray you like that.'

'You really are an idiot,' I tell him, half laughing, half furious. 'You think you can fix me like you fixed everyone else. "Oh, I'll show Cleo not everyone is going to cheat on her," blah blah blah. Except my ex didn't cheat on me. He betrayed me, yeah, but it wasn't another woman. It was at work. For a job. He screwed me over to get ahead at work. So, yes, thank you for proving to me that you're just like him.'

'I didn't know that,' he says. 'But that's not—'

'Your time is up,' I tell him. 'Here comes the cavalry.'

A speedboat charges towards the shore, with Arabella standing on the front, waving at us. Behind her, there's a small crew – a cameraman and a sound guy. Of course there is.

Arabella looks flawless, which is just perfect when I look like this.

'There you two are!' she says brightly, like we've been avoiding her. 'The others are okay, they're on the way to the yacht. We just need you two and we can have ourselves a final. What do you say?'

What can I say? All I can do is force a smile and climb aboard. It's my ticket off this island, no matter what happens. I just need to put my brave face on, get through this finale, and then I'm done. Contract completed. I can put all of this behind me.

'You must be relieved. I mean, what a journey,' Arabella says as we board the boat.

'I'm glad to be saved,' I say – I really am. Not just from the island, but from making any more mistakes with Lockie. When will I learn, eh? Now, hopefully. This is my rock bottom. It has to be.

35

I'm back on a yacht, lined up with the other survivors, cameras on us from all angles, waiting as Arabella talks to the public.

We're all national treasures, it turns out. Tara flashed me a couple of headlines on her phone while someone mic'd me up. Apparently the whole world is obsessed with us and our survival story. Simon playing the hero who 'worked tirelessly' to rescue us from a reality TV show gone wrong. Utter bollocks. You just know he strung it out for as long as he could before rescuing us.

Arabella beams at the cameras a little brighter than usual, like she knows her audience just got much, much bigger.

'We've had a number of votes to determine the winner, seeing as though this season has gone way off script,' she says to the camera.

Yeah, no kidding.

'The first vote was to pair the islanders into couples, seeing as though we couldn't do it on the show. And those couples are...' – she drags out the dramatic pause – '...Camilla and Tony, Honey and Ozzy, and Cleo and Lockie. Please stand in your couples.'

Ugh, fantastic. I wound up left with him.

I move as I'm told. Lockie steps beside me, his eyes fixed forward, playing the part perfectly. I just need to get through this bit and it's over.

'The winner of the popular vote is...' Another endless pause. '...Cleo and Lockie!'

My jaw drops down onto the deck. We won the popular vote? How? We weren't even a couple. Half the time we were fighting...

'Please stand either side of me,' Arabella tells us. We do as we're told. 'How are you both feeling?'

'Great,' Lockie says. 'And shocked and just... so glad everyone's safe.'

'Yeah, so glad we all made it, and that we're all here,' I say without thinking. I just need to play along for a little longer.

'Okay then,' Arabella continues. 'The moment of truth. If the public think it's true love, you win one hundred thousand pounds. If not, well, at least you know you're popular!'

Laughter all around. I don't even need to fake it. There's no way anyone is going to think it's love.

'The public have voted... and they think...' – longest pause yet – '...it's love! Congratulations, you've won a hundred thousand pounds!'

Now my jaw is on the deck below. There's music, the cheering, fireworks, a ridiculously oversized trophy that we don't usually have. Arabella thrusts it into our hands before turning to the camera to do the outro.

Then the red light on the main camera clicks off, and I drop my smile like a dead weight.

'Can we talk?' Lockie says. 'Before we do anything else.'

'Yeah,' I say, already walking off. 'Let's get it over with.'

We go down to a lower deck, where we can have some privacy.

'Well, you were right,' he begins. 'The secret to great ratings was normal people after all. It was you they loved.'

'Us,' I correct him.

'Look, I'm sorry,' he says, cutting to the chase. 'I thought I was doing the right thing, keeping the show alive. I knew you wouldn't want to lie to the others, so I... did what I thought was best. The truth is, Simon was going to fire you, after this season. He said with audience numbers dwindling, there were going to be cuts, they would only need one person in casting, and that if it came to it, they would be keeping me. I didn't want you to lose your job, least of all to me – especially not now I know what you went through before – so I just thought... I don't know, if we made it a hit, we'd both get to stick around.'

'Simon was going to fire me?'

'You know what Simon's like,' he says softly.

Unfortunately I do.

'I should have just been honest with you,' he continues. 'About everything.'

'I get that you were looking out for me, and that you were just doing your job,' I tell him, because I do. 'But it felt like a betrayal. And the worst part? I didn't know what was real and what was scripted.'

'What was between us was real,' he says quickly. 'Everything I did with you was because I wanted to. And everything I didn't do. I'm sorry if it felt like I was trying to fix you. The truth is, you've fixed me. I've been too into work, too obsessed with ratings. But that stops now. I want to live my life, not manage other people's.'

'I just...' My voice trails off.

'Things were going so well until the masquerade party, when something changed, but I didn't know what,' he says.

I know what to say to that.

'What changed was I overheard Elle Shaw bragging that sleeping with you got her a spot on the show. I was disgusted,' I tell him.

He looks baffled.

'That's not what happened at all, I don't know why she would say that,' he insists. 'I thought you were just pissed off that she'd weaselled her way in, and that I hadn't taken a stand against it.'

'Then what was she talking about?' I reply.

'I don't know. Simon asked me for a card, he said he wanted her back, she was one of the best contestants...' He trails off.

'So it was Simon she slept with,' I say flatly.

'It was just a misunderstanding, Cleo, I promise.'

'Except it wasn't a misunderstanding, not really,' I say with a sigh. 'I wilfully misunderstood the situation to protect myself. It was obvious it was Simon, thinking about it. He's done it before. But I let myself believe the worst of you, because I was scared. I was falling for you and it was easier to push you away.'

'It's all gotten messy,' he admits, stepping closer. 'But I've fallen for you too. In fact, I've already fallen. Can't we just start again?'

'How?' I reply.

I'd love to, I really would, but how do we just hit the reset button? It's not like we can just call out 'take two', is it?

He pulls out a chair at the table next to us and gestures for me to sit down.

'Ding!' he says as he sits down next to me. 'Hi, my name is Lockie, and I've never been speed dating before, so I'm pretty nervous. And you are?'

'I'm Cleo,' I reply with a smile. 'First time too.'

'There you are,' Simon's voice snaps, ruining our moment.

We get up to talk to him.

'So the show was a big hit,' he says. 'So were you guys. We need to figure out how to go harder next year – and obviously you're not keeping the prize money.'

I just knew that part was too good to be true.

'Actually, we were real contestants,' Lockie points out. 'We had a contract. We won so the money is legally ours if we want it.'

'And we do want it,' I add. 'And I quit.'

'Yeah, unfortunately, I quit too,' Lockie says.

Simon reddens with anger.

'You're making a mistake,' he tells us. 'You'll never get another job in TV. You'll see.'

He storms off before we can say anything else. Perhaps he thinks we'll come around.

'Is he insane?' Lockie says as he walks off. 'We just won the biggest series of *Welcome to Singledom* yet. We can get any job we want.'

I laugh, a real one this time.

'So,' I say, 'we're starting again?'

'Yeah,' he replies, stepping closer. 'But I can't wait as long to kiss you this time.'

And then he does. And for the first time in what feels like forever, I don't feel watched or manipulated or in danger. I just feel happy. Like everything might be okay.

I guess sometimes it takes a shitload of rain to wash over everything and make it like new again.

It might have been unorthodox and low-key traumatic, and we've had a lot to figure out, but it's led us to where we are now. It's opened new doors for us, and this time, I'm not afraid to see where the doors lead.

36

ONE YEAR LATER

I don't think I've ever seen a man looking so terrified – and I've seen a man rolling around on the sand in agony while he watches women argue over which one of them is going to pee on him.

'Relax,' I tell him with a smile.

'It's my first time,' he says, his voice wobbling. 'Doing anything like... this.'

'I was terrified, when I did it for the first time,' I reassure him. 'But you would be amazed how quickly you get used to it.'

'Yeah, yeah...' he says, each of his words coming out when he exhales. 'It's just speed dating, right? I've done that before.'

'How did it go?' I ask curiously.

'I'm here, aren't I?' he manages to joke.

I laugh. That's fair enough.

I still have mixed feelings about speed dating. There's something so weird about it, it's like an odd form of human interaction, like, if this were a nature documentary, we'd all just be standing by, watching the hyenas picking off and eating the baby antelope, letting it happen, because it's just a fact of life, one that we're here to observe, not intervene in.

But people aren't like animals – not entirely, at least – sometimes we need a little intervention, and push to go for what we want, and a helping hand to get it.

'Do you think you'll be giving him a tick?' a voice says from behind me.

'I don't think I'll be giving anyone a tick ever again,' I reply, turning round to face him.

Lockie takes me in his arms and peppers my lips with kisses.

'So you don't fancy sitting down and doing a few rounds, seeing if you can find someone better?' he jokes playfully.

'Do you?' I reply.

'I'm not going to find better,' he says with a smile. 'But... I am going to help this lot find love.'

'You're not going to script it for them, like old times?' I tease.

'We're on-air in less than a minute, so I'm going to leave that one hanging in the air,' he replies.

Soon enough, someone behind the camera signals that we're live in three, two, one...

'Hello, and welcome back to *Heartbreak Hotel*,' I say to the camera.

'We've got a new batch of guests checking in – but who do we think they'll be checking out?' Lockie replies.

'And, later in the show, we've got celebrity guests – and our reality TV camp mates, Ozzy, Honey, Tony and Camilla on the panel – talking about all things love, war and survival. They'll be giving us their thoughts on all the action in the hotel today.'

'There's going to be action?' Lockie jokes. 'I didn't think it was that kind of show.'

I give him a playful shove.

Our on-screen banter is just as good as it is off. In fact, *TV*

News magazine described us as having 'the best on-screen chemistry since *Breaking Bad*' and *Stylife* magazine wants to write a profile on us as 'the hottest new couple on TV'.

It's hard to believe that a year ago, pretty much to the day, I was lying on a beach convinced I was going to die, surrounded by coconuts and people I didn't think I liked. Now I'm in a luxury hotel, in Sicily, co-hosting a reality TV dating show that Lockie and I came up with together. *Heartbreak Hotel*, a show where people can come and find love. People who are sick of dating apps, who always seem to meet the wrong person, or who can't seem to meet anyone at all. And when I say people, I mean people, real people. Everyone said that Lockie and I were the best part of our short-lived season of *Welcome to Singledom*, because we were real, we were doing our best and – turns out – we were falling in love. So our show is open to anyone, no matter what their age is or how straight their teeth are or if they know what 'no cap' means.

No tricks, no scripting, no embarrassing challenges, no public votes. Just a gorgeous hotel, good food, better wine, and time for people to get to know one another. The only intervention comes from trained psychologists and matchmaking experts, who make recommendations on who might do well to spend time with whom, to see if anything develops. We've only been on-air for a couple of weeks and, honestly, it's already making captivating viewing. We've even had our first kiss – between Helen, eighty-two, and Jonas, seventy-eight.

As the show goes on, Lockie's doing his usual rounds, chatting to contestants, turning on that easy charm of his. The producers love him. The guests love him. The hotel staff love him… I love him too.

When we cut for a break, Lockie and I head into the shadows, where the crew lurks, to grab a drink.

'You know Lucia, who manages the hotel?' Lockie says. 'She says we're the perfect couple.'

'Aw, that's nice,' I reply. 'Of course, she doesn't know that you snore.'

'She doesn't know because I don't,' he replies.

'How would you know, if you're sleeping?' I tease.

'I've slept with other people – Ozzy would've told me,' he jokes.

'He did actually snore,' I reply, the memory dragging my brain back to the island for a moment.

It's strange because, like with anything, the only things I can really remember now are the good parts. Any time you're going through a tough time, always focus on the glimmers of good, because when you're on the other side of it, they are the parts worth remembering.

Did I want to take part in *Welcome to Singledom*? No. Did I want to be stranded on the island, in full-on survival mode, fighting to get by? Absolutely fucking not. But was it a journey I needed to go on? It really was. I'd been carrying around so much excess baggage, and it turns out I didn't need any of it. So I left it on the island and made space in my life for Lockie. Plus, becoming an accidental TV star, it opens doors. I knew it was the right thing to do, quitting *Welcome to Singledom*, but I was terrified. The £100k helped, I knew it would buy us time, but I had no idea what I was going to do next. Then the offers started flooding in, but they only wanted me and Lockie – luckily, we only wanted each other too.

I still can't believe Simon wanted us all to stay there, and that he livestreamed the whole thing. I later found out that he at least reached out to our families, and let them know that we were safe, and willingly participating, and with everything going wrong, and us becoming main characters, he made a whole thing of the two of us being production members who were trying their hand at being contestants. I suppose we were in that we'd signed contracts to say we were taking part, and that 'anything goes', but it's hard to think I would have chosen to stay if we hadn't been stranded.

'Do you ever think about it?' I ask. 'Other than desperately clinging to the memory of sharing a bed with a hunk like Ozzy?'

Lockie laughs.

'The island?' he replies.

I nod.

'I do but, I don't know, it feels like another life, or a movie I watched,' he explains. 'But I thank Mother Nature for that storm every day, because without it, I don't know – I was going to say we wouldn't be where we are now but I like to think we would have found our way together somehow.'

'Either way, I'm glad someone or something, somewhere, scripted us a happy ending,' I say.

'Me too,' he replies, pausing to kiss me. 'But I think this might be just the beginning.'

I glance around at the busy set of the show that we built together and smile. It really does feel like the start of something great.

I spent all those years thinking love was something I found for other people – fake TV love – and that I didn't want any part of it. It took being stranded on an island, in danger, with a man I thought I hated, to realise that I wasn't only safe, but I was head over heels in love too.

The truth is that Lockie did save me – not from the island, because that was definitely a team effort – but from myself. He showed me what to let go of and what to pick up and hold tight.

It's funny, isn't it, that the public clocked that Lockie and I were in love before we did? But I'd like to think that even without the prize money, we would have caught on as soon as we spoke. I know we would have.

We got there eventually – to our happy TV show ending – but Lockie is right, as far as real life goes, this is just the beginning.

* * *

MORE FROM PORTIA MACINTOSH

Another book from Portia MacIntosh, is available to order now here:

https://mybook.to/NewPortiaBackAd

ACKNOWLEDGEMENTS

Thanks to Megan, Nia, Ross, Amanda and the rest of the team at Boldwood HQ for all of their wonderful work on this book.

I had a lot of fun writing it – thanks so much to everyone who takes the time to read and review not just this book, but all my books. It means so much to me.

I couldn't do any of this without the support of my wonderful family. Thanks so much to the amazing Kim, Pino and my incredible gran, Aud. Shout-out to my brilliant brothers – James and Joey. Thanks as always to Darcy for being by my side. Finally, huge thanks to Joe, my husband, for all of his love, support and hard work. I love you all so much.

ABOUT THE AUTHOR

Portia MacIntosh is the million copy bestselling author of over 20 romantic comedy novels. Whether it's southern Italy or the French alps, Portia's stories are the holiday you're craving, conveniently packed in between the pages. Formerly a journalist, Portia lives with her husband and her dog in Yorkshire.

Download your exclusive bonus content from Portia MacIntosh here:

Visit Portia's website: www.portiamacintosh.com

Follow Portia MacIntosh on social media here:

f facebook.com/portia.macintosh.3
X x.com/PortiaMacIntosh
[instagram] instagram.com/portiamacintoshauthor
BB bookbub.com/authors/portia-macintosh

ALSO BY PORTIA MACINTOSH

Just Date and See

Your Place or Mine?

Better Off Wed

Long Time No Sea

The Break Up Plot

Trouble in Paradise

Ex in the City

The Suite Life

It's All Sun and Games

You Had Me at Château

Wish You Weren't Here

Too Hot to Handle

Going Overboard

A Lot to Unpack

A Shore Thing

Boldwood

EVER AFTER

×♡×♡

JOIN BOLDWOOD'S
ROMANCE COMMUNITY
FOR SWEET AND SPICY BOOK RECS WITH ALL YOUR FAVOURITE TROPES!

SIGN UP TO OUR NEWSLETTER

HTTPS://BIT.LY/BOLDWOODEVERAFTER

Boldw⬤⬤d